THE GRAVESEND GRYPHON
AND OTHER
SHERLOCK HOLMES
STORIES

Robert V. Stapleton

Edited by David Marcum
and Derrick Belanger

Hardcover ISBN 978-1-80424-747-1
Paperback ISBN 978-1-80424-748-8
ePub ISBN 978-1-80424-749-5
PDF ISBN 978-1-80424-750-1

Published by MX Publishing
335 Princess Park Manor, Royal Drive,
London, N11 3GX
www.mxpublishing.com

Cover design by Awan

To my wife Rosemary, who has patiently supported my writing for many years.

Thanks to:

To our editors and publishers, David Marcum and Derrick Belanger for their wise editorial skills, and to Steve Emecz and all at MX Publishing, together with all others who have been involved in putting together this collection of previously published stories.

Contents

Once a Soldier

A cloud was hanging over the people of London. The year 1901 had begun with the passing away of the old Queen, and the whole Empire was currently in mourning. With the age of Victoria now at an end, the future looked as uncertain as the gloomy weather.

Ned was sitting at his usual place, on the bench on the Victoria Embankment, looking out across the River Thames. The diffused light of that spring morning was fighting against the murk that hung over the city and its people, and it showed no sign of winning that battle.

Wrapped up against the cold, and lost in the mists of his own thoughts, Ned failed at first to notice a tall figure come to stand directly in front of him, and he only looked up when a voice interrupted his meditations.

"A military man, I see," said the stranger.

"Ex-military," replied Ned, raising his eyebrows in surprise. It was unusual for anyone to stop and take the trouble to speak to him.

"You have the bearing of a soldier," continued the stranger. "Those ribbons on your chest stand testimony to a distinguished career. Your skin still shows the vestiges of a suntan, which you undoubtedly acquired in warmer climes. South Africa would be a safe assumption. Perhaps serving as a non-commissioned officer."

"That is very perceptive of you, sir," said Ned. "You are, of course, quite right. I returned from the war in South Africa only a couple of months ago. Edmund Hunter is the name, but now people just call me Ned. I was a sergeant, serving with Her Majesty's forces in the Transvaal. And I would still be out there now, fighting for my new king and country, if some Boer hadn't taken it into his head to explode a bomb which deprived me of my lower left arm." He looked down at the empty left sleeve of his coat and uttered a sigh of tired resignation. "Now I have neither dignity nor any means of earning a decent living. Instead, I now have to rely on the pity of others. It is utterly humiliating, sir."

"I can well imagine. But I have need of a man like you, Ned."

"Me? Whatever use can I be to a gentleman like yourself?"

"My name is Sherlock Holmes," said the man, "and I am currently assisting Inspector Gregson of Scotland Yard in his search for a certain villain. A small-time, persistent but illusive criminal who goes by the name of Owen Kencraig. In his own small way, he is a spider at the center of a web of crime. The recent spate of robberies from wealthy West End homes are the work of his gang. Extortion, blackmail, kidnapping, murder. They are all down to him. But neither Gregson nor I can locate this villain, to arrest him and bring him to justice."

"In that case, how do you imagine I can help?"

"A man like you can move around London without arousing much in the way of suspicion."

Ned sat up straighter. A light of interest now shone in his eyes. "You have a point there, Mr Holmes."

"And a small allowance might be arranged in payment for your services."

Ned scowled. "I have no wish to depend any further upon charity, Mr Holmes."

"I can assure you, Ned," continued Holmes, "that if you help apprehend this man, you would certainly have earned every penny of it."

"Very well," said Ned. "In that case, tell me more about this man, Kencraig. How could I recognize him?"

"From the few who have survived his clutches, and are not too scared to tell, we know that he is about five-foot three, two-hundred pounds, with dark curly hair and a black beard as thick as a jungle. He invariably wears a green jacket, corduroy trousers, and a bowler hat."

"And you want me to find this bloke for you. Is that it?"

"That is exactly it, Ned. But beware of his colleagues. They are a dangerous pair."

"My days are not as full as they used to be," mused Ned. "So, if you need somebody to help Scotland Yard out of this difficulty, then I am at your service, Mr Holmes."

"Good man," said Holmes. "But it might prove to be a dangerous assignment."

"I've faced worse in South Africa and survived it, too. Just about. But how can I get in touch with you again?"

"You will be contacted by a small boy. A street urchin by the name of Flax. He will remain our means of contact."

Before Ned could ask any further questions, the man had gone.

*****

As Ned mulled the matter over and considered how he might best set about his quest, he became aware of a small boy standing a few feet away. The child was barefooted and wore ragged clothing. The boy was watching him.

"You must be Flax," said Ned. "You have the right color of hair, anyway."

"That's me, mister."

"Who exactly was that man I was talking to just now? He said his name was Sherlock Holmes."

"Him? Don't you know nothing, mister? That there is the one and only Mr Sherlock Holmes. He's the greatest detective in all of London. And the entire world."

"He wants me to find this criminal mastermind for him. And it seems you're going to help me do it."

"That's the idea, mister. Mr Holmes's idea, at any rate. You see, people don't take much notice of street kids like me. They think we don't matter. That we don't know what's going on. But we know more than they think."

"In that case," said Ned, "where do we start looking for this man, Kencraig?"

"He'll be difficult to pin down," said Flax, "but his cronies might be easier to find. Perhaps we could start by looking for them."

"Do you have their names?"

Flax held out a small card.

"What's this?"

"It's a photograph," said Flax. "Mr Holmes told me to give it to you. You see, it's the only picture he has of Kencraig's two mates."

Ned studied the small two-tone picture. It showed a couple of men standing in an urban street, clearly unaware that they were being photographed. It was not the clearest photograph ever taken, but the men's features were distinctive and memorable enough.

"The one on the left is Reggie Braningham," said Flax. "He organizes things for his boss. Then there's the fellow on the right. That's Karlin Pikeman. Be careful of him. He's what you might call an assassin. He kills people."

"They sound a nasty couple. But how can I find them, let alone Kencraig?"

"You have to ask people."

"But that could be dangerous. For them and for me."

"Don't worry," said Flax, with a broad smile. "Mr Holmes will keep an eye on you."

*****

Giving his small companion a doubtful look, the disabled veteran soldier stood up and ambled his way along the Embankment, toward his other haunts. He had to start somewhere, but he was unhappy about putting his own friends in danger.

He began by visiting a man he thought might help. Harry the Hawker. But, as soon as Ned mentioned the names of the men he was looking for, Harry turned on his heel and walked briskly away.

Next, Ned turned his attention to another veteran soldier he knew, but this one flatly said that he couldn't help.

Ned realized he had to be more cautious about how he approached people. His next contact he found sitting at a table at the far corner of a dark and dingy bar. This was a Scotsman he knew, by the name of Angus.

"I'm looking for a couple of criminals, Angus," Ned began. "But I need some idea of where to find them. So, I'm hoping you can help."

Angus continued to sip his whisky, and to look into the unfocused distance. Ned wondered if the man had heard him at all.

"Braningham and Pikeman." Ned slipped the photograph onto the table in front of Angus.

The Scotsman continued drinking, until finally he turned his empty glass upside down on the top of the table and looked up at Ned. The message was clear.

Ned bought another scotch and placed it in front of Angus. It had cost him most of the cash he had to last him through the day.

The Scotsman gave Ned a long look. "So, you want to find Braningham and Pikeman, do you?"

"That's right."

"Why?"

"I'm trying to locate their boss. Owen Kencraig."

At the name of Kencraig, Angus reached for the glass, and drank down the entire contents in a single swallow.

"Ned," he continued, wiping his mouth on the back of his hand. "I am greatly obliged to you for the drink but listen to what I tell you. And listen carefully. You would be wise never to mention that name to anyone. And to stay as far away from him and his crew as you possibly can."

"I don't want to meet him," Ned explained. "I'm just helping somebody to find him. That's all."

Angus looked around, with an anxious expression on his face. After pulling a scrap of paper and a stubby pencil from the inside pocket of his jacket, he wrote something down and passed the paper to Ned. "This fellow might be willing to help you," he said. "Take this, and then take your leave. Good day, Ned."

Outside, and away from prying eyes, Ned looked down at the paper. It carried a name. George Coalfield. And an address which Ned recognized as one of the side-streets that ran almost literally under the shadow of St Paul's Cathedral.

He looked around for his young companion. But Flax was no longer anywhere in sight. So, he continued on his way alone to look for this man, Coalfield.

After several minutes, Ned reached the street where George Coalfield was supposed to live. The thoroughfare was busy, with people coming and going. One man was pushing a handcart covered with a tarpaulin sheet. Another was carrying a heavy stick and swaggering along with a gait that would have been more appropriate to somebody on the high seas. A tall man was leaning against the wall of a nearby building, holding a half-empty bottle of gin. Ned ignored them all, and carefully examined the doorways as he passed them.

Then, everything happened at once.

The carter drew back the tarpaulin cover and took out a heavy revolver from inside his cart. As this man turned and raised the gun, the drunk launched himself toward Ned, knocking him to the cobbles just as the gun fired and a bullet tore a chunk out of the brick wall behind them.

Noticing the other man's failure to kill his target, the seaman raised his heavy stick and advanced to where Ned was picking himself up again.

The man with the bottle, obviously not as drunk as he had pretended to be, hurried Ned along to the corner of the next alleyway. They looked back but could see nothing of the two would-be assailants.

Ned relaxed. "Thank you for coming to my aid," he said to the drunk.

"Glad to be of service, sergeant," said the other man.

"Mr Holmes," cried Ned. "I didn't recognize you in your disguise. But it's good to see you again, especially as you just saved my life."

"My irregulars have been keeping an eye on you," said Holmes.

"Your irregulars?"

"The street children. They are spread out all over London."

"Then you'll know that I've been looking for Kencraig's companions."

"Indeed," said Holmes, "and I think you just found them."

"Those two in the street just now?"

"Of course. But they were also heavily disguised."

Ned took out the paper that Angus had given him. "I've been given the address of a man who might help me track them down. He lives down here, somewhere."

"Then let us hope we are in time," said Holmes.

It turned out that George Coalfield was a cobbler, who made and mended shoes at his workshop farther along the street. But the shop where he worked was now empty.

"It is as I feared," said Holmes. "Those men in the street just now must have taken him. He was probably lying in the cart, unconscious and trussed up like a turkey."

"If those men were Braningham and Pikeman, then we must follow them and find out where they've taken him."

"I think we are too late for that," said Holmes. "They will be well away from here by now."

"Then my search must begin again," said Ned.

"No," said Holmes. "This business is becoming far too dangerous. You will have to keep a lower profile from now on, Ned. Keep out of sight and leave it to the professionals."

"But you told me the professionals are failing to make any progress."

"True."

"Then remember this, Mr Holmes. A soldier on an assignment never gives up on his mission."

*****

Sergeant Ned Hunter felt that the job of helping Scotland Yard to find a criminal mastermind was important to him. Finding the man would bring a much needed boost to his self-respect. How difficult could it be? He shrugged off the very idea of failure. It was true that his quest had nearly cost him his life. But he would keep on going.

When he returned that evening to the Salvation Army hostel which was to be his lodging place for yet another night, he talked with some of the men there. And showed them the photograph.

One man, by the name of Webber, a bargee laid off work with an injury, took the picture and studied it closely.

"I recognize the man on the left," said Webber. "My work has been mostly on the river, and from there you can see all sorts of things you could never notice from the land. I've seen this man, more than once, hanging around a boat moored at the Melavian Wharf."

"Can you take me there?"

"If you like. But you need to be careful."

"Tonight?"

"Certainly. As soon as the bloke in charge here locks the front door, I'll show you the way through the back entrance. We can be at the Melavian Wharf and back again in less than half an hour. Are you game?"

"Let's do it."

*****

In the night-darkened street outside the hostel, Ned was surprised to find Flax emerge from a dark corner.

"I've been waiting for you," the boy explained. "I knew you wouldn't give up so easily and that you'd surely be out again tonight."

Ned introduced Flax to Webber, as his personal minder. "He probably knows the docks as well as anyone."

"But not the whereabouts of those villains," said Flax.

Webber led the way to the entrance to a wharf a little way downstream from London Bridge.

The man on duty there stepped out in front of them. "What business do you have here?" he demanded.

But before Ned could come up with a convincing reply, Flax kicked the man in the shin, and ran away, laughing.

The man on guard chased after him, but by the time he'd given up looking for the boy, Webber and Ned had reached the far end of the jetty.

Webber led the way to a long and narrow vessel lying there. "This is the boat," he whispered to Ned. "A converted barge. You can see inside by looking down through the skylight. But be cautious."

Ned looked down into the saloon of the barge. In the light of an oil-lantern hanging from a beam, he could see a man lying on a couch. Ned recognized him as one of the men in the photograph. Reggie Braningham. The only other person there was a man tied to a chair. That had to be George Coalfield. Ned had never met him before, but he already felt responsible for the man's entrapment here. But at least he was still alive.

Webber moved closer. "That man you're looking for, is he in there?"

Ned shook his head. There was no sign of Owen Kencraig. And it was clear that the other man, Karlin Pikeman, was missing as well.

"All we can do is go back to the hostel, and come back again another time," said Ned, feeling disappointed.

On their return to the hostel, Ned and Webber found the place in an uproar. Everybody was now awake, and the warden in charge was in a state of anguish. They had had an intruder. Webber found his mattress cut to ribbons, the result of an apparently frenzied attack. And Ned found a dagger plunged deep into his own mattress, its handle just about visible.

Ned realized that one of the men in the hostel had betrayed him, and that somebody had come here to kill both him and Webber.

*****

With no chance of sleep that night, Ned made his way back down the stairs, and out into the fresh night air once more.

"I thought I might see you again," came a child's voice from the darkness. Flax.

"Why do you say that?"

"While you were at the wharf, I came back here. And that's when I saw him. That other fellow."

"Karlin Pikeman?"

14

"That's him. I saw him coming out of this very entrance. Anyway, I followed him back to where I'd left you and the other bloke. And I watched him go along to the boat at the far end. I knew he'd been up to no good, so I came back here to tell you."

"So, he'll be there now."

"That's what I said."

"They're holding George Coalfield on that boat," said Ned.

"That makes sense."

"But I can't help wondering where he fits into this business."

"He's one of their network of informers," said Flax. "Like I keep Mr Holmes informed of what's happening on the streets."

"One of the men in the hostel was an informer as well."

"Stands to reason."

"So why did they kidnap Coalfield?"

"They didn't trust him. They thought he was going to tell you where they were hiding out. Perhaps somebody heard you talking to the Scotsman."

"In that case, why is he still alive?"

"They're waiting for something to happen."

"Or for somebody else to arrive."

"Kencraig."

"Must be. In that case, we need to go back there and wait. See if their boss comes to join them. He's the one the Yard are really looking for."

Ned and the boy returned to the quayside, overlooking the Melavian Wharf. There they sat down and made themselves comfortable.

"Many a night I've gone without sleep," said Ned. "Keeping watch against those who would murder me and my colleagues. I had to stay alert and listening."

"Same as me," said Flax. "It's only at night that the backstreets of London really come alive, and we can see and hear things that Mr Holmes wants us to tell him about."

"And will he know what's going on here?"

"He will when I tell him."

At first, as the night dragged on, few vessels moved up or down the river, and nobody drew near to the Wharf.

Then, as the hour of four struck from a nearby church clock, Ned spotted something on the river. A small dinghy, with a square sail, set to catch the gentle pre-dawn breeze. He watched it draw closer to the wharf. And to the boat at the far end.

Ned turned to Flax, who nodded that he had seen it as well.

From where they were sitting, Ned and the boy watched a man step out of the dinghy and climb up onto the wharf. In the darkness, it was difficult to make out much about the man, except that Ned could see he had a beard, and that he was wearing a jacket and a bowler hat.

"Stay here until I get back," said Flax, as he hurried away into the night.

Life on the river was beginning to stir into action by the time Ned next heard Flax sit down beside him.

"Mr Holmes says you're to go and arrest the lot of them," came the boy's voice.

Ned was horrified. "Me? On my own?"

"Here," said Flax, pushing something heavy into Ned's hand.

The soldier looked down and recognized it as a service revolver.

"But I only have the one hand."

"No need to worry, mister. It's loaded, and they say you're a good shot."

Ned nodded. "I used to be. Very well, but I hope Mr Holmes knows what he's doing."

Holding the firearm in his right hand, Ned stood up from his place, stretched his stiff limbs, and strode off toward the wharf.

The caretaker shone his lantern, took one look at the revolver and allowed Ned to pass. "It's about time you was here," he said. "Something bad is happening along there."

Ned made his way quietly to the place where he could look down into the boat. Yes. Four men were there. George Coalfield was still tied to the chair, whilst the other three were gathered around him. Ned recognized Pikeman and Braningham. The other man standing there, he could now see in the light of the oil lantern, had to be Owen Kencraig.

Looking around, but unable to see anybody who might back him up, Ned Hunter, the injured veteran soldier, recently returned from South Africa, stepped down onto the deck of the boat, and pushed open the saloon door. The men inside were making so much noise with their shouts and threats that they failed to notice him at first.

"Owen Kencraig," barked Ned, standing in the doorway and raising the revolver. "I am here to place you under arrest. You and your mates."

In an instant, the atmosphere in the saloon turned from threatening shouts to stunned silence.

Kencraig turned and glowered at the intruder. "Who is this?" he demanded.

Karlin Pikeman laughed. "It's that old cripple who hangs out on the Embankment. We tried to kill him yesterday, just like you said. But he got away."

"Oh, so this is the man Sherlock Holmes is relying on to bring me to justice, is it?"

"That's right. That other bloke at the hostel, Webber, must have brought him here when I went there to kill them. Otherwise, they'd both be dead."

"In that case, you'd better finish off the job." Kencraig's face twisted into a nasty grin. "He isn't going to shoot. The chances are the gun isn't even loaded. Kill him."

Pikeman reached into his jacket for his gun. But Ned's reflexes were quicker. The old soldier had the gun, and the nerve to use it as well. The moment Pikeman raised his gun toward him, Ned squeezed the trigger of his own revolver.

The bullet tore into the other man's hand, causing him to cry out with alarm and pain, and to drop the gun onto the floor. The sight of the man's injured hand gave Ned some consolation for the loss of his own lower left arm.

Before the others had time to recover from the shock of the gunshot, the door burst open, and the boat rapidly filled with armed Scotland Yard men. The reinforcements had arrived.

"You did a good job, Ned," came the voice of Sherlock Holmes from close behind him. "Inspector Gregson will take charge here now."

"They came at exactly the right moment," said Ned, handing back the revolver.

"Now that he has Kencraig and his friends, Gregson will make sure to unravel the rest of the spider's web within hours."

As the first rays of sunshine forced their way through the early morning haze, Ned smiled. "But it took a one-armed soldier and a small boy to finally bring those criminals to justice."

Pipes, Bonnets and Pieces of String

I am obsessed. At least that's what my uncle Charles keeps
telling me. The truth of the matter is that I have taken to
spending my lunchtimes, at a fashionable and busy London
teashop, in the company of a most peculiar old man. My fiancé,
Richard Frobisher, tells me it's an unhealthy interest. Perhaps
he's jealous. But then I really cannot see why he should be.
I'll readily admit that the old man at that corner table is not
the sort of person any ordinary young woman is likely to
spend much time with. But then again, I am no ordinary young
woman. No. I am a journalist.

"You're still interested in detectives, are you, Polly?" said
Uncle Charles when he came round to my lodgings early one
morning.

"It's just part of my job, Uncle," I replied defiantly.

"Nonsense. It's starting to take over your life, girl."

"What can possibly be wrong with making friends with
an amateur detective?"

"Oh, you consider this fellow to be a detective, do you?
Some boring old man in a tea-room?"

"You know I do, Uncle. And he's not boring. Far from it."

"It's high time you met a proper detective for a change.
Now, as it happens, a man at my club has managed to arrange
for you to meet an investigator of a very different order."

I bridled. "It really is extraordinarily good of your friend
to go to all that trouble, Uncle, but I am really not interested."

"You might regret not accepting the offer, my dear."

I hate it when people try to organize my life, especially
when they claim to have my best interests at heart. But my
curiosity can sometimes overcome even the most
temperamental aspects of my personality.

"There might even be a story in it for you," he added.

"Very well," I replied without enthusiasm. "Let me have the address, and I'll see if I can fit in a visit there sometime this week."

"You must understand, Polly," said Uncle Charles, pointedly, "this detective is an extremely difficult man to pin down. We are particularly fortunate that the appointment has been made for you to meet him this very morning."

I realized I would have to see this matter through, even if it turned out to be a complete waste of my time. I decided that, if I was going to meet this detective, then at least I would need to make a good impression. With that in mind, I put on one of my more stylish bonnets; the one with the feathers sprouting out of the middle. A few minutes later, wearing a coat against the cold March wind, and a hatpin securing this bonnet to my mop of brown hair, I set off to attend this unexpected appointment.

*****

A corporation omnibus brought me to Baker Street, where I made my way to 221B, and rang the doorbell. A woman opened the door, who told me her name was Mrs Hudson, and that she was the landlady of the property. I handed her my card and told her I was there to meet the famous detective. Mrs Hudson smiled, told me that I was indeed expected, and immediately led me up a flight of stairs. On reaching the landing, Mrs Hudson knocked upon the door, and opened it to reveal a most extraordinary room. A table in one corner of the room was laden with laboratory paraphernalia, whilst another held a large aspidistra, together with a copy of the *Evening Observer* newspaper. Beside the fireplace stood a tall, thin man, with an aquiline nose, and sharp facial features. I estimated him to be somewhere in the middle years of his life.

All this I observed through a cloud of tobacco smoke, rising from the briar pipe that the man was smoking in a contemplative manner. As a newspaper reporter, I am of course quite used to men smoking. I have even occasionally indulged in the practice myself, so I resisted the temptation to cough loudly.

Mrs Hudson, on the other hand, proved to be rather less indulgent. To the amused gaze of the man with the pipe, she gave a theatrical splutter, crossed the room and threw open the window.

With fresh air now chasing the smoke around the room, and finally pursuing it outside to mingle with the fumes of the Baker Street traffic, Mrs Hudson introduced me. "Miss Margaret Burton to see you, Mr Holmes."

As the landlady left, Mr Holmes invited me to take a seat beside the glowing fire. I sat down, watching Mr Holmes as he took his seat on the other side of the hearth. Then I waited for something to happen. This visit was not my idea, so I saw no reason why I should initiate the conversation.

"You are certainly a young lady of the most unusual abilities, Miss Burton," said the man.

"It is very good of you to say so, Mr Holmes."

"A lady whose business quite clearly lies in the handling of words."

I raised an eyebrow in surprise, inviting him to explain this comment.

"That is quite evident from the ink-stains on your right hand, and from your stories published regularly in the daily Press. He indicated the copy of the *Evening Observer*.

"My work is always keeping me busy, Mr Holmes."

"Indeed. And you possess a special interest in detectives. I understand from your uncle that you are interested in meeting a proper detective for a change."

I returned his gaze. "That is entirely my uncle's idea."

Mr. Holmes smiled as he recognized my evident discomfort at having been coerced into this meeting. "Quite. But whether I might be described as a proper detective or not is for others to decide, although I have had some experience over the years in the art of detection. However, I have to tell you, Miss Burton, that I am no longer active in public life. I am semi-retired even from my work as a private consulting detective."

"In that case, it is extremely good of you to agree to meet me this morning, Mr Holmes."

"I am intrigued by what little I have learned of your apparent predicament, Miss Burton. Tell me, what exactly does your uncle expect you to gain from this meeting?"

"He hopes you might deflect the attention of this innocent young girl away from another detective she has taken to meeting, and whom her uncle considers totally unsuitable for her."

"Another detective?" Mr Holmes raised an eyebrow in what I took to be mock surprise. "And where exactly do these meetings take place?"

"At an ABC teashop."

"ABC standing for the Aerated Bread Company," noted Holmes.

"That's right. They have a teashop in Norfolk Street. Just off the Strand."

"An emporium for serving hot drinks and light meals."

"Conveniently within walking distance of my newspaper's offices in Fleet Street. Merely an ordinary, though quite fashionable, tea-room. But the man I meet there is far from ordinary."

Holmes sat back in his armchair, drawing deeply upon his smouldering pipe. "Unlike myself, of course." His eyes sparkled with subdued mirth. "Pray, tell me more about this detective. For example, can you give me his name?"

"I have no idea of his name," I replied. "He has never told me it. To me, he is simply the old man in the corner. He wears a rather loud tweed suit, and an extraordinary shapeless hat. He is elderly, pale in complexion, thin in both face and limb, balding, but with mild blue eyes that show a keen intellect. And he possesses decidedly large ears. In fact, he looks very much like a human scarecrow."

Mr Holmes chuckled. "You are an extremely observant young lady."

"I am a journalist, Mr Holmes, employed by the *Evening Observer*. It is my job to be observant."

"Quite." He nodded. "And what does this man have to say that so intrigues you?"

"He analyses crimes reported in the daily newspapers, considers the facts and, with myself as his audience, he solves those crimes which have left Scotland Yard completely baffled. He loves to show the professional detectives in an extremely poor light."

Mr Holmes laughed. "That would not be a very difficult task."

"But he tells the stories with such powerful insight that I imagine he can almost read the minds of the people recorded in the newspaper articles. He sometimes even attends court hearings, in order to gain a better insight into the crimes and the offenders."

"This man sounds like a most fascinating character," said Sherlock Holmes. "When will this detective of yours next be at the Norfolk Street teashop?"

"I generally meet him at around lunchtime. I have been doing so fairly regularly for several weeks now."

Sherlock Holmes consulted his pocket watch. "Then I suggest we repair to that tea-room for our own luncheon. If this man is there today, then I would certainly like to listen to what he has to say, and then come to my own conclusion about him."

* * * * *

Mr Sherlock Holmes led the way downstairs, and out into Baker Street. There he hailed a cab, which bore us through the crowded streets of central London, until we alighted in Norfolk Street.

At such a popular hour, the teashop was crowded with patrons, but my own customary corner table was left unoccupied, save for a single solitary figure. The weird old man was sitting reading a newspaper, with his usual glass of milk and cheesecake on the table in front of him. He looked up as I led Mr. Holmes toward him, but remained seated, holding in his scrawny hands a length of string which he was absentmindedly tying into a series of complicated knots.

Before I had time to introduce my guest, the shrunken old man in the corner said, "You must be Mr. Sherlock Holmes."

"Indeed, I am," replied Mr. Holmes, taking the seat directly opposite the old man. "And, although I have no idea of your name, I can immediately tell that you are a man with an interesting life. Your coat and trousers are in need of a brush and an iron, and your shirt requires the tender care of a launderer. I must therefore conclude that you live on your own. Your mind is usually upon matters requiring a great deal of attention, since the eyeglasses you wear have seen better days, and the right side-arm has been repaired in a decidedly utilitarian manner."

The man in the corner remained almost completely impassive, except for a twitch at the edge of his mouth, which I took to be his appreciation for the keen mind he had now encountered.

I ordered my usual midday meal: coffee, a roll with butter, and a plate of meat. Mr. Holmes declined to order, but continued to sit, observing the withered old man. I sat watching the two men, with keen interest.

Abruptly, the man in the corner put down the string, opened the newspaper he had been reading, and spread it out upon the table.

"Mr. Holmes," said he, "allow me to ask you what you make of this recent burglary; the one reported in the latest edition of the *London Mail*. It is supposed to have happened at number 24 Melgrove Gardens."

"It seems a very commonplace crime to me," replied Mr. Holmes. "On the surface."

"Aha! On the surface." The man in the corner reached for his glass of milk, and immediately drank down half its contents. Then he picked up his piece of string, and continued to tie knots along its length. "You have clearly read about the incident. Now, you will recall the fact that the burglary occurred only a couple of nights ago. At the home of Admiral Pulverholm and his wife. It appears that somebody entered the building by breaking a window in the scullery downstairs. According to the newspaper reports, the intruder, whoever it was, then proceeded to make his way upstairs to the bedroom, where the admiral and his wife, lay fast asleep in bed. The thief then removed an ornament from the mantelpiece, a figurine in the shape of an elephant, a souvenir of the admiral's time serving in the Indian Ocean, and escaped with it into the night. In the morning, although a thorough search was conducted of the premises, it was discovered that nothing else in the house had been either touched or taken. Except that the admiral reported that the door of the safe in the corner of his room had been unlocked, and left ajar. He declared that nothing whatsoever was missing from the safe."

I watched as Mr Holmes fixed his attention upon the man in the corner, intrigued as the eccentric old man continued to fidget with his piece of string and tied it into ever more complicated knots.

"Odd, would you not agree?"

"Singular," replied Mr. Holmes.

"Puzzling," I added, attempting to remain a part of the conversation.

"The newspapers recorded the proceedings that took place at the magistrate's court on the following day," continued the old man. "Lady Pulverholm revealed that she had been out shopping later on the day following the overnight robbery, when she happened to pass a certain pawnbroker's shop, and her eye was caught by an item on display in the window. It turned out to be the missing statue. The one taken from the bedroom. The owner of the pawnbroker's shop, a Mr Walter Hallibred, provided a detailed description of the person who had brought in the object. Within the hour, the local police who had been investigating the break-in and theft, had arrested a young small-time crook by the name of Danny Crumb. This was the man who now stood before the magistrate in order to answer the charge of burglary. Although admittedly no saint, young Danny Crumb claimed to be completely innocent of this particular offence. Yes, he had indeed pawned that object, but no, he had no idea that it had come from the home of Admiral and Lady Pulverholm. He claimed to have discovered the missing figurine in the garden of a neighbouring house. What he had been doing in that garden remained a matter for speculation, upon which Crumb refused to elucidate. Then came the question of the open safe in the bedroom. The defendant appeared puzzled by the suggestion that he might have opened it, and once more claimed that he had nothing whatsoever to do with the matter. And, with nothing having gone missing from the safe, the investigation passed over that particular charge. With no further evidence to consider, but with his suspicions by no means assuaged, the magistrate felt he had no choice but to remand the accused into custody, whilst further investigations were made by the police."

"Which will of course take them nowhere," said Mr. Holmes.

The man in the corner nodded. "But now we come to the point of it all. Tell me, Mr. Holmes, why would anyone do something so strange?"

"What exactly do you mean?"

"Of all the things that were vulnerable to being stolen from that house, including from the open safe, why would anyone choose to take a ceramic elephant, and why not, at the same time, take the opportunity of stealing some or all of the other valuable items and ornaments in the house?"

"Did the elephant have any particular value?"

"None at all, above a few shillings."

"I agree. It is very strange. The only conclusion has to be that, whether or not this was a burglary, then it was no mere common or garden crime. We might safely set aside the improbable scenario suggested by the Press, and investigated by the police, that this rather naïve young man, Danny Crumb, actually carried out the robbery."

"Agreed. Then consider this proposition, if you will," continued the man in the corner. "This apparently minor crime could well have been a cover for the theft of some other item in the house. Danny Crumb was the hapless petty criminal who was used as a scapegoat to divert attention away from some much more serious crime."

I was now completely fascinated by this story. "If so, then what else was taken?" I asked.

"Precisely the question we need to ask."

The two men sat quietly watching each other, until Mr. Holmes concluded, "It is too early to propose any conclusion about that matter. We must make further inquiries."

The man in the corner finished off his milk, stood up, and left like a shadow, stopping only to settle his bill at the counter.

"I must also leave," said Mr. Holmes.

"Are you going to follow up the case?"

"Oh, yes."

"Then may I come with you?"

"Most certainly."

The moment we stepped out through the front door of the teashop, Mr. Holmes and I immediately noticed a vehicle draw up beside us. The door of the brougham opened, and a head looked out. "Ah, there you are, Sherlock. Mrs. Hudson thought I might find you here. Would you care for a lift?"

"Where are you going?"

"Melgrove Gardens."

"Then we should be delighted to join you."

We climbed into the vehicle, and as the carriage set off again, I found myself sitting opposite a man I vaguely recognized as someone I had once interviewed at the Foreign Office.

"This is my brother," explained Sherlock Holmes. "His name is Mycroft, and he works with several government departments, including the Foreign Office."

Mycroft leaned closer. "And I recognize you, young lady. You are Miss Polly Burton, of the *Evening Observer*. A journalist. And an expert busybody."

"You are quite correct, Mr. Holmes," I averred.

"Then, if you are going to accompany us, I hope you will be circumspect in your reporting of today's events."

"I can make no promises," I told him, "but I am a professional reporter."

"Then remember this, if you allow your creative imagination to run away with you, I shall be forced to deny everything."

"Naturally."

Sherlock Holmes sat back in his seat. "Now, Mycroft, what is this all about? Why are you interested in such a minor infringement of the law as occurred, or did not occur, in Melgrove Gardens?"

Mycroft Holmes took a deep breath. "We have received information that a certain European power, who in view of Miss Burton's presence here I shall refrain from naming, has obtained a stolen document giving details of a new steam propulsion system being developed for use on our new generation of torpedo-boat destroyers. These details are extremely sensitive, and are of course in the highest category of secrecy."

I felt baffled by this revelation, but tried not to show it. Which foreign power was he talking about? As though I and my prospective readers could not make an educated guess. And what was so important about this new propulsion system? Here were matters far above my head.

"Only three copies of these plans exist," continued Mycroft Holmes. "One set is kept at the admiralty, whilst a second is under lock and key in my own office."

"And the third is undoubtedly kept at the home of Admiral Pulverholm," concluded Sherlock Holmes.

Mycroft Holmes chuckled, and turned to me. "Do you see now why my brother is considered to be the greatest detective in the world?"

"You exaggerate, Mycroft," objected Sherlock Holmes.

My eyes lit up as I came to the obvious conclusion. "And one of these sets of plans has gone missing."

"That is precisely the matter we are investigating," said Mycroft Holmes.

The brougham rolled into Melgrove Gardens, and stopped outside the front of Number 24, a large town house with well-maintained lawn and shrubbery in front.

The housemaid admitted us to the building, and Mycroft Holmes led the way inside. We were immediately greeted by Lady Pulverholm. A tall, respectable woman in her later years. "An Inspector from Scotland Yard has arrived," she told us, "and is talking with my husband upstairs."

"Who is this man from Scotland Yard?" asked Sherlock Holmes.

"An Inspector Hopkins."

"Ah, yes. I know the fellow well."

"Then we must join them upstairs immediately," said Mycroft.

"No," asserted Sherlock Holmes. "I should first of all like to examine the site of the break-in."

The housekeeper, Mrs. Wellenough, a lady who apparently carried a great deal of weight in the household, in more ways than one, called for the kitchen maid to take us to the scullery.

This storage room lay close to ground level, and the single window, still jagged with broken glass, had now been covered over with a sheet of canvas, and was awaiting the attention of a glazier.

I joined the two Holmes brothers, together with the kitchen maid whose name was Prue, as they made their way into the scullery.

Sherlock Holmes examined the floor. "There appears to be very little in the way of broken glass inside this room," he noted.

"That's right, sir," said Prue. "Mrs. Wellenough told me I needn't bother brushing up in here just yet. She says I shall have plenty to sweep up after the glass has been replaced."

Sherlock Holmes nodded. "Now, may we proceed outside?"

Prue led the way out into the backyard, and there we came across the main debris left by the break-in.

Sherlock Holmes pointed to the glass lying on the ground immediately outside the shattered window. "As you can see, the window was broken by the use of a sheet of newspaper, covered in molasses, which had been pressed up against the glass in order to keep it largely in position as the intruder broke it."

"That seems simple enough," said Mycroft. "That way, the intruder would not have woken up the rest of the household."

"Or so it would appear," continued Sherlock Holmes. "But look at this. When we examine the glass which is still attached to the newspaper, we find that it is the wrong way round. Observation, and a moment's thought, will tell you that glass on the outside of a window attracts dirt which is quite different from that on the inside of the window. I am sure that Prue does an excellent job of cleaning the window. But only on the inside."

"Yes, sir," said the kitchen maid. "It's the job of the window cleaner to clean the outside. But he often misses this part of the building."

"Even so, if the glass had been broken from the outside," continued Sherlock Holmes, "we should expect to find a scattering of shards of glass inside the scullery. Both fallen from the glass itself, and scraped from the window frame by the intruder as he climbed inside."

"But it isn't there," I exclaimed.

"Which is why," continued Sherlock Holmes, "we can be certain that the window was broken from the inside rather than the outside.

I gasped. "But that means that somebody inside the house must have broken the window, and made it look as if it had been done by an intruder."

"Bravo, Miss Burton."

"And Danny Crumb has to be innocent."

"At least of breaking and entering."

I now had at least one newspaper story from today's activities. But the day was far from over yet.

"Now we must find out what Inspector Hopkins has to tell us." With a look of satisfaction upon his face, Mr. Sherlock Holmes led the way back to the entrance hallway of the house, from where the butler escorted us up the main staircase.

In the master bedroom, we found Inspector Stanley Hopkins talking with another man, seated in a comfortable armchair. This man's air of authority indicated that he was the owner of the house.

"Inspector Hopkins," said Sherlock Holmes, with a knowing smile.

The policeman did not look happy. "Ah, there you are Mr Holmes," he said. "I am glad you are able to join us here."

"And Admiral Pulverholm. Allow me to introduce myself. I am Sherlock Holmes. And this is my young friend, Miss Polly Burton."

The admiral did not seem impressed.

"My brother has provided me with some background information on this case," Sherlock Holmes told him, "but I sense that there is more going on here than meets the eye."

"Maybe less," replied Inspector Hopkins dolefully. "That is what we are here to determine."

"In that case, be kind enough to explain yourself, my dear Inspector."

"As Mycroft will have told you, certain pieces of secret information have been leaked to a foreign, and possibly aggressive, military power."

The admiral stirred in his chair. "And your brother, in the company of half the detectives at Scotland Yard, is accusing me of being responsible for leaking this information."

"Certainly not you personally, Admiral," said Mycroft Holmes defensively. "As I have already explained, it is just that yours is one of only three possible sources of the leak."

"And why could it not have been leaked from your own home?" demanded the admiral.

"Because my papers are still inside the safe at my house."

"And so are mine," roared the admiral. "Let us see, then, shall we?" With that, the admiral stood up, removed a key from the watch-chain attached to his waistcoat, and approached the safe in the corner of his bedroom. "See, gentlemen," he announced. "Apart from one held for security purposes by my bank, this is the only key to this safe." He slid the key into the lock, rotated the mechanism, turned the brass handle, and pulled the safe door wide open.

The admiral examined the contents. "Here, on the top shelf, I keep loose cash, which is necessary for meeting everyday expenses. I use it to pay the servants, the outside utilities and the shopkeepers and traders who supply us with our daily dietary and other necessities."

He turned to the second shelf. "And here I keep items of greatest value, including the papers entrusted to me by the Admiralty. See. Here they are, safe and sound." I watched him push aside some other documents, and lift out a cardboard folder, which he held up for us all to see. The folder carried the words "Top Secret" stencilled in red letters on the outside. He opened the folder, and removed a pile of official-looking papers.

"Gentlemen, and the lady present," he announced with exaggerated grandeur, "these are the papers we are talking about, and they are all here. Every one of them."

Inspector Hopkins looked embarrassed, whilst Mycroft Holmes gave the impression of being confused beyond reason. Only Sherlock Holmes remained impassive, pensively watching the papers, whilst I shrank back into the shadows.

"It certainly looks as though we owe you an apology, Admiral," Inspector Hopkins replied sheepishly.

"It does indeed look to be that way, Inspector," replied the admiral, with an expression of triumph upon his face.

"In which case, we must extend our investigations elsewhere in our search for this leak of information," admitted Mycroft Holmes.

Mumbling their profuse apologies, both Mycroft Holmes and Inspector Hopkins turned, made their way back down the stairs, and hurried out into the fresh air.

The admiral turned to face Sherlock Holmes. "Well, Mr. Sherlock Holmes, are you going to join them? If not, then why are you and the young lady still here?"

"We shall of course take our leave of you shortly," said Sherlock Holmes. "But first I have a few questions I would like to ask you, Admiral."

The admiral glowered back. "Very well. Ask your questions, and then be off with you."

Unperturbed, Sherlock Holmes asked, "How many sheets of paper are in that Top-Secret folder, sir?"

"In the folder? Half a dozen. Why?"

"Do you check those papers every day, sir?"

"Of course, I do. Religiously. Every single day, without fail."

"And do you count them every time you check them?"

"No, sir, I do not. I usually have better things to do with my time."

"Then you would never know if just one single sheet had been removed."

"True enough, I suppose."

"In that case, perhaps you might agree that somebody could have removed a single sheet one day, and then replaced it again on the following day. If this were to be done every day for a week, then you would never have been any the wiser."

"Do you always make such wild guesses, Mr. Holmes?"

"I never make guesses, Admiral. I employ the science of deduction."

"But you have no evidence whatsoever that such a thing as you suggest has taken place."

"True."

"And, much more to the point, who would do such a thing, and why?"

"I have not yet come to a definitive conclusion about those matters," said Mr. Holmes.

As the Admiral turned his attention to reattaching the key to his watch-chain, Sherlock Holmes asked if he might examine it for a moment.

The admiral handed over the key without objection.

Sherlock Holmes then held the key to his nose and sniffed it gently. His eyebrows rose slightly, and the hint of a smile appeared upon his face. He knelt down beside the safe, and sniffed at the lock.

"This lock has been recently oiled," he observed.

"Not by myself," declared the admiral.

"Nevertheless, the aroma of lubricating oil is strong here. As it is upon the key."

"With the two having recently been in close contact, that would hardly be surprising," returned the admiral.

"Except that the key carries another scent."

He passed the key to me. "What is your opinion, Miss Burton?"

I took the key, and held it close to my nose. I sniffed. "Yes, oil," I decided.

"And?"

"It also carries another smell. Wax. Distinctive."

"Suggestive."

"Of what?"

Holmes said nothing.

"Wax?" demanded the admiral.

"Oh yes," replied Sherlock Holmes. "Now, let us try to imagine what might have occurred here. Somebody gained access to that key."

"Impossible," declared the admiral. "That key is upon my person at all times."

"Except when you are in bed."

"Even then, it is always close at hand."

Sherlock Holmes brought out his magnifying glass, and studied the key in greater detail. "There are even traces of wax adhering to the side of the key. That too is suggestive."

"What are you proposing, Mr Holmes?"

"It is clear that the perpetrator of the crime, or an accomplice, would need only a moment's contact with this key in order to make a wax impression, so that a copy could be made."

"This is a preposterous idea, Mr Holmes," cried the admiral.

"Not really. If the person involved in this crime were to be a member of your own household, they might have plenty of opportunities to gain access to your bedroom, and to the safe."

The admiral sat down heavily on the side of the bed. "Then I shall have to sack every one of them."

"I would advise against that," said Mr. Holmes. "No. Leave the matter with me, Admiral, and I shall endeavour to solve the problem. Though exactly how many of those pages I shall be able to recover is a matter of some doubt."

"Now I must ask you to leave, Mr. Holmes," said the admiral.

"One final question, if I may," said Mr. Holmes.

"Very well."

"Why did you report the open safe to the police when you knew that nothing had been taken?"

"It was entirely my wife's idea. She considered a full disclosure to the police to be essential."

"And the attempt to lure the young thief, any young thief, by planting the elephant in your neighbour's garden?"

The admiral scowled. "Please go, Mr. Holmes."

It was late the following morning when I met Sherlock Holmes again. At my habitual corner table in the ABC teashop. Today, I was wearing a more workaday bonnet. We were alone, and I had already begun my luncheon, when the diminutive figure of the amateur detective arrived, and took pride of place in the corner seat.

The man in the corner then took a piece of string from his pocket, and began to tie knots along its length. "The presence of Mr. Holmes here suggests that you are making progress in the case involving 24 Melgrove Gardens."

As Sherlock Holmes remained in pensive silence, I tried to explain. "It seems that somebody in the household has made a copy of the key to a safe containing top-secret government documents. We even discovered traces of the wax when we examined the key."

"I find your mention of the smell of wax intriguing."

"Mr. Holmes thinks that whoever did this may have gone on to make copies of those government papers, so they could be passed on to some foreign power without the knowledge of the admiral."

"This is undoubtedly the more significant case I was suggesting the last time we met."

Sherlock Holmes now leaned forward and riveted the little man with a steely stare. "If the information carried by those documents were to fall into the hands of some foreign power intent on gaining military superiority over this nation, then this might become a matter of the greatest importance."

"And for the thief. Who do you have in mind, Mr. Holmes?"

"It is still too early to say."

"But you have some ideas."

"Indeed. Although I would need further information before I can be certain."

"Then permit me to supply that information," said the man in the corner, with an evident sense of arrogant pride. "Allow me to provide the single piece of information which will prove to be the key factor in unravelling this entire mystery."

I sat watching these two men as they faced each other across the corner table. Two detectives with so much in common, and yet with so much difference between them. I was intrigued. My journalist's ears were alert. I wondered what great pearl of wisdom would now be revealed. I bit deeply into my bread-bun.

"Let us consider the household in general," said the little man. "They have a fairly modest array of servants. Including cook, kitchen maid, housemaid, footman, chauffeur, gardener, valet, butler, and housekeeper. But let us concentrate upon the housekeeper."

"Mrs. Hester Wellenough."

"That is indeed her name now. But it was not always so."

"Really?"

"Certainly not. I have spent a great deal of time, both yesterday and this morning, looking through newspaper archives and public records. It seems quite clear that Mrs. Wellenough was previously married to a man by the name of Mulberg."

Sherlock Holmes sat deep in thought. "Tell me, does she have any connection with the firm of Milton and Mulberg, the brewers?"

The man in the corner continued to tie ever more complicated knots into his piece of string. "German immigrants," he said. "The Mulberg brothers. Heinrich and Joseph. Both proved to be intelligent and resourceful young men. They arrived in this country two-and-twenty years ago, met up with the Milton family, and went into business together. Brewing beer."

"A profitable business, one would suppose," opined Holmes.

"Perhaps. But it seems that Joseph Mulberg had a huge row with both his brother and the Milton family. Over some trivial matter. The two brothers never spoke again. Joseph found employment with a publishing company, met a young woman from Stepney, married her and settled down to a life of domestic bliss. They had only one child. A boy called Samuel."

"But Joseph died."

"That's quite right. After ten years of happy marriage, Joseph succumbed to pneumonia, leaving his widow with a young boy to raise and feed. However, within a year, she had met this man, Wellenough. A clerk at an insurance office in the city. They married and settled down. Then, after another four years of what we might assume to be a happy marriage, the new husband died. Of a stroke."

"A very tragic situation."

"Indeed. It was very sudden. Hester Wellenough was once more left to fend for herself. Taking in washing and ironing amongst other things. And the son, who had until now been an assistant to an odd-job man, looked to his father's family for assistance. The other Mulberg brother wished to help the young man. Whilst he was not prepared to assist the mother, he found his nephew a job at the coopers' workshop that supplied the brewery. Samuel's job was to make the barrels which were used by the brewery to hold and transport their beer."

"But that was an independent firm."

"Just so. To stand or fall on its own merits. However, the young man did very well there, and rapidly rose to a position of responsibility and seniority within the firm. At the same time, young Samuel kept in touch with his mother, and helped her to find employment at the home of Admiral and Lady Pulverholm. As housekeeper. A highly respected and responsible position."

I now felt bold enough to make my own comment on the story. "Good for her. It seems that everyone was now happy."

Mr. Holmes nodded slowly. "But recently things began to go wrong." He stared at the man in the corner. "What can you tell us about that?"

The little man had come to the end of his piece of string, so he put it down, took out his notebook, and removed from it a couple of photographs. These he laid out upon the table, in full view of Mr. Holmes and myself. They showed a young man, dressed in a smart suit and a bowler hat. "It was in the newspapers earlier this year," said the man in the corner.

"This must be Samuel Mulberg," I decided.

"Quite right. These two pictures were taken of him on the occasion of a court case. A sawmill firm was seeking settlement for a delayed payment from the coopers' workshop at which the young Mr. Mulberg was employed."

"They were having financial problems," concluded Mr. Holmes.

"But the matter must have been settled fairly quickly," I added, "or else we would have heard more about the matter in the Press."

The scarecrow sat back, with a self-satisfied grin upon his face. "That is the intriguing part of this whole business. Within a couple of weeks, the debt was settled, and nothing more was heard of the matter."

I watched as the man in the corner smiled, slipped quietly out of his place, and scuttled across the floor of the tea-room. A moment later, he had disappeared through the front door, and was gone about his own business.

Whilst my own mind was awhirl with so much new information, I turned to see Mr. Sherlock Holmes, also sitting deep in thought. After a couple of minutes, he stood up abruptly, and also headed for the door. I adjusted my bonnet, picked up my notebook, and followed in his wake.

*****

I returned with him to his lodgings in Baker Street, where Mr Sherlock Holmes declared that he needed time to think.

"This will probably be a three pipe problem," he declared, as he took a clay pipe down from its place in a pipe-rack beside the fireplace, filled it with a plug of tobacco, then then lit and drew heavily upon the lighted pipe.

"I suppose you would like a cup of tea, my dear," came the voice of Mrs. Hudson from the doorway.

I turned, and smiled. "Yes, that would be a nice idea. My cup at the ABC went cold before I had time to enjoy it."

Down in her own living room, Mrs. Hudson sat talking with me for the rest of the afternoon, until I realized I was going to be late for a meeting with Dickie Frobisher, and would have to leave at once.

It was at that moment that Sherlock Holmes burst into the room.

"Ah, there you are, Miss Burton," said he. "Are you up for an adventure this evening?"

My plans for the evening were about to receive a shattering blow. "I'm always up for anything exciting, Mr. Holmes," I told him.

"Even if it might involve breaking the law?"

I hesitated, until Mrs. Hudson, with a twinkle in her eye interposed, "Your young man will be able to visit you in prison."

That decided the matter. "Of course."

"Splendid." Sherlock Holmes smiled, and led the way outside.

The hansom cab we hailed took us to the southern outskirts of the city, and dropped us off at the gates of a building which described itself as the "Milton and Mulberg Brewery Company".

The smell of hops and barley hung heavy in the cold atmosphere, but Mr. Holmes reminded me that we had no argument with either Mr. Milton or Mr. Mulberg, but only with the latter's nephew.

After speaking with the man on duty at the gate, Mr. Holmes followed the directions he had been given, and we shortly found ourselves standing outside another collection of buildings. This time the gates were locked, and solid iron railings protected the place against entry by anyone who ought not to be there. Like us. The place betrayed itself as a coopers' and barrel-makers' workshop, not least by the presence of lengths of wood, metal hoops, and half completed barrels standing outside in the yard.

With dusk now falling rapidly, Mr. Holmes discovered a small door in the side of the building, and used his pick-lock to gain us entry that way. Then we were inside the main building itself, where a strong smell of sawdust greeted us.

Having broken into the place, I felt less inclined to object when Mr. Holmes used the same method to gain entry to the main office of the premises. A brass plate fastened to the door declared it to belong to Mr. Samuel Mulberg. I looked around, and discovered that the building was supplied with electric lighting, so I flicked the light-switch, and bathed the office in the glow of an overhead lightbulb.

After a search of the filing cabinets, Sherlock Holmes found a document detailing exports, both accomplished and planned. "They are expecting to complete a shipment of beer to Europe within the next few days," he told me. "We need to take a closer look at the barrels they intend to use for that purpose."

By the dim light of overhead skylights, together with an electric torch Mr. Holmes had discovered in the office, we made our way through the rest of the building. We narrowly avoided tripping over half-finished wooden barrels left in the construction workshop, and finally reached the storage room at the far end.

There we looked around at two rows of wooden barrels, each barrel three or four feet in height, containing, so I estimated, approximately thirty-six gallons apiece, and all branded, "For Export".

"What exactly are we looking for?" I asked my companion.

"If Mulberg is supplying copies of those documents to some foreign power, then the best way would be to employ some channel of communication already in use. That way, no suspicion would be aroused."

"Mulberg was using his trade in beer. But how exactly?"

"Use your imagination, Miss Burton," replied Sherlock Holmes. "If you wished to hide a sheet of paper, where would you conceal it?"

"Inside a barrel?"

"Perhaps. But the liquid contents would inevitably render the paper unreadable."

"Then where?"

"Possibly a secret compartment hidden inside the top of the barrel. The entire purpose of this place is to construct wooden containers. It would take very little extra labour to construct a false cavity in the top of one or more of these barrels."

"Then how can we discover which one it is? There must be a dozen of them in here."

Sherlock Holmes removed an iron crowbar from beneath his coat. "When struck, the noise made by a gap containing air will sound very different from one which carried only liquid."

He walked along the lines of barrels, striking the top of each as he came to it. The dull sounds emitted by the barrels showed that each contained only liquid. Until he reached the far end of the second row.

"Aha! Now, listen to this, Miss Burton."

I listened with great care as he again struck the top of the wooden barrel. The sound was indeed different. Distinctive. I could imagine the gap of air immediately beneath the wooden top.

Using the sharp end of the crowbar, Sherlock Holmes broke open the top of the barrel. As the wood gave way, with a crack, and a sigh which sounded almost human, we saw, in the light of the torch, a cavity separated from the liquid below by a secure wooden base.

Mr. Holmes put his hand into the cavity, and drew out a bundle wrapped in waxed and sealed leather. As I held the electric torch and directed its beam, I watched as he opened the bundle, to reveal a small stack of papers, each carrying diagrams and technical formulae which meant nothing at all to me.

"This is better than I had hoped," said Mr. Holmes. "These are copies of the papers taken from the safe of Admiral Pulverholm. Somebody has gone to extraordinary lengths to reproduce the information in exact detail."

"But only five of the six."

"Then we must conclude that Mulberg was paid on delivery of the first sheet, with a promise to supply the rest in due course."

"Quite right, Mr. Holmes," came a voice from the doorway.

We turned as a light switch clicked on, and the incandescent lightbulb above our heads glowed into life, flooding the room with illumination. In the entrance, we saw three men. I gasped when I saw them. Two were armed with metal tools used in the coopers' trade. One carried, what I later discovered to be a flanging iron; a length of iron with a pair of claws at one end. The other man held a heavy hammer. They both carried their implements in a threatening manner, which made my blood run cold. The third man, I recognized from the photograph shown to me by the man in the corner of the teashop. It was Samuel Mulberg.

"So, you have managed to work out our little subterfuge, have you?" said Mulberg.

"You are a dangerous man, Mulberg," cried Sherlock Holmes. "You are selling the interests and security of your country to an enemy power."

"In view of our financial problems, it was a sad necessity, Mr. Holmes. As indeed is your unfortunate death. And that of the young lady."

"And, if you fail to deliver these other papers," said Mr. Holmes, "your own life will be in grave danger."

Mulberg said nothing in reply, but remained standing in the background as the other two men approached us. The one with the hammer closed upon Sherlock Holmes, who leaned the crowbar against the side of the barrel, turned to face his attacker, and began to give a good account of himself using his wits and bare fists.

In fear for my life, I backed away as the other ruffian approaching me.

Almost at once, I tripped over the crowbar, and fell backward between the barrels.

The man with the flanging iron continued to approach me, with a nasty expression distorting his face. I scrambled to my knees and picked up the crowbar. As the man raised his iron, in preparation for striking me dead, I grasped the crowbar in both hands and held it up to defend myself. The flanging iron struck the crowbar with great force, jarring my wrists painfully. But, despite the pain, I gripped the crowbar with both hands at one end, and swung it with all my strength. The man was too slow to move out of the way, so the crowbar made painful contact with his right arm.

I heard a bone crack.

The man fell back, uttering words that no young girl should ever be expected to hear. Mostly disparagingly about my parentage. So, I hit him again.

Another shadow now fell across me, and I looked up to see Samuel Mulberg himself standing between me and the light. Before I had time to react, the man kicked the iron bar out of my hands, and reached down to grasp hold of me by my collar. What he might have done to me next, I hardly like to imagine, but, at that moment, the air was filled with the piercing sound of a police-whistle.

Uniformed policemen emerged through the doorway, and soon had the two thugs in custody. Samuel Mulberg, on the other hand, had slipped away through an outside door, leaving it open, and himself nowhere to be seen.

Inspector Hopkins now took center-stage. "Ah, here you are, Mr. Holmes and Miss Burton. A strange little old man left us a message. He said we should come down here and arrest you two both for breaking and entering into these premises. I don't suppose you know who that might have been."

"I can hazard a reasonable guess," said Mr. Holmes, as he dusted himself down. "But I must say, it is extremely good to see you, Inspector."

"And Miss Polly Burton here, as a reporter with the *Evening Observer*, will have to explain herself to the editor of her newspaper."

"But first we must hurry off in pursuit of Mulberg," said Sherlock Holmes. "We now have clear evidence of his involvement in the theft of government secrets. And now he is on the run."

Adjusting my bonnet, I followed Sherlock Holmes and the policemen outside. "He must have taken the footpath across the common," shouted Mr. Holmes. "Quick! We must catch him before he reaches the roadway and finds a lift."

I was determined not to let the man get away. Now, emboldened by the presence of so many policemen around me, I gathered up my skirts and hurried on blindly into the darkness. After another minute I ran full-tilt into somebody hidden in the darkness, and felt rough hands grasp hold of me. I looked up, and saw, to my horror, that it was Samuel Mulberg. The man turned me round and held me firmly from behind, with his arm across my throat, almost throttling the life out of me. As the policemen gathered around us, he shouted his defiance.

"Call off your men, Inspector," he yelled, "and give me time to escape. Otherwise, I'll kill the girl."

"I don't think you'll do that, Mulberg," shouted back Hopkins.

"I wouldn't be so sure if I were you, Inspector. If I have to face an accusation of treason, and then in all probability the hangman's noose, I have nothing further to lose by taking her life."

I knew I had to take the initiative in this standoff, so I lifted my right foot, and raked the edge of my boot down

Mulberg's shinbone. The man holding me yelled in shock and pain, and momentarily loosened his grip on my throat.

At that moment, from out of the darkness, a huge fist collided with Mulberg's face, sending the man who had been holding me in a death-grip collapsing stunned onto the ground.

I looked up, and saw Richard Frobisher step out of the darkness and into the torchlight.

"Dickie!" I yelled. Then, with my insides turning to mush, I ran into his outstretched arms, and burst into tears. There are times in life when a girl is allowed to do that sort of thing, and this seemed to me the most appropriate moment ever.

"You were late," he scolded me.

"I know," I sniffled. "I'm sorry. But we had some villains to catch."

"So I see. A lady called Mrs. Hudson sent me a note, telling me to contact Scotland Yard about you. So, here I am."

"Good for Mrs. Hudson." I hugged him more tightly, whilst the policemen set about taking charge of the situation, and placing our three villains under close arrest.

*****

The man in the corner continued his nervous habit of tying knots in the length of string he was holding in his thin bony fingers. "You understand," he told me, "that it was very much against my nature to approach the police at all, and Scotland Yard in particular. But I knew exactly where you were going to be that evening, and I wanted to make sure they captured the chief miscreant. Samuel Mulberg."

"And you saved our lives in the process," I added, adjusting the new bonnet I had purchased in celebration of our success.

He merely smiled indulgently.

Sherlock Holmes had told me that, compared with the antics of that evening, he considered the keeping of bees to be much less hazardous to the health of a middle-aged man like himself. So, I was not particularly surprised when he failed to join us at the ABC teashop.

"The full story, or as much of it as we have discovered, can now be revealed," I told him. "Having been given extra time in which to raise the money he owed, Samuel Mulberg agreed to sell military secrets to a foreign power in exchange for enough money to solve all his financial needs. It seems that somehow, his mother managed to make a copy of the key to the admiral's safe, and so gained access to the folder containing the secret documents. Over a period of several days, Mrs. Wellenough would remove the pages from the document, one at a time, and give it to her son. After he had made a careful copy of that page, he would bring the original back, so that his mother could return it to its place in the document file, removing a further page for similar treatment. The first page had already been sent, but we managed to rescue the other five." I felt proud that I had finally gained a proper understanding of the affair.

"All very neat and tidy," observed the strange old man sitting in the corner across the table from me. "So, the police are happy."

"Indeed."

"And what about the other business? How do you explain the supposed break-in by the burglar, Danny Crumb?"

I blinked, and tried to remember the details of that case. "Mrs. Wellenough and her son made it look as though a break-in had occurred, to distract attention after all of the sheets had been copied, and the originals returned to the safe. It can only have been a way for them to cock a snook at the police."

"If true, then it would certainly be an attitude which I myself would applaud. But there appears to have been more going on here than you have so far grasped."

"More?"

The wizened old man leaned forward, his long neck and beak-like nose reminding me of a stalking bird. He opened up his newspaper, and laid in out across the table in front of me. "Now, Miss Newspaper girl," he said in a scathing tone. "What do you make of this latest entry in the Stop Press column of this morning's newspaper?"

I looked down at the column before me.

The old man explained. "It reports that, earlier today, Admiral Pulverholm was arrested on charges of passing government secrets to agents of a foreign power."

In complete amazement, I read, and re-read the article, just to assure myself that he had indeed revealed its contents correctly. He had.

"It was, of course, quite obvious," the man in the corner told me.

"Was it?"

"Of course, it was. And it all had to do with the wax."

I blinked in amazement. "The wax?"

"You identified the presence of wax by its distinctive smell."

"Yes, certainly."

"Then consider this. If the key had been impressed into a bed of wax, then returned to its place among its fellows on the keyring, then spent much of its time in the pocket of the owner's waistcoat, being brought out each day for practical use on numerous occasions, and all this for the entire seven days, then it would no longer carry any residual trace whatsoever of the original wax. If what you said really did happen, then you would never have been able to detect the smell the wax at all."

My brain was working rapidly now. "In that case, the presence of the wax must have been staged. Somebody put it onto the key at almost the last moment, specifically so that we should find it there."

The old man chuckled. "Perhaps by the admiral himself."

My eyes opened wider, in even greater amazement. "Then there never was any second key."

"Even your friend Sherlock Holmes realized the truth of it. He should be at Scotland Yard this very minute, helping Inspector Hopkins detail the charges against the admiral. They are going to need every bit of help he can give them."

"You can be a very cynical man at times," I told him.

"Cynicism is the very first requirement necessary for any detective. But consider this, what if the point of the supposed break-in, which was blamed on that foolish young burglar, was to place something in the safe rather than take anything out?"

I buried my face in my hands. "I find this whole business utterly confusing."

"But it all becomes as clear as day the moment you introduce the idea of blackmail."

"Blackmail?"

"Supposing Mrs. Wellenough and her son had secured possession of some letters which proved the admiral guilty of marital infidelity. He would be willing to do almost anything to secure the return of those letters."

"Certainly."

"Think back, Miss Burton, to the occasion when you saw the inside of the admiral's safe. Did you see a bundle of letters in there?"

I thought carefully. "Yes. I think I did. He had to move it to the rear of the safe in order to reach the government documents."

"Now, suppose the mother and son promised the return of those letters in exchange for access to those top-secret papers, albeit one sheet at a time. With all the documents now having been copied, they returned the final page, together with the incriminating letters, leaving the door open as a sign that they had done as they had promised."

"How intriguing."

The man in the corner grinned. "Not really. It's all quite simple when you admit the possibility. Now the situation is about to erupt into a full-scale scandal, and I can hardly wait to see how the newspapers report the unfolding public humiliation of the admiral."

I continued to study the newspaper article, trying to come to terms with this latest turn of events. Had we all been wrong about those thefts from the admiral's home, or was it just I who had been too slow to realize the truth? As a journalist, I am used to humbug, but here I had found deception at every turn. Had the admiral's unsuspecting wife let the cat out of the bag by insisting upon reporting the open safe to the police? And, more interestingly, would I be the one called upon by my editor to cover the case when it came to court? I hoped so.

I finally looked up again, only to discover that the man who had been sitting in the corner seat had slipped away, and was already stepping out into the fresh afternoon air. I was alone, with nothing more than this newspaper article, and a piece of string, twisted into complicated knots, from one end of its length to the other.

Fishy Business

"Science," opined my friend Sherlock Holmes one sunny summer's morning in the year 1900, "is merely one of many tools in the service of investigative logic."

I looked up from my reading of the *Telegraph*, and watched my friend as he studied the pages of the *Times*. "For my part, Holmes," I replied, "I regard science as the very bedrock of all such investigation."

He turned his steely eyes upon me. "And yet, in your occupation as a physician, you invariably utilize a whole variety of other tools in order to arrive at a diagnosis suitable for your sick patients."

"True. Close observation and smell, to name just two. But always in a strictly logical manner."

"But if all of those tools of logic failed to produce an adequate solution, what would you do then?"

I shrugged. "I would refer them to a specialist. Naturally. Somebody who has more knowledge of their specific subject than I do."

"And that is where we part company, my dear fellow," replied Holmes. "When I have eliminated all other possibilities, even after consulting with others, I am forced to assume that whatever is left over has to be the truth."

"Even if it defies all logical investigation."

"Certainly. Because it would then add to our ever-accumulating sum of knowledge."

He observed my skeptical expression, and burst into a subdued chuckle.

The sharp and insistent ringing of the front doorbell interrupted our discussion.

"We have a visitor," observed Holmes, standing up and repairing his attire in preparation for receiving this unexpected arrival. A moment later, the door to our living room at 221B Baker Street opened, to reveal a young lady whose physical beauty attracted my attention in no uncertain manner. She was wearing a long blue dress, which matched the deep-sea blue of her eyes. A charming creature if ever I saw one.

Again, Holmes fought to restrain his mirth as he considered my reaction. "You still have an eye for the ladies, then, Watson."

"Only the most attractive ones, I can assure you, Holmes."

Turning his attention to our visitor, Holmes indicated the armchair positioned between where Holmes and I had been sitting. "Please come in and take a seat."

The young woman thanked him, smiled, and sat down.

"Mr Sherlock Holmes, I presume," said our visitor, removing her pinned hat, and allowing a mass of golden hair to cascade around her shoulders.

"I am Holmes," replied my companion, dropping his newspaper onto the hearth of the unlit fire beside him. "And this is my friend and companion, Dr John Watson."

"I am glad to have found you," said our visitor as she looked around at us. "My name is Doris Thalassa Waters."

"Is that your married name?" asked Holmes.

"No," said Miss Waters. "But why do you ask?"

"You are wearing what might be taken for a wedding ring on your ring finger," Holmes pointed out. "Which suggests that you are indeed attached. But it is an unusual ring. Coral, if I am not mistaken. From the South Seas."

The young lady nodded. "You are indeed an observant man, Mr Holmes."

"Some would merely say that I possess an unhealthily inquisitiveness," he replied.

Miss Waters folded her hands on her lap. "My husband's name is Harry Chatteris."

The name rang a bell deep inside my memory. "Is that not the young man who died in an unfortunate swimming accident?" I asked. "About a year ago?"

Miss Waters nodded, and became visibly agitated. "So it appeared, and so it was reported in the newspapers at the time. But there are some who prefer to call it murder." She sat forward, to fasten her keen eyes upon Holmes. "And it is for his murder that a policeman from Scotland Yard is coming here to arrest me."

Holmes and I looked at each other in astonishment and deep concern.

"But the coroner declared the death of Chatteris to be a tragic accident," I replied.

She bit her lip, and nodded. "Nevertheless, you may expect a visit from Inspector Lestrade at any moment."

"And how do you wish me to assist you?" inquired Holmes.

Miss Waters grew even more troubled. "I didn't kill him, Mr Holmes. The matter is complicated, and there are ignorant people who refuse to accept the truth. But, to cut the matter short, Mr Holmes, I need somebody to stand beside me when I am accused."

"Hmm." Holmes sat deep in contemplation.

Once more, the front doorbell rang, and our room was invaded by a flustered Inspector Lestrade. He was accompanied by another woman. She was perhaps nearing her thirties. Her dark hair, gray eyes and austere expression contrasted with the blonde countenance and lively eyes of Miss Waters. A musky scent surrounded the new female visitor like a cloud.

Lestrade was breathing hard. "Good morning, Mr Holmes. You too, Dr Watson. I must say those stairs seem to be getting steeper every time I come here."

Holmes chuckled. "Welcome, Inspector. And the lady with you."

"Ah, yes. This is Miss Adeline Glendower."

Miss Glendower glared at Miss Waters with a vicious scowl. The two women clearly knew each other.

The newcomer extended her finger.

"That's her, Inspector," she growled. "I would know her anywhere. Even without her tail."

Lestrade looked astounded. "Tail?"

"Oh yes. That woman is a mermaid."

"Poppycock!" I exploded. "Utter nonsense!"

"I am a Lady of the Sea," replied Miss Waters enigmatically.

Miss Glendower ignored these interruptions. "And she is responsible for murder."

"So you keep telling me," said Lestrade. "But what exactly did she do?"

"During the time she lived with us in Folkestone, as a guest of the Bunting family, I was engaged to be married. To Mr Harry Chatteris. The up-and-coming Liberal politician. But that woman, that mermaid, lured him away from me. She turned his mind against all that I held dear. She wanted to take him away from me, so he could live with her in the deep ocean. At least, that's what she told him. The two of them were last see together one night, leaving the hotel, with him carrying her away into the darkness. She had a tail in those days."

Lestrade appeared confused. "And you think she killed Mr Chatteris?"

"Of course she did. That woman, that mermaid, is the bringer of death to normal human beings."

"But the coroner decided his death was by drowning," countered Holmes. "Misadventure. So what happened to make you think she murdered him?"

"His body was washed up on the beach a couple of days later," she replied.

"Yes, but what evidence do you have that she murdered him?"

"None, beyond the blindingly obvious."

"No!" All eyes turned to Miss Waters, who returned our gaze with a look of horror. "I did nothing to hurt him. I never would. I loved him. I still love him."

"I don't believe you," shouted Miss Glendower. "Now that you are without your tail, you are just as vulnerable as any other woman. Your neck will snap as easily as that of any other human being, at the end of the hangman's rope."

Miss Waters touched her throat, as the horrible prospect loomed in her mind that she might be hanged for murder.

"Now look here, Miss Glendower," said Lestrade in his no-nonsense tone of voice. "If you want me to arrest this young woman for murder, then you are going to have to come up with some definite proof. If we go before a court of law and tell them that all you have against her is that she is a mermaid, not only will you most likely be put into jail for bringing the court into disrepute, but the whole of the Metropolitan Police Force will be held up as a laughing stock before the entire nation, if not the world. The criminals would have a field-day."

Adeline Glendower turned her hatred onto the inspector. "So, you will do nothing about it. Is that the way of it?"

"Not without more substantial evidence."

"In that case, Inspector," she snarled, "I shall have to see to the matter myself."

"Do anything illegal," cautioned the Inspector, "and you will find yourself up against the law."

The embittered woman turned, and hurried down the stairs and out into the morning air in a flurry of crinoline and fury, leaving the rest of us to collect our thoughts.

Heaving a sigh of relief, Inspector Lestrade turned to follow, but Holmes stopped him.

"Please sit down, Inspector. Before we go any further, let us find out a little more about Miss Waters here."

Lestrade once more took his seat.

"Thank you for your support just now, Inspector," said Miss Waters.

"There's no need to thank me, miss," the policeman returned. "There is simply no evidence to back up the case against you. Whatever you did. There is nothing illegal about being a mermaid," he said dolefully. "If such a thing really exists."

"My thoughts precisely," I told him.

Holmes turned to face Miss Waters, who was still sitting in the armchair.

"Now, Miss Waters. We need to hear what this matter is all about."

She looked him full in the face. "About a year ago, after spending some time as a guest of the Bunting family in Folkestone, I persuaded Mr Chatteris to give up his engagement to Miss Glendower, Adeline, or Addy as he called her, and instead, to come with me and share my life. This human life is, after all, merely a tissue of dreams. I was offering him a better dream. Together. With me. When he came to join me, he no longer had any need of his human body, so he allowed it to float away with the tide, until it ended up on the beach a few miles away. But when Addy heard that his body had been discovered, she became insanely bitter. She declared that she could have married him, and would have made him happy. Instead, I had taken away any chance of happiness from both of them. This is of course completely untrue, but it is how she saw the matter. Now, after twelve months of allowing the matter to fester in her mind, she has become even more bitter. Toward me. When I arrived again, unexpectedly, at Folkestone a few days ago, I caused quite a stir among the Bunting family. Addy saw that I no longer had my tail, so she assumed I was no longer immortal. She realized she could kill me, and so her deranged mind caused her to accuse me of murdering Harry. Now that she has failed to see me arrested for murder, she still intends to see me dead. One way or another."

My blood ran cold as I listened to her.

Sherlock Holmes nodded, as if he believed all the nonsense she was telling him.

"So now, Miss Waters, why exactly are you here, and not at the bottom of the sea with your lover?"

"This is a matter of genuine murder, Mr Holmes," she replied. "You have to understand that under the sea we are not entirely cut off from the events of the human world above. Books, newspapers and documents of various sorts drift down to us from the surface. On top of that, we can hear what is being said by people inside the ships as they pass by on the surface. We have noticed that, from time to time, and more especially in recent months, ships have been deliberately sunk by their crews. Scuttled. Mostly old ships. Ones whose wooden hulls are in danger of falling apart during the next storm. But these ships are being deliberately sunk during calm weather, allowing their crews to take safe passage by small boat to land. This has always happened in areas of sea close to the coast of England. Their purpose, so it seems, is to collect insurance money."

"Fraud," I muttered, with a knowing nod.

"Such fraudulent activities are not unknown to us at Scotland Yard," Inspector Lestrade told us.

"But this is much more than simple fraud," she continued. "It involves murder. When we dive down to examine these wrecks, we often find people trapped inside. Men who have been deliberately left inside those wrecked ships. Abandoned to drown."

"How do you know their drowning was deliberate?"

"Because each time, they had been kept inside a locked cabin. With their hands tied up. And they have all drowned. The latest sinking took place only a couple of weeks ago. I remember the faces of those drowned men. Three of them in all." She ran her hand over her eyes, as though hoping to erase the memory. "Horrible."

All of this seemed to me nothing but daydreaming. Perhaps a good long rest, together with some decent medication, would solve her problems.

For several minutes, Sherlock Holmes remained in quiet contemplation. The rest of us looked on, with an air of expectation. What would the great man decide to do? Would he believe this demented young woman, or send her packing?

Holmes finally stood up. "Gentlemen, and Miss Waters, I believe we need to investigate this matter further, and to do so with the utmost urgency. We are entering dark waters here, so to speak, and we must call upon Scotland Yard to support us in our endeavours." He looked to Lestrade, who made an enigmatic shrug.

"What exactly do you have in mind, Holmes?" I asked.

"Miss Waters," he began. "Do you remember the name of the ship you investigated? The one that was sunk most recently."

The young lady thought for a moment. "I seem to remember it was the *Chauncey Smith*, or something like that."

Holmes rummaged through a pile of old newspapers cuttings for a few minutes, and then uttered a cry of delight as he retrieved the news report of the vessel's loss. "Indeed. The *Chauncey Smith*." He turned to me. "Watson, I want you to find out all you can about this vessel."

I sighed as I resigned myself unwillingly to this crazy adventure. Inspired by one madwoman, and under insubstantial threats from another.

"I'll go to the Royal Exchange building, and find out what Lloyds of London can tell us," I replied.

"Capital!" exclaimed Holmes. "In the meantime, I shall accompany the young lady and Inspector Lestrade to Scotland Yard, where I hope Miss Waters might be able to identify those men she saw in the sunken wreck."

*****

Like a schoolboy sent on a mission for which he has no passion whatsoever, I set off on foot toward the oddly shaped Royal Exchange building in Cornhill. I thought the walk would do me good, and help clear my mind of all this nonsense. It did nothing of the sort.

I arrived at the Royal Exchange in a confusion of mind, and sought out there the premises of Lloyd's of London, the center for insurance and financial dealings, particularly regarding maritime matters.

There I set about my inquiries, which led me to an Insurance Broker by the name of Maidstone. He seemed a decent enough chap, and we were soon talking about acquaintances we had in common. Then our discussion turned to the subject of lost ships.

"We have had quite a spate of them lately," Maidstone told me.

"I am particularly interested in the *Chauncey Smith*," I informed him.

He raised his eyebrows. "Are you indeed?"

"There seems to be something peculiar about the sinking of that particular vessel," I continued.

"You don't have to tell me that," grumbled Maidstone. "The loss of that ship is proving to be a costly business all round. And that is just one of many similar sinking over recent months. I have been organizing the insurance for many of them. And it has cost my insurers a pretty packet, I can tell you. It has also not done much good to my own reputation as a broker."

"What ships do you have in mind?"

Maidstone pulled out a ledger, and flipped through it, stopping occasionally to draw my attention to one or other of the ships for which he had arranged insurance.

"And the *Chauncey Smith*?"

"Much the same. It seems that this was just one more ship, a twenty-year old brig that had been rescued from the scrapyard. But she was then insured for a massive amount of money. Far more than the vessel was worth."

"That has to be fraudulent," I told him.

"Certainly highly unethical as far as the owners are concerned."

"And who are the owners?"

Maidstone gave a sick smile. "Wouldn't we all like to know? It seems the owners are hiding behind an offshore holding company called Corvillo Holdings."

"The owners must have their offices in London."

"If you can find them, I'd be happy to know where they are."

*****

I left the offices of Lloyds, having achieved very little. It seemed now that something dishonest had certainly been going on, and I had a name to follow up which meant nothing to me.

At Scotland Yard, I found Holmes and Miss Waters sitting at a desk where they were scanning through a pile of photographs.

"Modern nineteenth century technology," Lestrade explained proudly. "Whenever possible, we keep photographs of criminals who pass through our doors. Which is how we have managed to give names to those men Miss Waters saw drowned."

Miss Waters looked up at me, and pointed to two photographs lying on the table. "Those two men. I definitely recognize them," she told me.

"Through the young lady's description, we have also managed to identify the third man," said Lestrade.

"And these three are the ones that Miss Waters found dead."

"So she assures me," said Lestrade. "We know that a war is currently being waged between several East End gangs, and these men were all members of one of those gangs."

"But where does that take us?"

"That all depends," said Holmes, "on what you have managed to find out from Lloyds."

"Very little," I replied dolefully. "It seems there have been other ships sunk in similar circumstances. Calm seas. Old vessels insured for vast amounts of money, which has been claimed from the insurers upon their loss."

"And who owns these vessels?" demanded Holmes.

"I asked, but my contact at Lloyds could give me only the name of a holding company. Corvillo Holdings."

"Then we must find out who they are and, more significantly, where we can find the ship's owners."

"Agreed."

Sherlock Holmes consulted the clock on the wall. "We have had an interesting few hours," he decided. "So I suggest we call it a day, and see what the morrow brings."

"What about Miss Waters?" I asked him.

"I am sure Mrs Hudson can find a corner where the young lady may settle down for the night. But first I am also sure that Miss Waters would be well served by one of our landlady's most excellent evening meals."

Mrs Hudson was delighted to have a new charge to fuss over and, after a healthy meal, the two women set about sharing gossip and opinions.

Later that evening, seated in my chair, replete and ready for a nap, I was interrupted by the arrival of Mrs Hudson.

"Excuse me, gentlemen," she said. "But that is a most unusual young lady you have there."

"Miss Waters?"

"A suitably apt name, if ever there was one."

"How do you mean?"

Our landlady placed something onto the dining table. "I found this in the bath after she had finished there."

It appeared to be a fish scale.

"Most unusual," said I.

"Most interesting," said Holmes. "Leave the matter with us, Mrs Hudson."

She nodded and left.

I sat studying the fish scale, but I could make no sense of it.

Holmes changed his attire and headed for the door.

"Are you going somewhere, Holmes?" I asked.

"Merely to make arrangements for tomorrow," he told me, and was gone.

*****

The following morning, I appeared in the living room, ready for a decent breakfast, only to find that Holmes was already there, as indeed was Miss Waters. Both had a sparkle in their eyes, which made me wonder what they had planned.

"Where do we go now, Holmes?" I asked as I tackled a slice of toasted bread.

"This morning we have an appointment," he informed me. "To interview a certain gentleman. Although that might not be a completely fitting description of him."

"Has this anything to do with this gangland war?"

"Indeed," said Holmes. "Those three who were drowned must have been sent to their deaths by one of their rival gangs. All I had to do was to find out who was in charge of that rival gang."

"And did you?"

"Oh, yes. A nasty character if ever there was one, by the name of Jack Kavan."

"But why do we want to speak to him?"

"Remember, Watson, we are trying to find out who owned that vessel. The *Chauncey Smith*. And who better than a man who has an interest in using the vessel to dispose of his unwanted rivals. However unpleasant, he is the only person we know of who can tell us. He asks us to go and visit him this morning. All three of us."

We took a cab to a street which lay deep within London's East End. There we were stopped by a gang of men, all armed with cudgels. They looked a rough and vicious lot.

"Mr Holmes?" grunted the one wearing a bowler hat.

"I am Holmes," replied my companion.

"Yer brought the girl wiv yer?"

"Indeed. Just as Kavan demanded."

The ruffian gave a toothless grin.

I climbed down, and helped Miss Waters out of the cab.

Bowler Hat spoke to the cabbie. "You wait 'ere."

He then led the three of us through a narrow gap between two rows of houses. We emerged into a courtyard, where another carriage stood, ready to depart. "Get in," growled our guide.

A couple of other men climbed into the vehicle, and tied blindfolds around our eyes.

"What's this for?" I demanded.

"Yer wanna see Kavan, don't yer?"

This vehicle then rumbled away. I could feel every cobblestone, but I had no idea where we were heading.

After several minutes, we stopped. The door of the vehicle was opened, and hands removed our blindfolds.

I looked around. We had arrived at the entrance to a dim and dingy alleyway, where the air was thick with the stench of decay.

"Out!" demanded Bowler Hat. And we all three stepped down onto the filthy cobbles.

With three other thugs prodding us from behind, we followed Bowler Hat down the alleyway, to a door at the far end.

This was pulled open as we arrived, and those behind us pushed us inside.

Here we found ourselves in a long, dark room, with gas-lights on the walls, and a long table preventing us from advancing any farther.

A voice behind us told us to place our firearms onto the table.

Holmes and I did as we were ordered.

At the far end of the table sat a small man. Fat and repulsive. He was flanked by thugs even more vicious than the ones who had brought us here.

I wondered what on earth we were doing in such a place.

It was Sherlock Holmes who spoke first.

"You must be Jack Kavan."

"And you Sherlock Holmes," came the man's grating reply.

"Indeed."

"Now, to what do I owe the pleasure of having you under my roof, Mr Holmes?"

"We have been investigating the deaths of three men, drowned in the ship the *Chauncey Smith*."

"Is that supposed to mean something to me?"

"I am convinced that their deaths are part of the conflict presently in progress between you and your rivals."

"How interesting."

"We are currently trying to identify the owners of that ship. And of others which have gone down in similar suspicious circumstances during recent months."

"Why would you want to know?"

"We want to put an end to the activities of those who are defrauding honest people who are forced to carry the resulting high insurance payments."

"That is hardly my problem, Mr Holmes."

"Perhaps not. But I imagine that you use these people to dispose of your unwanted enemies, without leaving any trace."

The man called Kavan was clearly becoming bored by our conversation. He shifted in his seat and declared, "I am not a charity, Mr Holmes. I see no reason why I should assist Scotland Yard in their investigations."

"I am not Scotland Yard," declared Holmes, "merely a private consulting detective. So giving me the name of the shipping owners would do little to damage either your own reputation or your many other activities."

Kavan leaned forward and fixed his dark eyes upon Holmes. "What's in this for Jack?" he demanded. "What do I get out of it?"

"I am here neither to bargain nor to beg," said Holmes. "Merely to invite you to do the right thing."

"Hah! If you are trying to save my soul, Mr Holmes, then I have to tell you that you are far too late for that." The two men stared at each other for a full minute. Then the man seated at the far end coughed. "Very well, Mr Holmes. You don't know where you are now, so you can hardly return with half the constabulary of London in tow."

"True."

"Those people are criminals, Mr Holmes. They are trying to put pressure on me to pay them more for their services. As a result, I am considering ending my relationship with them. In that case, it is no skin off my nose to give you their name."

"That is all I am asking."

"Very well. The name of the firm you are looking for is Maldemoor and Jones."

"And where do I find this firm?"

"They have an office above a warehouse somewhere down by the river."

"Where exactly?"

"That is for you to find out. I'm sure you will have little trouble finding them through the many contacts you have. Now I must ask you to leave."

"Thank you for your help, Mr Kavan," replied Holmes finally.

"One more thing." Jack Kavan leaned forward "Mr Holmes. I allowed you in here on the strength of your reputation as a fair man. But getting out of here will be a very different matter."

"Different? How so?"

"The price for you and Dr Watson leaving this place unharmed is that you leave the young woman here. Her job will be to amuse my men."

The other men in the room shared cruel grins with each other.

"You unutterable swine!" I shouted. "How dare you!"

"If you want to leave here in one piece, Dr Watson, then I suggest you go now. But not with the girl."

I looked at Miss Waters. But her face showed a calmness which was entirely absent from myself. "Don't you realize what they are going to do to you?" I asked her.

"I do realize the dangers," replied Miss Waters. "But go now, while you still can. I'll be fine. Really I will."

I turned to Holmes. But he was remaining coldly aloof from our discussion. What was going on here?

"I shall join you both shortly," whispered Miss Waters. "Give me ten minutes."

Bowler Hat picked up our firearms from the table, removed the ammunition from each of them, and then handed them back to us.

Whilst one of the ruffians dragged Miss Waters through one doorway, others pushed myself and Holmes outside through another.

With my mind so obsessed with concern about the young woman, I hardly remember the journey back, once more blindfolded. We arrived at our cab and retook our seats.

"How can you remain so calm?" I asked Holmes. "Think of what they are doing to Miss Waters."

"We wait."

"For what. She is hardly going to turn up here safe and sound again."

But that is exactly what she did do a few minutes later.

Miss Waters opened the door, and pushed her way inside. Holmes called to the driver to take us back to Baker Street.

I looked in amazement at Miss Waters.

Holmes passed her a handkerchief. "You have blood on your chin, Miss Waters. You had better wipe if off before Mrs Hudson sees you."

She favored us with a blooded smile. It might have been my imagination, but I thought her teeth seemed more canine than those of normal people. "Relax, gentlemen; this is not my blood. That fellow bled like a sea cow."

But my blood still ran cold as ice. "And is he dead?" I asked.

"Oh, yes. But he only had himself to blame, after threatening to cut my throat and dump my body in the sewers."

"And how did you manage to find your way back here again?"

"Dr Watson, you have to realize that a girl like me has many more skills up her sleeve than even you can imagine."

I dared not ask any further questions, for fear of what the answers might be.

*****

Leaving Miss Waters and me at Baker Street, Sherlock Holmes went his own way to spend the rest of the forenoon making inquiries amongst his many contacts. He returned in time for luncheon. A meal of which I partook very little, following the events of the morning, which had robbed me of my appetite for food.

I finally broke the silence on the matter of our next step. "Well, Holmes, what do we do now?"

"The firm of Maldemoor and Jones occupies an office in the Montmorency building a little way below London Bridge. I suggest we continue our inquiries there."

We left almost immediately, with Miss Waters as eager as Holmes to be on the chase. Myself somewhat less so.

Our cab deposited us beside a large warehouse down by the River Thames, and Holmes led the way in through the main doorway.

A sign on the wall, with a finger pointing up a flight of steps, indicated that we were on the right track. We found the office we were looking for on the third floor.

Holmes knocked upon the beige painted door and, when a man in a dark suit answered, Miss Waters and I followed him inside.

"Now, gentlemen, how may I help you?" asked the man who had answered the door. He was clearly a secretary.

"We would like to see Mr Maldemoor," said Holmes.

"Do you have an appointment?"

"No."

"Or else, Mr Jones," I added.

"Oh, I am sorry. Mr Jones is merely a sleeping partner in the company. But Mr Maldemoor is available. Who shall I say is asking to see him?"

"Tell him Sherlock Holmes, Dr Watson and Miss Doris Waters would like to speak to him."

A moment later, we were standing in the inner office, a room with a window facing out onto the river, and a wall covered in paintings of foreign places most of which I was unable to recognize. On the other side of the central desk stood a man of perhaps forty, with thinning hair and bushy sideburns.

"Good morning, Mr Maldemoor," said Holmes. "It is good of you to meet us."

"I hardly had any choice, given the circumstances. One cannot refuse an interview with a man of such reputation as yours, Mr Holmes."

"Indeed."

"So, how may I help you?"

"Am I correct in saying that your company deals in shipping, Mr Maldemoor?"

"Not really," he replied with a smile. "We deal mostly with real-estate. We trade in property."

"But you have in the past purchased vessels which were close to the end of their useful lives."

Maldemoor scanned our faces, and seemed to be thinking carefully how to reply.

"Who told you that?"

"It is true, is it not, that you take out insurance on such ships. Vessels such as the *Chauncey Smith*, for example. No doubt purchased for next to nothing in price."

"There is nothing illegal about that." The man's attitude had turned decidedly frosty.

"And you do all this through your holding company. Corvillo Holdings. An organization which I suspect you yourself control."

The man now grew belligerent. "I am not sure what you are getting at, Mr Holmes. But if you had any real evidence that I am involved in something illegal, then you would have brought the police with you. I suggest that you leave now."

"But there is more to the matter than mere shady dealings," continued Holmes. "You also help a certain East End gang to dispose of their rivals. At a price."

The man from the outside office came in, and handed Maldemoor a paper, and left. Maldemoor read through the paper, and then returned his attention to us. His expression had altered. From belligerence to sweetness, in a heartbeat.

"It is true that we purchase elderly vessels. As a matter of fact we have one, a rather elderly ship, ready to sail today. Her holds are filled with machine parts, bound for France. I would be happy for you to see around that vessel, and satisfy yourselves that all you are suggesting is nonsense."

Holmes nodded. "Very well."

"Splendid. I shall arrange for our steam-launch to take you downriver to the docks, and there you can inspect her for yourselves."

The weather was fine and the air was clear as we made our way by launch down past the hundreds of ships berthed in the Port of London. I watched carefully as we passed the vessels, until my eyes fixed upon one, a small, ancient, wooden schooner. Here we drew alongside, and I was able to read the vessel's name: *Ocean Mischief.*

"Here we are, gentlemen and lady," said the man at the wheel. "Be careful as you step on board. The woodwork can be slippery."

A moment later, we all three were standing on the deck of the *Ocean Mischief.* Preparations appeared to be underway for the vessel to sail.

A man stepped out from the shadows. "Good afternoon," he said with a chuckle. "I am Marsden, the ship's captain. Welcome to this splendid vessel of mine."

"She has clearly seen better days, by the look of her," I told him.

"We have not had her for very long, so I can give no guarantee as to her seaworthiness. But now that you are here, I would like to invite you to inspect her. We can begin with the fo'c'sle."

We followed him to the bows of the vessel, and down a short companionway, into a cabin that was furnished with simple and well-worn seating. The atmosphere there felt stuffy, and smelt of tar and stale human sweat. Two men dressed in dark sweaters stepped forward and fastened a length of rope around the wrists of each of us.

"Here," I cried. "What do you think you're doing?"

"You are going on a voyage," came a woman's voice. A voice I recognized.

We all three looked round, and found ourselves in the presence of Miss Adeline Glendower.

"I suppose you are all surprised to see me again. Especially you, Miss Waters. When Scotland Yard refused to prosecute you, I promised you I would deal with you myself. And now the time has come. Without your tail, you are just as vulnerable to drowning as any other human being."

"Kindly explain yourself, Miss Glendower," said Holmes. "You may have a complaint against Miss waters, but why are we all three here?"

"Blame it on your insatiable curiosity," she replied bitterly. "You just could not keep your nose out of my business, could you? Now that I have you in my power, I am able to do whatever I wish with you. But to explain, let me tell you that from the moment Miss Waters returned to Folkestone a couple of weeks ago, she has been talking about a ship called the *Chauncey Smith*. Searching for any news of it. I decided to make my own inquiries into that vessel, and my investigations led me through some unsavory backwaters of underground London, and finally to the firm of Maldemoor and Jones. I found out about their little scheme, to sink ships and claim on the insurance."

"And their murdering of East End gangsters."

"You are hardly in a position to criticize those men, Mr Holmes. Not after what Miss Waters did to one of Kavan's men earlier today. Oh yes, I heard about that. Jack Cavan is livid and has ordered that she be killed. And I am responsible for making sure that it happens."

"It was entirely a matter of self-preservation," growled Miss Waters. "And you know that."

Adeline chuckled. "Sit down and make yourselves comfortable," she told us. "As I told you, we are going on a journey."

We took our places sitting on the bunks. This had obviously been the haunt of the ship's crew until recently, but tonight this would be our prison. The others would have to sleep elsewhere.

As Miss Glendower left the fo'c'sle, somebody closed the hatch and secured it with a lock on the outside. The only light we now had was filtering in through the dirty skylight above us.

We sat together, thoughtful but saying very little. When the daylight had grown perceptibly dimmer, we heard another boat pull up alongside. From up on deck, the crew led two other men down into the fo'c'sle. These also had their hands tied. They were rough looking men, and it was reasonable to assume that these were Kavan's latest consignment of unwanted rivals from London's underworld. The men chose to take their seats on a bunk at the far end of the fo'c'sle, and watched the three of us with a mixture of scorn and extreme displeasure. They recognized Holmes, and relished the idea of him sharing the same fate as themselves.

Miss Glendower scanned our gathering with contempt.

"I am sorry to have to inform you that there is no room-service operating on board this ship, but I can assure you that your time here will be limited."

She then turned, and climbed back up on deck, leaving us to our own contemplations.

With my hands tied, I was feeling helpless, but Holmes appeared to be occupying another world entirely. With the prospect of impending death, his face showed a serenity which I certainly did not share. No doubt he was using meditation techniques he had picked up during his travels in Tibet. Techniques I had never been able to master.

Miss Waters sat with her eyes closed, at least giving the impression of being on the verge of sleep. Only I was left awake and alert, with my attention fixed upon the two men at the far end of the limited space available. Once the two thugs had tired of shouting insults, they settled down. But I still kept them in sight. I had no doubt that, if anything untoward happened, Holmes would have sprung to life immediately. But I was used to sitting up alone all night. My time in Afghanistan had often demanded my attention throughout the night, in order to keep safe the encampment of our soldiers. As a physician, I had often had to stand vigil over the sickbed of those nearing the end of their lives. This night was little different from many of those.

*****

The schooner sailed in the small hours, but since the only view of the outside world was through that dingy overhead sky-light, it was difficult to follow the course of our journey downriver.

By the time the light of the sun had turned the visible patch of sky from indigo to a rich cerulean blue, I assumed that we had traveled downstream for many miles. Apart from the passage of time, there was little way of telling how far that might be.

For several hours, the only sounds that reached us were of water splashing against the hull, and the creaking of the ship's rigging. At least the water appeared to be reasonably calm.

I finally heard the sails being lowered, and realized that we had stopped, apparently in mid-ocean.

My companions were now awake.

Holmes looked up, and also listened to the activity up on deck. "I think we have arrived," he announced.

"But where?" I demanded.

"Perhaps several miles off the coast of Essex. Several fathoms above our intended final resting place."

A shudder ran down my spine. "At least they have chosen a pleasant day for it."

Sounds now came to us from below.

"The crew will be making preparations to scuttle the ship," said Holmes. "Opening the vents to allow seawater to flood in."

The men at the far end of the saloon, having no doubts now about their intended fate, resumed their shouting and cursing.

"I think the time has come, Miss Waters," said Holmes, "for you to deal with the situation."

"What are you expecting me to do, Mr Holmes?"

"Use your singular skills, of course," he replied.

"Oh, those." She raised her bonds to her mouth and began to gnaw at the strands of rope. The sight of such unnatural behaviour by an apparently civilized young woman made my blood run cold. And not for the first time during those days. Within a very short space of time, her bonds were severed and her hands were free.

Miss Waters then proceeded to release Holmes and myself.

I offered my thanks, and asked, "What about those other men?"

"They probably deserve to go down with the ship," replied Holmes. "But you had better cut them free, and let them swim for their lives, if they can."

He handed me a knife from concealment deep within his clothing.

Whilst I was busy releasing the other men, Holmes had little difficulty in opening the saloon door. Miss Waters and I followed him out into the daylight, where I took a deep breath of sea air, and relished the salty tang.

I looked around. The only sign of land was a line on the horizon to the west of us. A white sail was also visible, a couple of miles astern.

"That will be the coastguard cutter I arranged to follow us," said Holmes. "I only hope Lestrade doesn't suffer from seasickness."

A few feet away from us, off the port quarter, we saw the ship's boat bobbing in the ocean swell. It was full of the ship's crew. A half dozen men, and one woman.

The head of Adeline Glendower appeared over the gunwale. "I'm going to sit here and watch you all drown," she yelled.

"I don't think so," shouted back Miss Waters. "You now have a choice to make, Addy. You can wait for the police to arrive in their cutter, or you can come and join me in the depths of the sea. Or else you can drown."

The other woman's face twisted into something resembling a demonic mask. "If you go free, I shall have both Kavan and Maldemoor after my blood. Jack has engineered the death of several young woman in recent years, and I have no wish to be found tomorrow morning in the gutter with my throat cut. I think I would rather drown." With that, and a loud curse, she stood up and threw herself into the water, where she immediately sank from view. I never saw her again.

Beneath our feet, the ship began to heel over, preparatory to sinking below the surface. The men from the saloon now joined us up on deck. They too would have to wait for the cutter, or else drown.

With a loud creaking sound, a spar from the mizzenmast collapsed across the deck, and something heavy landed on my head.

*****

"Watson! Watson!" A voice seemed to be calling to me from far away, as I gradually regained consciousness. It was a voice I recognized.

I opened my eyes, and saw that I was now lying in a hospital bed, a substantial iron-framed construction, recumbent between clean white sheets. My head was hurting, and I discovered a bandage wrapped round it. I looked around. To one side of the bed stood my friend, Sherlock Holmes. Beside him, in a bath-chair, sat Miss Waters, looking as charming as she had upon our first meeting.

"Holmes?" I croaked.

"Yes, my dear fellow. You are quite safe now."

"What happened?"

"Utter chaos broke loose," replied Holmes. "One of the spars hit you and knocked you into the sea. Miss Waters had to dive in and rescue you. Then we had to pump you free of seawater, and bring you here to be assessed by the medical staff. But they say you are suffering from nothing more serious than mild concussion."

"In that case, Miss Waters, I am truly grateful to you for your swift action," I said, smiling at the young lady. "But where is here?"

"Southend-on-Sea," replied Holmes. "The nearest port we could reach which had a hospital."

"How about everyone else?"

"Adeline Glendower drowned. I fear she must have lost her mind, particularly with the prospect of being murdered by one of Kavan's mob. But we managed to rescue the others when the coastguard cutter arrived a few minutes later. They took everyone else on board. Now it will be up to Scotland Yard to decide what to do with them all."

"And Maldemoor?"

"He seems to have disappeared."

Miss Waters gave me a delightful smile. "The time has now come for me to go home, Dr Watson. Mr Holmes has been kind enough to arrange transport for me."

"Home? You mean, to Folkestone?"

"Maybe a little farther away."

"In that case, farewell to you, Miss Waters. Or Mrs Chatteris as I ought to call you."

"And farewell to you, Dr Watson. Have good dreams." Holmes turned the bath-chair toward the door. Then stopped. "I keep telling you, Watson, when you have rejected all other possibilities, the one remaining, however unlikely it might be, has to be the truth."

I nodded, still not sure what he meant by such a remark.

Miss Waters gave me a wicked grin, cocked her head to one side and lifted the edge of the blanket which until now had been covering the lower part of her body.

I expected to see a pair of shapely female ankles. Instead, I saw a tail, a fluke, of which any self-respecting whale or porpoise might be justly proud.

A moment later, she was gone. And I was left to reassess all that I had seen and witnessed during the last couple of days, in the light of that parting revelation, and in the light of the wisdom of Mr Sherlock Holmes.

The Gravesend Gryphon
(Sequel to The Man with the Twisted Lip)

My notes fail to properly express the intense curiosity I felt that morning. I have to admit, I was intrigued. I had arrived at the sitting-room in Baker Street which I had formerly shared with Mr Sherlock Holmes, only to discover my friend standing before a black chalkboard, white marker in hand. A few feet away from him stood Scotland Yard's Inspector Lestrade, staring intently at the markings that Holmes was still making upon that board.

I only had myself to blame, of course, since I had arrived at such an early hour, completely unannounced and unexpected. Or so I imagined.

"Come along in, Watson," said Holmes cordially, as I appeared in the doorway. Nor did he appear the least bit surprised at my spontaneous arrival. "I have been expecting you."

"You have?" I had become accustomed to the extraordinary turns of my friend's mind, most notably his ability to arrive at astonishing deductions from the most trivial of facts, but this particular statement seemed to stretch the limits of plausibility even for him.

"It is no mystery whatsoever, my dear fellow," said Holmes, innocently. "Consider the facts. Your wife is away from home, visiting her sister, I believe. And, with the summer now upon us, many of your patients will be feeling the benefits of more clement weather, whilst others will inevitably be taking the waters at some fashionable spar town or other, and making rather fewer demands upon your time."

"All true," I admitted, feeling slightly crestfallen by the simplicity of his explanation. "But why today?"

"Such a bright and sunny morning is sufficient to tempt outside even the most housebound of physicians. Besides, with your wife away, you will no doubt be attracted by the recollection of Mrs Hudson's excellent cooking."

I chuckled to myself, and changed the subject. "Now, tell me, Holmes, whatever are you up to here?"

Sherlock Holmes stood back from the board, to admire his own handiwork. "As you can see, Watson, I have drawn a rough map of London, and pinpointed certain locations and dates upon it. These represent the particulars of the most notorious crimes committed within the Metropolitan area during the last four months."

"So I see, but what makes this precise period of time of special interest to both you and Scotland Yard?"

"Allow me to explain," said Lestrade. "As you may have read in the newspapers, Dr Watson, the Metropolitan Police force has recently seen a significant increase in the number of the more serious crimes committed within the city of London itself: the murders of influential people, break-ins at properties owned by prominent citizens, and theft from high-profile public buildings. These and other crimes have all grown significantly both in gravity and in frequency during that period of time. Serious crime here within the last four months has become rampant, and demands for the attention of Scotland Yard have grown alarmingly."

"It is therefore in order to shed some light upon the reasons for this disturbing increase that we have marked the site of each of these crimes upon our plan of London," said Holmes.

I looked closer, almost squinting at the map. "If you are looking for some pattern to those crimes, then I certainly cannot discern one."

"Then allow me to explain further," continued Lestrade. "In almost every case, we have been able to identify the perpetrator, each within only a couple of days of the crime taking place. Such is the result of dogged and vigilant police work… together with occasional help from Mr Holmes here. There are only so many men in London who are capable of committing some of these more serious crimes. And each man has his own peculiarities, which enable us to identify him: the murder instrument chosen… the method of entry selected… the particular items stolen. Together or separately, these all point to a small pool of criminals, most of whom are already known to us. In each case, we have been able to identify our suspects, and follow their movements across town. However, by the time we are ready to arrest the man and bring charges against him, my men can find no trace of our quarry. Each one appears to have vanished from the face of the Earth."

"Great Scott!"

"Quite so."

"Is there nothing at all that these crimes have in common? Some pattern, perhaps, that I have failed to detect?"

"That is the purpose of our current consultation, and of my map," declared Holmes.

"Indeed," continued Lestrade, stepping closer to the map, and holding another piece of chalk in his hand. "In each case, our suspect was last seen in the vicinity of Upper Swandown Lane. One was observed in the street itself." He marked the position of the lane on the chart. "Two others disappeared from a nearby tavern called the *Blue Unicorn*." This he marked with a cross. "And two others have vanished from adjacent alleyways. Here and here." He marked them also on the map. "We are rapidly coming to the conclusion that we might be dealing with an organized gang, perhaps of professional criminals."

As Lestrade stepped back, Holmes took his place at the map and chalked a white circle around the infamous thoroughfare now identified upon his carefully drawn map.

"There, within that circle, we shall undoubtedly find the common factor in all of these cases."

"Upper Swandown Lane," I concluded. "In such a place as that, the most likely explanation for these disappearances has to be that they have all been murdered, and their bodies dropped into the river."

"But for what reason?" demanded Lestrade. "None that we can discern."

"Thieves are not known for their comradely fellowship," I opined. "Perhaps the various gangs are settling outstanding disputes."

"Unless perhaps some more powerful mind is at work here," said Holmes, mysteriously. He then turned to the Inspector. "Is there any further information you can provide us with, Lestrade?"

"Only that these crimes, and the subsequent disappearances, take place at regular intervals."

"Regular?"

"Indeed so. Every ten to fourteen days."

"A coincidence?"

"These crimes are happening too regularly for that to be the case."

"Then we must conclude that the events are synchronized in some way."

"That is how it seems to us, Mr Holmes."

"Which brings us back to the possibility of some sophisticated criminal organization being at work here."

"To summarize," said I, attempting to consolidate my grasp of the situation. "There has been neither sign nor sight of these villains since your men lost them in the backstreets of that notorious end of the metropolis. And no bodies have been discovered?"

"Neither alive nor dead. Neither in the river nor out of it."

Holmes sat down, concentrating his attention upon the map he had drawn. He reached for his old briar pipe, the slipper containing his tobacco pouch, and a box of matches.

The signs were now inescapable. My friend was withdrawing into one of his meditative moods. In order to allow him sufficient time and space, I dismissed Inspector Lestrade with the promise that we would be in touch with each other in the event that anything significant transpired.

I made my own way down to Mrs Hudson's rooms, where our landlady greeted me warmly. "It really is good to see you again, Dr Watson," she exclaimed.

"And I to see you, Mrs Hudson."

"I have your breakfast all waiting for you."

"Exactly what I need. But however did you know I would require feeding?"

"A little of Mr Holmes's powers of deduction have rubbed off onto me over the years, Dr Watson. Along with a certain second-sight that becomes natural to women over a certain age."

I nodded, not entirely certain of her meaning.

"Besides," she added. "I recognized the distinctive sound of your feet upon the stairs."

"Yes, I admitted, "my tread is one of my most distinguishing features."

"And is your wife well?"

"Oh, yes, but she is away visiting her sister at the moment."

"Then breakfast it has to be."

*****

As I was finishing off my last slice of toast, and my final cup of coffee, I was alerted by the abrupt arrival of Sherlock Holmes, now bright eyed and seemingly ready for action.

"Come along, Watson," said he. "We have work to do. Are you with me?"

"Today, Holmes, if anything needs doing, then I am definitely your man."

"Splendid. But you will need to change into something less formal, you will find some of your old clothes in your room. Then let us make our way down to Upper Swandam Lane."

After all that I had learned whilst listening to Holmes and Inspector Lestrade, I was not surprised to learn the identity of our destination, although admittedly I remained apprehensive about what we might discover in such a disreputable area of town. A hansom cab ride, followed by a brisk walk, brought us finally to that vile alley, the condition of which I had been trying to forget. Holmes was now dressed in a navy-blue working jacket and cap, and I had on a bottle-green cord coat, with a cravat around my neck.

We concealed ourselves in the entrance to a disused building on the opposite side of the lane from the establishment bearing the name the Bar of Gold. The place smelled of mildew and rats.

"There is that accursed opium den," I said, keeping my voice low. "The entrance lies down those steps, does it not? Are we to go inside?"

"Not this time, Watson. We already know that toward the rear of that building lies an opening in the floor, sealed by a heavy trapdoor. I am convinced that Lestrade's missing villains are using that as a means of escaping the clutches of the law."

"But that must lead directly to the river itself."

"I have carefully considered all the possibilities," declared Holmes, "and I am persuaded that this is the best and only secure means of escape open to our absconding villains."

"If so, then they must be desperate men."

"Desperate, perhaps, but also confident of their ability to evade the clutches of Lestrade's men."

"What can we do now?"

"We make our way down to the river Thames," said Holmes. "Come along, Watson."

Keeping to the shadows, and watching where we placed our feet, Holmes and I made our way through the far-from-fresh air, and along a narrow alleyway which led down to the riverside. Here we could see the river traffic, serving the busiest port in the world, passing us in both directions. Keeping to the deeper stretches of the river, vessels powered by sail or steam crowded the waterway, together with a bevy of barges and their flat-bottomed lighters. Here was the hub of a vast empire of trade. Along the river, and among the numerous dock systems lining its banks, we could see dockers, lightermen and stevedores going about their work, like a vast army of industrious ants.

Holmes made his way down on the shingled foreshore which still lay exposed and awaiting the rising tide. I took my place beside him, pulling my coat collar up tighter around my neck. Even with the sun shining, a chill breeze was blowing up the river and ruffling the water into a myriad wavelets.

"From here, we can observe the underside of Upper Swandam Lane," said Holmes. "The less respectable side."

"I find it difficult to imagine that there can possibly be a less desirable side to such a dreadful thoroughfare," I told him.

Holmes pointed to a section of the building directly above us, overhanging the position where we were standing. An uninterrupted wooden wall rose from there, and cast its menacing shadow across the riverside.

"Now. Can you see it?" said Holmes.

"See what?"

"That trapdoor, of course."

"Ah, yes. Now I see it." The door, situated on the underside of the overhang, was almost invisible in the shadows, discernible only by the variation in the way the grain extended at right angles to the rest of the discolored woodwork. "When the tide is in, and this area is under water, that door will be situated directly above the river."

"I can imagine that door being used to discard many a human body over the years," I told him, with a shudder.

"But, in this case," said Holmes, "I rather think they are being lowered down, very much alive, through that hatchway and into a small boat waiting exactly where we are now standing. It almost certainly occurs during the hours of darkness, depending upon the tide."

"Most ingenious. But where do those scoundrels go from here?"

"That is the next question to be considered," said Holmes. "The nearest riverside landing-stage is Paul's Wharf. You can clearly see the near end of it from here. It has to lie no more than a few oar-strokes away from this very position."

I followed his indication. "Yes, but the nearest berth appears to be completely empty."

"Worthy of investigation, then."

I accompanied Holmes as he set off from this hidden position, made his way back up into Upper Swandam Lane, turned down a series of even dingier back-lanes, and finally emerged close to the entrance to the wharf itself. With his cap pulled down to conceal his high forehead, his pipe gripped firmly between his teeth, and his hands thrust deep into his coat pockets, he led the way as we approached the wharf caretaker.

"What can I do for you, gents?" the caretaker challenged us as he stood with arms akimbo, and his eyes hooded with suspicion.

Holmes looked around at the vessels occupying the many berths along that part of the riverside. "I am looking for a steamship, *The Grand Duchess*. I was told that her berth lay along here somewhere."

The caretaker rubbed his stubbled chin, as though it would stimulate his concentration. "You must be mistaken, pal. We don't get no steamships on this wharf. Mainly brigs, schooners and the occasional sailing barge. Mostly serving ports along the Thames estuary, and occasionally farther afield."

"But you've plenty of space at the moment," said Holmes as he indicated the vacant mooring.

"Ah, now that'll be for the schooner *The Gravesend Gryphon*. Curious name for a boat, and she's not much to look at either, but she's very particular about where she berths. It has to be here, or nowhere else on the face of the Earth."

"But she won't be back again for a couple of weeks," suggested Holmes, clearly fishing for information.

"Now that's where you are definitely wrong, pal," said the caretaker pointedly. "She'll be back at her berth here by Saturday of this week. She's only gone as far as Harwich. Her usual run. And, if her place ain't ready here at this wharf the very moment she returns, then there'll be real trouble, I can tell you."

"Bad skipper?"

"Oh, he's alright. Old Jack Smithers. No, it's that mate of his. A bloke going by the name of Codworon. Believe me, the mate is the fellow who runs *The Gravesend Gryphon*, and that's the truth of it. Always up to no good, that one. Not that anybody from Scotland Yard can ever catch him at it."

*****

"Mrs Hudson," called out Sherlock Holmes the moment he and I stepped in through the entrance to 221B Baker Street.

"There's no need to shout, Mr Holmes," came our landlady's firm but reassuring voice as she appeared in the hallway.

"I have to warn you to expect a group of street children to appear shortly."

Her manner cooled. "Are you sure about that, Mr Holmes?"

"Indeed. I was the one who invited them to some here. I would be obliged if you would kindly allow the tallest of them to come up to our rooms."

Mrs Hudson sighed, and turned away. "Whatever you say, Mr Holmes."

Within five minutes, the leader of that scruffy little gang known to Holmes as the Baker Street Irregulars, was standing, cap in hand, in the middle of the apartment's sitting-room floor.

He closely resembled an animated scarecrow, with a broad grin lighting up his face.

"You wanted to see me, Mr Holmes?"

"Indeed I did, Wiggins."

"A job, perhaps? I'm sure we can oblige with whatever you have in mind."

"I'm sure you can," replied Holmes, "So listen carefully. This coming Saturday, a schooner called *The Gravesend Gryphon* is due to dock at Paul's wharf."

"I know the place. But I'm surprised you do, Mr Holmes. It's definitely not a place for a gentleman like yourself."

"I want to know as much as you can find out about that vessel. And her crew. I know that the skipper is a man called Jack Smithers, and that the mate is a difficult fellow who goes by the name of Codworon."

Wiggins looked thoughtful. "Finding out things like that might be easy enough for a gentleman such as yourself, Mr

Holmes, but how do you suggest we might get hold of it for you?"

"The boat will have a ship's boy amongst its crew," said Holmes. "I suggest you separate him from the rest of the crew, and have a quiet word with him. But be sure to impress upon him the need to remain silent about your meeting. Not least for the sake of his own skin if the mate gets his hands on him."

"Saturday, you say."

"The day after tomorrow. But time is limited. She will inevitably be sailing again for Harwich within the week."

"It might take us a few days."

"Just so long as you get the information I need."

"Usual rates?"

"Of course."

Over the subsequent few days, Sherlock Holmes studied the daily newspapers with even greater attention than usual.

At first, the only news we heard from the Baker Street Irregulars was that the schooner had indeed arrived at her berth late on the Saturday afternoon. But this made Holmes even more restive, and keen to learn the information he was confident would eventually come his way.

Several days after the arrival of the schooner *The Gravesend Gryphon*, I happened to call in to see my friend once more. This time, I found Holmes in a much improved frame of mind.

"Finally, Watson," he declared with great glee. "A robbery worthy of a front-page mention. It took place at the premises of a large retail store in the West End. The criminal went on the run, but has now disappeared. Scotland Yard are baffled. Nothing unusual there, then."

A sound like thunder upon the stairs alerted us to the fact that we had visitors. The Baker Street Irregulars had arrived. A host of small faces vied with each other for the limited space provided by the open door frame, their enthusiasm pushing at the boundaries of Holmes's hospitality. But as long as they remained outside the doorway, Holmes made no objection.

Wiggins stepped forward with an expression of delight upon his young face.

"It took a long time, but we got what you wanted, Mr Holmes."

"Information about the schooner *The Gravesend Gryphon*?"

"That's right, Mr Holmes."

"Splendid. Well then, come along. What do you have to tell me?"

Wiggin coughed, and began. "It took some doing, but we managed to get the ship's boy, Sniffy Symonds, all on his own for long enough to get some useful information out of him. There's definitely something fishy going on in that vessel."

"And her crew?"

"You told us about the skipper, Jack Smithers, and about the mate, Codworon. Now we know there's the cook. A Chinese bloke, who has the name 'Moo'. But he isn't very popular among the crew, on account of his being not very good at his job. Then there are the deck-hands. And this is where it gets a bit odd, Mr Holmes."

"Pray elucidate."

"Do what, sir?"

"Tell me what's so odd."

"Oh, right. Sniffy says that there are two regular deck-hands, working as permanent members of the crew. But, on their regular voyages, both going and coming back, another man joins them. The crew are told to call this bloke Joe. Always just Joe. But, every time, it's a different fellow. Except that, every so often, they recognize one of them as having sailed with them a few months before. But the mate threatens horrible revenge if anyone ever mentions this fact to anybody else. Even the skipper."

"And it's the mate's job to provide the crew."

"That's right."

"Go on."

"At this end, one Joe gets off, and another Joe gets on. The same happens when they get to Harwich, one Joe gets off, and another Joe gets on."

"And what does young Sniffy think is happening?"

"We asked him about it, but that's when he made his quick getaway. He scarpered like the hounds of hell were after him, and was back on board his ship before we could ask him any more questions."

"And that's it?"

"That's all I can tell you, Mr Holmes."

"Will you be able to have a word with him again before they leave?"

"I don't think so. You see, the schooner *The Gravesend Gryphon* sails for Harwich, and wherever else she has to call in, this very evening."

Holmes passed Wiggins a handful of coins. "Just one thing more."

"Yes, Mr Holmes?" said Wiggins, gleefully pocketing the coins.

"Let me know the very moment that schooner returns to her berth at Paul's wharf."

"Indeed, I shall do that, Mr Holmes."

Holmes turned to me. "It looks as if I might be right about an organized gang, Watson."

"That is certainly how it seems," I told him.

*****

The moment Wiggins and his gang had left, and Mrs Hudson had shut the front door behind them, with her customary sigh of relief, Sherlock Holmes gathered his coat. "Come along, Watson," he said. "We have work to do, and not much time to spare."

"Where are we going at such short notice?" I demanded, looking at my watch and discovering that the evening was already drawing on.

"Why? The Cedars, near Lee in Kent, of course."

I was shocked. "The home of Mr Neville St Clair?"

"The very same."

"But we have sworn to leave that poor man strictly alone following that unfortunate event last summer."

"That cannot be helped, Watson. He is the only man whom I am confident will rise to the challenge I have in mind for him. It might even provide him with a story for his newspaper."

Dusk was turning to night when we reached Lee in Kent. Mr Neville St Clair and his wife welcomed us warmly when we arrived at The Cedars, entirely unexpectedly, at the front door of their home.

"It really is good to see you again, Mr Holmes," exclaimed Mr St Clair. "And you too, Dr Watson. And completely out of the blue as well. I cannot imagine what errand has brought you here tonight. I can only assure you that my old way of life is well and truly over."

"But your skill at applying make-up and taking on the appearance of somebody else was truly remarkable."

He seemed flattered. "Did you really think so?"

"Indeed. And that is the very reason we have come to see you tonight. I am here to discuss with you a matter which would utilize your skills of deception to the fullest."

Mr Neville St Clair raised his eyebrows in surprise. "I thought all that business had been well and truly buried in the past."

"That is true," said Holmes, "but it has now become necessary for Hugh Boone to make one final bow."

"If you wish to revive that painful matter once more, then it is best we do this in a more congenial setting," said Neville St Clair. "Please, gentlemen, make yourselves at home. Take a chair and accept a drop of wine. Both of you."

I accepted the kind invitation, whilst Holmes declined.

"Now, Mr Holmes," said Mr Neville St Clair, taking up his glass of wine. "What exactly can I do to help you?"

"Scotland Yard are currently in their normal state of utter perplexity. Some of the worst criminals in the land seem to be running rings around them. They appear to be losing these wretches like sand through a sieve. My investigations have brought me to believe that a certain schooner called *The Gravesend Gryphon* is the key to this whole business. But I do not yet know what exactly is going on."

"Please expound your theory, Mr Holmes."

"In each case, within a few days of perpetrating some horrendous crime in London, it seems that the criminal makes for the building known as the Bar of Gold."

"A place with which I was once shamefully connected."

"It is my belief that, in each case, the fugitive is lowered down through the trapdoor at the rear of the building into a small boat waiting below, and is immediately taken to a nearby wharf, there to board the schooner. Having arrived on board, he then takes on the guise of a member of the crew. One of the three deck-hands, in fact. At the final destination of the schooner, in Harwich, the criminal leaves, and disappears into the night."

"Ingenious," said Neville St Clair. "And even more resourceful of you to have unravelled the mystery."

Holmes shook his head. "At the present moment, this is all pure speculation, based upon certain information I received only this day. I need proof. I need somebody I can trust on board that schooner, to discover exactly what is going on there."

"And you want me to volunteer to be one of those deck-hands?"

"Show me your hands."

Neville St Clair held out his hands.

"It is obvious to me, Mr St Clair," said Holmes, "as indeed it would be to any other member of the crew, that you are not a working man. Your hands are too soft to have done much in the way of laboring work. The only possibility therefore is that you take over the position of cook."

"Cook?"

"The present one is causing some discontent among the crew. Not just because he happens to be Chinese, but because he is untrained in preparing meals within the confines of a small boat's galley."

"But I am totally unable to cook a meal even here in my own home, Mr Holmes," objected St Clair.

"That's true, Mr Holmes," said Mrs St Clair. "My husband would be more likely to poison than to feed the crew of any ship he served on."

Sherlock Holmes smiled, and rubbed his hands. "Then you will have to learn your cooking skills. I can provide for you an excellent instructor, who will teach you all you need to know. At least for the single voyage I have in mind for you. And that will be sufficient for our needs. If you are willing to be my ears and eyes on board *The Gravesend Gryphon*, then you have between seven and ten days in which to learn your skills. How say you?"

Mr Neville St Clair stood up abruptly and clapped his hands. "I am up for the challenge, Mr Holmes. Hugh Boone will indeed rise again. But just this one last time."

"Good man," said Holmes. "But you will need a disguise."

"If you mean the clothing of a seaman, I seem to remember noticing a slop shop next to the Bar of Gold."

"Capital!" exclaimed Holmes. "I can arrange for the cook to go absent when the schooner returns. Sometime within the next seven to ten days. But you will then need to make contact with the skipper yourself. A certain Jack Smithers. I believe he drinks at a tavern called the *Blue Unicorn*. He will undoubtedly refer you on to the mate. But beware of that man. Codworon. He may well prove be the real villain in this business. He will inevitably try to make life difficult for you. So, be particularly careful of him."

Neville St Clair laughed. "The mate would have to be extremely careful if he chooses to bully the cook. He might well pay for it in the quality of his next meal."

"Very well, then," said Holmes, decisively. "Our landlady, Mrs Hudson, will make the arrangements for your training, and, by the time the schooner returns to her berth, you will be equipped to replace her present cook, and reign supreme in the galley."

The following day, whilst Mrs Hudson was taking our trainee cook in hand, Sherlock Holmes withdrew into his own world of contemplation, filling the entire apartment with a thick cloud of tobacco smoke. I was obliged to take to my erstwhile room, and lose myself in an old medical bulletin. The hours passed without any sign that Holmes had returned to us.

I must have finally fallen asleep, because the next thing I knew, Holmes was shaking me into wakefulness.

"Come along, Watson," said he. "The time has come for us to make our plans, and we need to do it in consultation with our colleagues at Scotland Yard."

I was fully refreshed by the time we sat down opposite Inspector Lestrade, and Holmes leaned forward to explain matters.

"Lestrade, I need your cooperation in apprehending a handful of criminals."

"That would be most helpful, Mr Holmes," said Lestrade guardedly. "We have plenty of felons in our sights just at the moment. Are you thinking of those we were discussing at your rooms the other day?"

"The very ones," said Holmes. "The criminals who seem to be slipping through your fingers at regular intervals, Lestrade."

"And how exactly do you intend to help us capture them, Mr Holmes?"

"I believe that the schooner *The Gravesend Gryphon* is being used as a means of escape for these men. Taking them away from the city, and from the hands of Scotland Yard. I am convinced that these criminals make their escape through the opium den situated beneath the Bar of Gold in Upper Swandam Lane. I believe that each one is lowered down through a trapdoor in the floor. At the same time, another criminal makes the return journey, and is then left to integrate once more into the local criminal fraternity."

"*The Gravesend Gryphon?*"

"Indeed. And, by raiding that infamous building, I can hand over to you not just one but two of the most notorious criminals in London. But leave the schooner alone until I we have a better chance of capturing the entire gang of them."

"And when exactly did you have in mind to make this raid, Mr Holmes?"

"On the night of the schooner's return to her berth on the Paul's Wharf. I intend to take the place of the fugitive and then, with my own man taken on as cook of the vessel, we shall unveil this trickery the moment we reach its destination at the port of Harwich. If you are ready to meet us there, together with a contingent of officers from both the London and the local force, then I am confident of being able to deliver the entire gang into your custody."

"It could be dangerous, Mr Holmes. Are you sure you're doing the right thing?"

"If you can keep the owner of the opium den from calling the alarm, then I believe everything will be well."

"You say you intend to replace the cook with your own man."

"Indeed, but that would require you to take the current cook, a Chinese called 'Moo', into custody. If you keep him for questioning, you might be able to extract the whole story from him. Although I can give no guarantee about that."

*****

News of *The Gravesend Gryphon's* return came so rapidly from the Baker Street Irregulars that Holmes and I were able to watch the schooner make fast to her habitual berth at the Paul wharf. She looked to be a vessel well past her better years. Her sails, on both main and mizzen masts, were stained and showed signs of having been frequently patched. The men on board were already preparing for the unloading of one cargo and the receiving another for the outward journey.

"It will be dark within the hour," said Holmes, "looking up at the now overcast sky. "By then, we must make sure Lestrade has the attendant of the opium den completely under his thumb."

"Are you really going to take the place of this fugitive villain?" I asked him.

"Certainly. It is the only way to reach the bottom of this mystery. And to keep a protective eye on our friend St Clair."

Once Inspector Lestrade sets his mind to something, he can be relied upon to do his very best to bring it to pass. So it was that we met him and a handful of uniformed officers at the entrance to the Bar of Gold. As we made our way inside, and down to the den, the sickly smell of opium, which exuded from the premises and indeed from the very walls themselves, struck us with a blow that was almost physical. The shuffling sound of rapidly moving bodies came from the darkness all around us, as clients hurried to escape disturbance by the law. But, on this occasion, they had no need to worry. We were there for other purposes. Holmes and I accompanied Lestrade down into the bowels of the building, and to that abysmal room where we found the trapdoor, topped by a huge iron ring. A door such as a man might come across in his darkest nightmares, as the gateway to Hell.

The Lascar who ran the den, an unreformed rogue if ever I saw one, appeared in the room in great agitation, giving Lestrade a glare of absolute hatred. I have no idea what threats Lestrade had made against the man, but it was sufficient to make the caretaker cower in the corner of the room.

Now, in growing agitation, I checked the revolver in my pocket.

"What exactly is it you want here?" demanded the Lascar.

"We wait," said Lestrade.

"We wait? For what?"

"You are expecting two guests to pass through this trapdoor tonight."

The Lascar's face betrayed nothing, but neither did he hurry to deny the Inspector's accusation.

Despite their instinct to escape this place, Lestrade and his men waited in silence, with baited breath, as the minutes slowly passed. The Inspector darkened his lantern, and the blackness of night gripped the soul of every sane man amongst us.

The sound of scuffling from the entrance, followed by the noise of footsteps upon the stairs, betrayed the fact that our waiting would shortly be at an end.

A moment later, I became aware of another presence in the room with us.

Lestrade opened his lantern, and raised it to illuminate the face of our newcomer. "Jeremiah Twist, and no mistake," hissed the Inspector.

The man, who had now been taken completely by surprise, let out a bitter cry, and uttered a curse that turned my blood to ice.

As Twist turned to escape, the hands of half a dozen policemen descended upon him, holding him so fast that the man had to gasp for breath.

"Jeremiah Twist," said Lestrade. "I am arresting you for your part in the theft of jewels from the home of Sir John and Lady Langstondale, and the murder of a member of their household." Turning to the constables holding him, he added, "Right men, take him away."

"There goes our first villain," said Holmes, from the darkness.

"What now?" asked Lestrade.

"We need to signal to the schooner that we are ready to receive one criminal and dispatch the other. The signal has to be the opening of this trapdoor, and the emitting of light out into the darkness of the riverside gloom."

A glance at the Lascar's scowling face confirmed that this was indeed the signal that was expected.

Two of the policemen grasped the iron ring, and pulled it. The iron hinges made no complaint, having no doubt been greased liberally every couple of weeks for at least the last four months.

A light flickering through the gloom below, together with the sound of swilling water, declared that somebody was waiting some twelve feet below. But a mist rising from the river was now beginning to obscure our view of the rowboat which undoubtedly lay directly beneath us.

A brief but shrill whistle came from the darkness below. "That must be the signal," declared Holmes. "They are ready for the exchange to begin."

"Now what?" whispered Lestrade.

"Let down the rope."

The Inspector looked around the tiny room, and found a length of rope coiled up in one corner of the room. This he fastened to another iron ring fastened to the wall and dropped the other end of this rope through the open trapdoor, so that it disappeared into the darkness.

A moment later, the rope pulled taut, as somebody below seized it, and began to climb. A head appeared in the trapdoor opening, together with a hand. This, Lestrade grasped, and hauled the man up into the room.

"Here, what's going on?" demanded the newcomer, looking around in alarm.

Lestrade laughed. "Skinny Hardisty. Well, well. We've been looking for you for months. Whatever are you doing back in town?"

"Obviously got my timings wrong, Mr Lestrade," said the man. "But the Boss told me it would be alright."

"Obviously we have outsmarted him. Who is this Boss of yours?"

"I'm not saying."

"Never mind," said Lestrade. "You're coming with me, my lad. I've some questions to put to you about a certain burglary."

Sherlock Holmes now stepped up to the open trapdoor. It is just as well that we had until now been hidden in near darkness, as Lestrade would never have recognized him apart from his voice. Holmes was dressed in a dark linen shirt, working-man's jacket, peaked cap and canvas trousers, assuming a very different persona, one that might better suit him in his guise as an escaping criminal.

I was apprehensive about his safety, but I knew that if anybody could look after himself, it had to be Sherlock Holmes.

"Now I must take the place of our friend Jeremiah Twist," he said as he grasped the rope and began to lower himself down, hand over hand, into the darkness. "Watson and Lestrade, I hope to see you both in Harwich."

*****

The narrative which follows was later told to me by Sherlock Holmes himself, as I attempted to piece together the events of the extraordinary few days that followed.

According to Holmes, he reached the small boat below, and was whisked away across the dark and murky water to the side of the schooner *The Gravesend Gryphon*.

Holmes climbed aboard, stood on the deck and looked around.

"You'll be Jeremiah Twist," came a voice from the misty shadows.

By way of answer, Holmes took out his pipe, filled it, lit it and gave his inquisitor a dark stare. But said nothing.

"Now listen," continued the other man, "on this boat it doesn't matter what your name is, because it will always be Joe. Got that?"

Holmes nodded. "You must be Codworon, the mate."

"Aye, and don't you ever forget it," said Codworon, as he stepped forward and prodded Holmes in the chest with his index finger. "I call the tune around here, so don't you go causing no trouble among the crew, or complaining to the skipper, or else you'll answer to me. And that's something no man ever does more than once. Do you hear?"

"I hear you."

"We've got a new cook with us this voyage. I don't know what happened to Moo, so I'll have my hands full looking after him."

"We should be getting some decent meals, then," said Holmes.

"You'd better hope so."

"And what cargo are we carrying this trip?"

"It's no business of yours, but if you must know, we're carrying engine parts."

"Bound for Harwich?"

"Mostly. Same as you."

"And where's my berth?"

"Down in the fo'c'sle, along with the rest of the vermin. We've two permanent deck-hands, but you'll be expected to pull your weight on board this vessel as well as them."

"No need to worry. I'll do my share of the work."

"We'll be sailing before dawn, catching the morning tide, so your first job will be to make sure the side lights are lit, and the masthead light is in place."

Going now by the name of Joe, and substituting for the criminal known as Jeremiah Twist, Sherlock Holmes, took his place among the crew of the schooner, remaining quiet, and absorbing all that transpired between the members of the crew, the skipper and the mate. He kept his true identity from St Clair, believing that ignorance of his presence there might be enough to keep them both alive until they reached Harwich. Not that there was much chance of meeting the cook alone.

There also seemed to be little sign of the skipper, who kept himself mostly to his own cabin whilst, as expected, the mate ruled the roost on board that vessel.

Although the mate acted the bully to the rest of the crew, making their lives more difficult than they needed to be, he remained wary of Holmes. The news that Jeremiah Twist had killed a man in London gave him enough notoriety to keep him fairly safe for the duration of the voyage.

The two regular deck-hands introduced themselves as Henry, the tall one, and Albert, the one who had put on a few too many pounds during his frequent visits to the local taverns.

That morning, with a steady breeze blowing away the mist, the schooner made steady progress down the River Thames, past the many docklands, and reached the estuary later in the day. A light rain had begun to fall, bringing a chill as it blew across that wide expanse of water.

Holmes kept a special watch as the schooner drew toward her home port, the coastal community of Gravesend, in the estuary of the River Thames. Here was a busy town, in need of a delivery of engine parts from the schooner's hold.

Down in the fo'c'sle that evening, deck-hand Henry looked a pleased as a bullfinch, carrying a bag which he opened to reveal a pair of brass candlesticks and a silver fruit bowl. All taken, so he told the others, from the home of some local rich businessman. These he hid away beneath his bunk.

The men shared stories, of life on the coastal trading run, and in their various lives before that. Holmes remained as silent as possible.

Albert turned to Holmes. "You must have a good few tales to tell, Joe. You must have met a good few villains in your time."

"Indeed I have," said Holmes, calmly drawing on his pipe. "During the last few years I have come across some of the most notorious thieves in the land, along with a few murderers as well. Bombers, poisoners and cutthroats."

"Much like yourself."

"But my greatest skill," replied Holmes, "is to mind my own business, and to keep my own counsel."

Four days later, the schooner came in sight of the east coast of Essex. Now, on the evening before the schooner was due to dock at Harwich, Holmes was up on deck, smoking a late evening pipe, when the boy emerged in a state of great excitement.

"Hey, Joe."

"What is it, Sniffy?"

"I thought you ought to know. There's trouble in the galley."

Holmes hurried down into the domain of the cook, and found the mate holding St Clair by the throat.

"What's the trouble?" demanded Holmes.

"We have a spy in our midst," said the mate. "This fellow, Boone. I was suspicious about him before we left London, but now I'm certain of it."

"Surely not."

The mate held the cook in an even more deadly throat-choke hold. "What are you doing on board this schooner, Boone?" he growled.

"Keeping an eye on you lot," wheezed the poor cook.

"Who are you spying for? Who sent you?"

"A man called Sherlock Holmes."

The mate relaxed his grip on the man's throat, and stood back. "I've heard the name. But what exactly are you looking for here?"

The cook massaged his throat. "I'm looking for evidence that you're carrying stolen goods."

"You are, are you? And now tell me, what have you discovered so far in your search for these stolen goods?"

"Nothing at all. I've been far too busy cooking, washing up and bringing you mugs of coffee and tea at all hours of the day and night."

Codworon laughed. "This fellow Sherlock Holmes is going to be disappointed when he hears what you have to tell him."

"Leave him alone, Codworon," said Holmes, still hiding behind his assumed guise. "He gives us decent enough meals, so if you have anything against the man, you should save it until we get into Harwich."

"You're right, Joe. He's too good a cook to kill before we reach port." With that, Codworon turned sharply, and stalked out of the galley.

Still concealing his identity from St Clair, Holmes also slipped away into the darkness.

The schooner reached Harwich during the following afternoon. The port looked busy, with a cross-channel ferry standing at the Continental pier, and a paddle steamer from London unloading its cargo of passengers at another pier across the harbor.

The unloading of *The Gravesend Gryphon* began, and it was not until darkness fell that this activity abated for the night.

In the gloom of that moonless night, Codworon called for both their passenger and the cook to join him up on deck. "You two come along with me," he told them. "We have certain business to conduct."

As the three men reached the landward end of the pier, another man stepped out from the shadows of a nearby warehouse. He was holding a lantern; the only source of light on the pier at that moment.

"Codworon?"

"Aye. And that'll be you, Petrov."

"None other. What have you brought us this time?"

"Now here's a pretty kettle of fish," said the mate, once more grasped the cook firmly by the throat. "I find we have a spy in our midst, Petrov. He goes by the name of Hugh Boone. And here he is. Our stand-in cook."

"What happened to the Chinese bloke?"

"Probably telling the Yard all about us by now."

"No, not Woo. He's scared stiff of what might happen to him if he does. So he has good reason to keep his mouth shut."

"Well, this fellow tells me he's looking for stolen goods concealed on board our boat, and that he's doing it for some cove called Sherlock Holmes."

"Cut his throat, and drop him into the harbour," snapped Petrov. "But wait a moment, who else have you got with you?"

"This is Jeremiah Twist," added Codworon, pointing to Holmes.

"You fool!" shouted Petrov. "I know Twist, and this is not him." The man stepped forward, and shone the lantern into Holmes's face. "But I have seen him before. This is that fellow you were talking about just now. Congratulations, Codworon. You've managed to bring, right into the heart of our operation here, the one man in the world that our Boss is really worried about. This is Sherlock Holmes."

Holmes stood back, and scowled menacingly at those around him. "And I should be obliged if you would release my man without further harm being done to him," he said, pointing to St Clair. "When we were docked at Gravesend, our deck-hand Albert happened to come back drunk one night. In his sleep he kept muttering that a man was chasing him. He mentioned a name: Moriarty. Now, after spending a week on board *The Gravesend Gryphon*, I am convinced more than ever that the boat has been acting as an escape route for those working for that prince of crime, Professor Moriarty. It also allows him, a few months later, to feed some of the worst criminals in the land back into the heart of London."

Petrov scowled back at Holmes. "One day, my Boss will crush you, Sherlock Holmes."

"But not yet, I fancy," said Holmes looking around at Petrov and Codworon. "You should all now consider yourselves under arrest."

Holmes took out a police-whistle from his pocket, raised it to his lips and blew it long and hard.

A bitter curse cut through the darkness, the lantern was extinguished, and policemen's boots thundered on the woodwork. Chaos broke out across that night-shaded pier.

*****

Sherlock Holmes had been gone for nearly a week, and I was becoming anxious for his safety. So it was with a mixture of relief and concern that I responded to Lestrade's call, by meeting him at London's Liverpool Street Station to catch the mid-afternoon boat-train to Harwich. A journey which lasted more than three hours.

"Everything is arranged at the other end," said Lestrade, consulting the notebook he was holding. "The local Essex police have plans to surround the entire dockyard area, and to await Holmes's whistle. We ought to be able to take the entire bunch of these villains."

The local police Inspector, who had been assigned to support our visit to the town, met us at the railway station.

"Are your men in their places?" asked Lestrade.

"Indeed they are. Ready and waiting," replied the local man.

"Very well, then," said the Scotland Yard Inspector. "Lead the way."

As the darkness deepened, and my anxiety increased, I accompanied Lestrade and his men as they followed the local police Inspector into the shadows cast be a nearly warehouse.

"That's *The Gravesend Gryphon*," announced the local man. "She's at her usual berth. Whatever is going to happen tonight will take place in that area of the harbour."

We could see the men gathered on the quayside, and listened to the dialogue between Sherlock Holmes and a man hidden from our sight by one of the warehouses. We heard the whistle, which was the agreed signal to alert the waiting policeman to make their move. As they converged on the gathering on the pier, we heard a loud scream, and noticed somebody fall to on the ground.

I drew my revolver, and ran into the warehouse. In the darkness, I could hear the sound of scurrying feet, and caught a glimpse of a dark figure vanishing round a distant corner. I was more concerned about Holmes than to follow this man, and had to accept the fact that he had made his escape.

I returned to the pier, and hurried over to where Holmes was crouched over the prone body of a thick-set man.

"Holmes, you are alive!" I cried. "I am truly delighted to see you."

"And I to see you, my dear fellow."

I crouched down beside Holmes, as he turned the fallen man over onto his back. The man had been stabbed, and he was swiftly bleeding to death. There was nothing we could do to save his life.

"This is the mate of *The Gravesend Gryphon*," explained Holmes. "Codworon. He was the real villain on board the schooner. As well as being a bully, he is also the one who put into operation this escape route for fugitives from the law. But his misfortune was to be caught up in the web of intrigue and crime whose center is that rogue, Professor Moriarty, and to allow himself to become infected by his evil scheming."

The dying man opened his eyes. "This is the price of failure, Mr Holmes," he croaked. "But promise me, if you ever get the chance, kill Moriarty. For the sake of us all."

"That will be a huge undertaking," sighed Holmes. "But I promise to do whatever I can to put an end to that man's empire of crime."

Codworon relaxed, and gently expired his final breath.

"And how is our friend and highly proficient cook, Mr Neville St Clair?" asked Holmes, rising to his feet again.

St Clair stepped forward. In the dim light of the relighted lantern, his face looked pale and his eyes appeared wide with shock. "Mr Holmes. I had no idea it was you traveling with us."

"Keeping an eye on you, Mr St Clair," replied Holmes.

St Clair gave a smile that failed to do justice to the gratitude he felt at that moment in his heart. "Is this an end to the matter, Mr Holmes?"

"I think it probably is. At least as far as you are concerned. We can leave Scotland Yard to tidy up here, and the local force to search the schooner from stem to stern for those illegal goods which I know for a fact the crew have concealed on board. Professor Moriarty, if he has been here at all, will by now be far away, and Scotland Yard will never be able to capture the man. Moriarty is slippery as an eel, the Napoleon of Crime, and the mastermind of all that is evil in the City of London. And far beyond. His dastardly plot to use that schooner to ferry his villains to and from the center of London, has been brought to an end. But no doubt it will prove to be only a temporary setback for such a resourceful man, who will no doubt be seeking diabolical revenge for my meddling in his criminal affairs."

I joined Holmes and St Clair on the milk-train back to Liverpool Street Station, and finally all three of us arrived at Baker Street in time to make a feast of Mr Hudson's splendid and much needed breakfast.

"We must celebrate the completion of our mission with an evening meal," declared Holmes. "I am sure Mrs Hudson will agree with me when I say that Neville St Clair and his wife should both join us this evening here in Baker Street."

"It is very good of you to invite us," said Mr Neville St Clair. "I am sure that we will both be highly honored."

"Also, that Mrs Watson should come along here as well. Now that she has returned home from visiting family. The ladies deserve to hear the tales of our adventures, whilst partaking of one of Mrs Hudson's finest gastronomic triumphs. I think we all deserve it."

"On one condition," declared Mrs Hudson.

"Name it."

"That Mr St Clair helps me with the preparation of that meal. After all, he has undergone a most thorough and excellent course of training, followed by a demanding week of practical hands-on experience on board *The Gravesend Gryphon.*

Dead Man's Hand

In all the years I was acquainted with him, I never knew Mr. Sherlock Holmes to refuse assistance to any victim of a cowardly attack, even if this brought him into confrontation with the most violent and unprincipled criminals in London. Such was the case that morning in the middle of Baker Street.

We were returning from an errand to Scotland Yard, and had just alighted from our hansom across the road from Number 221. Our attention was immediately attracted by a commotion, as two men were submitting one another to a noisy and vicious physical onslaught.

The victim lay on his back in the street, with his top-hat rolling in the gutter.

I immediately laid about the nearest thug with my sturdy Malacca, while Holmes squared up to the other attacker, ready to knock seven bells out of him.

With the tables now turned on them, the two assailants revealed their cowardly natures by turning tail, climbing into a waiting four-wheeler, and driving off in great haste, leaving their victim lying in the dust.

"That was curious, do you not you think?" asked Holmes.

"What was curious?"

"The fact that they fled so readily."

We picked up the fallen man, retrieved his top-hat, and dusted down his long black frock-coat. Then we took him inside and up to our rooms. The fellow was so dazed from his rough handling that he made no objection to being led into our sitting room and being seated before the fireplace.

As Holmes collected our decanter of brandy, our landlady appeared in the doorway, looking concerned and carrying a bowl of hot water, while I commenced a thorough examination of our man. He was tall and slim, with dark hair and trim goatee beard.

After several minutes of my careful ministrations, he looked around with urgent eyes.

"You must take it easy," I told him. "You've had a nasty blow to the head, resulting in profuse bleeding. Dramatic, but fortunately not serious. It's a good job we came along when we did."

When I had finished bandaging the man's head, Holmes offered him a glass of brandy and sat himself down on another chair facing him.

"I see you are a Frenchman," said Holmes.

The man raised his eyebrows in surprise.

"And that you have been in this country for only a short while – perhaps only a day or two. And that you are in search of something of great value."

"How can you tell so much about me?" asked the visitor. His accent showed that Holmes's initial assessment of his nationality had been correct.

"Simplicity itself, Monsieur. The cut of your clothes shows you to be from the Continent. They immediately indicate that you are a man of importance, and that you are here on business. What more pressing business could there be than a personal matter?"

"True enough."

"The fact that you sought my door suggests that you consider the matter pressing."

"Then you really are Sherlock Holmes." The man's face lit up. "I'm so relieved to have found you."

"The man who is attending to you is my friend and colleague, Dr. John Watson."

The Frenchman smiled his gratitude.

"Now," said Holmes, "you need to tell us the nature of your business here."

Our visitor looked down at his hands, and tried to concentrate. "Where shall I begin?"

"Perhaps by giving us your name."

"Naturally. I am Henri, Comte de Sancoubrey, and I am searching for something that was stolen from a relative of mine many years ago."

"Something personal?"

"Extremely so."

"Pray continue, your Grace."

"My great-grandfather – for that is how he is related to me – while serving with the army of Napoleon Bonaparte, was slain on the battlefield of Waterloo in Belgium. His horse was shot from beneath him, and he was quickly finished off by an English bayonet."

"But that was seventy years ago. Almost to the month."

"Indeed, so all I have had to go on is family gossip."

"Hardly the most trustworthy of sources," commented Holmes. "But pray continue."

"It seems that while his body lay unburied upon the battlefield, somebody removed an item of great importance from it."

We both looked on with profound curiosity. "And what was that?"

"His left hand."

"Interesting," said Holmes. "And do you have any idea what became of the hand?"

"That has been the abiding mystery in my family for all these years, Mr. Holmes," said the Frenchman. "The man who took the hand must have been a member of the victorious British army, serving under the Duke of Wellington."

"But why has this become such an issue now?" asked Holmes. "After so many years have passed."

"It was my own decision, Mr. Holmes. I realized that if I did nothing to resolve this issue now, then it would remain a mystery forevermore. I therefore began to use all my contacts and influences to discover what really happened to that hand."

"Just the hand?"

"That is all I am looking for."

"So what lay behind the attack made upon you out in the street just now? And why did those men flee so quickly when challenged?"

De Sancoubrey appeared embarrassed by the question. "They are cowards. My search for the missing relic of my great-grandfather has led me to encounter some particularly unsavory characters. Those men wanted to know the location of the hand, but I was quite unable to tell them."

"Mysterious," replied Holmes as he thought deeply about the matter. "Which suggests that perhaps you haven't revealed the entire matter to me. You are holding something back."

"What more do you wish to know, Mr. Holmes?"

"Only the thing that you are hiding from me."

After a tense pause, the Count leaned forward. "Will you help me, Mr. Holmes, or do I have to find somebody else who will assist me in my search for the missing hand of my relative?"

"I am inclined to refuse your request," growled Holmes, "on the grounds that you haven't furnished me with all the facts. But the mystery intrigues me. On consideration, I think that I shall accept your request for help, but be assured that, as a private consulting detective, I shall charge the appropriate rate for my services."

"Of course."

"Now, can you at least tell us how far your research has taken you?"

"I am happy to do that," said De Sancoubrey. "Since my ancestor's regiment was known to us, together with the elite cavalry unit to which he belonged, I thought I might be able to identify the regiment of foot that opposed the French attack on that part of the battlefield."

"But the man who took the hand might not have been the one who killed him."

"That is certainly possible, Mr. Holmes, but I had to follow up the only lead I possessed."

"With what result?"

"In Paris, I came across an expert on the Battle of Waterloo. He gave me the names of two men I should consult in London. One was yourself, Mr. Holmes. The other goes by the name of Aloysius Clark."

"Watson?"

"I'm already looking up the fellow," I told him from my place at our shelf of reference books. "Ah, yes, here he is. Aloysius James Clark. He is the proprietor of a small museum dedicated to the battle itself, and is an expert generally on the wars against Napoleon. His address places him at Carlington Green, Richmond."

"Have you already been to see him?"

Clark shook his head.

Holmes stood up. "Then we must pay this man a visit. But first we must at the very least warn him of our intention to visit him later this morning."

Mr. Clark was already standing at the front door of his home when we arrived. Holmes introduced each of us in turn, but our host seemed particularly impressed to have a member of the French nobility to visit him, even with his head wrapped in bandages.

"Welcome, gentlemen," Clark said. "You will have to forgive my casual attire. I'm not used to having so many visitors descend upon me in one morning."

"It is good of you to see us at such short notice, Mr. Clark," said Holmes, "but our visitor from France is anxious to pursue his investigation without delay."

117

Clark gave us a questioning look. "How exactly may I assist you, gentlemen?"

Count Henri explained. "I am looking into certain events which took place immediately following the Battle of Waterloo. With you being an expert on the subject, I have naturally come to consult you on the matter."

"Naturally. Then you had better come with me to my museum," said Clark, leading us down a flight of steps to the basement. "Here is my little repository of artefacts and information concerning the Battle of Waterloo, which was fought in June 1815 between the French Emperor's troops and the British Army, ably assisted by the timely arrival of Marshal Blucher's Prussians."

The museum was impressive. Maps and illustrations covered the walls of that underground room, and in the middle stood a table with a model of the battlefield laid out illustrating the turning point of the entire affair.

"Now," said Clark, "please tell me more."

"It is a matter of record in our family," said Count Henri, "that my great-grandfather fell on the battlefield there. But, when his body was returned to the family after the battle, they discovered that something was missing from the body. His left hand had been cut off at the wrist. *Post mortem*, I would hasten to add."

"That is a grisly tale," returned Clark, "but after all this time, wherein lies the urgency?"

"As you say, all this took place a long time ago, so that anybody who still remembers the events of those days will be of a great age now. Consequently, time is short if I am to conclude my investigations."

"And you wish me to consult my extensive collection of records. Is that your intention?"

"That is certainly my hope."

"But with what purpose?"

"I wish to identify the person who took the hand and, if possible, to retrieve that missing item from the person who stole it, so that it can be laid to rest along with the body."

"Intriguing," commented Clark. "In that case, it will be the identity of the particular British soldier involved that you are looking for."

"That is indeed my next step."

"Since I received your telegram," continued Clark, "I have undertaken a little preliminary investigation into the matter. From the brief description you gave me, I've managed to identify the British regiment that was operating on that section of the battlefield. We have no way of knowing who killed your ancestor, but further investigation has come up with an intriguing lead concerning the missing hand. With so many corpses having to be identified and removed, a large number of wooden coffins had to be constructed. One of our soldiers later put in a request for a much smaller box – with ample space for a human hand. There may of course be any number of explanations for this, and the carpenters were so busy at the time that they had no occasion to ask about details. But it remains in the records as an unexplained oddity. However, I have discovered a name mentioned in the records at the time: A fellow called Jotham Kidd."

"That could well be the man we are looking for," I suggested.

"Perhaps," said Holmes, "but we need solid facts to go on."

"That name is a solid enough fact for me, Mr. Holmes," said Count Henri. "We have little choice but to follow up on it."

"But I must caution you, gentlemen," added Clark. "These records date back seventy years. If you could ever locate Jotham Kidd, the chances are that he will have been in his own grave for many years now."

"And yet he may have family who are still alive," I said.

"True."

"As His Grace has pointed out, Mr. Clark," said Holmes, "we need to follow up on that information. Do you have an address for Jotham Kidd?"

Clark remained strangely silent.

"Mr. Clark," repeated Holmes, "am I correct in concluding that somebody else has been asking about this man?"

"How can you tell?"

"Deduction from what you said earlier about being busy this morning, and the fact that you are reluctant to tell me."

Clark nodded. "Two men. Foreigners. They came here much earlier this morning."

"And their names?"

"I am sworn to secrecy on that matter, Mr. Holmes."

"You say they were foreigners," said Count Henri.

"Indeed. They spoke much like yourself, Your Grace."

"Then they were Frenchmen," concluded Count Henri. "Were they brothers? And were their names perhaps Jean and Hubert Clemice?"

Clark coughed. "I see I have no need to break the promise I gave them."

"What more can you tell us?" asked Holmes.

"You have to understand, Mr. Holmes, that these two men gave me a handsome payment to obtain that address in double-quick time. And to remain silent about it afterwards."

"So you paid a visit to the War Office in Whitehall earlier today."

"Again. How can you know that, Mr. Holmes?"

"The bottoms of your trousers are showing signs of white dust – more precisely, dust associated with Portland Limestone, the kind being cut in Dorset to build and repair so many of the public buildings in London. Since such building work is currently being undertaken in Whitehall, employing precisely this kind of stone, then it is reasonable to conclude that you paid a visit to that locality recently."

"But why are you so sure I was there this morning?"

"That is simplicity itself, Mr. Clark. If this dust had been left on your clothing overnight, somebody this morning, perhaps yourself or your wife, would have employed a clothes brush to remove such an obvious sartorial disorder prior to your leaving home this morning."

"Since you already know the truth," said Clark, "then I wouldn't be betraying any confidences if I refrained from replying. But since the money was already in my hand, I was committed to helping the men. I made contact with a colleague of mine who works at the War Office, and he supplied me with the address I needed. They keep all their old records with meticulous care. He and I agreed to split the money between us."

"In that case," said Holmes, "are you able to supply us with that address?"

"As a matter of fact, I have the address right here," said Clark. "And I am more than willing to let you have it, but whether it is still relevant to your investigation, or whether the man has moved on, or has died, I shall have to leave you to discover."

"And the address?"

"Goodluck Manor, in Leicestershire."

"Quite propitious," commented Count Henri.

"Then let us hope it lives up to our expectations," concluded Holmes.

The following morning, Count Henri was feeling much recovered from his head injury, and felt able to accompany Holmes and myself to Goodluck Manor in the Midland county of Leicestershire. At first sight, the building appeared to be much the same as any other country house: Solid, large, and rambling. Closer examination revealed that money had undoubtedly been expended on the building, with added rooms, details, and embellishments.

As we stood together in front of the main entrance doorway, I tugged on the bell-pull and was rewarded by a loud bell jangling somewhere deep inside.

A moment later, the sound of footsteps resulted in the door being opened, to reveal a man in his late-middle years standing on the threshold: The butler. His expression betrayed the fact that he hadn't been expecting us.

"Do you have an appointment?" he asked.

"No," said Holmes. "We are hoping to find any living relative of Mr. Jotham Kidd."

The butler's countenance returned to its normal, impassive expression.

"Please come inside," he told us, "and I shall find the mistress."

He escorted the three of us into a front reception room, where we stood waiting to discover what might transpire. The room felt cold, and the blue decorations added nothing to the uncomfortable feeling I had from being in such an austere place.

Once more the door opened, but this time a tall, elegant young woman entered. I was taken aback by her beauty, as indeed were my two companions, although Holmes would never have admitted to the fact.

"I am Adelaide Kidd," she said, casting her cold eyes round at us. "How may I help you, gentlemen?"

"My name is Sherlock Holmes," my friend informed her. "These gentlemen with me are my friend, Dr. John Watson, and our visitor from France – Henri Comte de Sancoubrey."

Miss Kidd looked around at each of us in turn as she pushed a lock of her dark-brown hair from her face.

"Ashbourne, the butler, tells me you are here to inquire after my grandfather."

"If your he is indeed the late Jotham Kidd."

"You appear to be misinformed," said the young lady. "I can assure you that my grandfather is still very much alive – though maybe for not much longer, considering his advanced years."

"He must be over ninety years of age by now," said Holmes.

"Ninety-five, to be precise, Mr. Holmes."

"Then may we be allowed to speak with him?"

"What exactly do you wish to talk with him about?"

"Waterloo."

The young woman nodded. "After so much time? Well, I suppose you had better come along with me and meet him. Although what he might choose to tell you will be entirely up to him."

"Quite so."

With a rustle of crinoline, Miss Kidd led the three of us out into the corridor and along a passage to a doorway situated toward the rear of the building. There she knocked on the door, and entered.

We followed.

I have visited many a sick room during the course of my medical career, and not a few to see people who were nearing the end of their lives, but I have to admit this was a refreshing change. Drapes covered much of the walls, so that our voices sounded somewhat muffled. An open fireplace occupied one wall, with a pair of crossed swords mounted above it. Where these might have come from was open to speculation. A French window on one side of the room stood slightly ajar, so that the air in the room felt fresh and carried the smell of the countryside with it. The room itself was large, and filled with daylight, bearing none of the usual depressive atmosphere of a sickroom. Apart from the bed. This solid wooden structure was situated at one side of the room, and in it lay a figure propped up into a sitting position by a stack of pillows piled up him. He was an elderly man. His face looked thin, with the skin drawn tight across the skull. The hands were twisted with rheumatism, and the thin skin was the color of parchment, tarnished with age-spots, and with blue blood vessels standing out on the surface.

"You have some visitors to see you, Grandfather," said the young woman as she straightened the pillows behind the old man and laid him once more against them.

"Visitors? Whatever do they want?" he shot back, glaring up at us. Then he sighed. "Very well, I suppose they had better get on with it."

We gathered around the bed and introduced ourselves.

Count Henri took center stage in the questioning.

"According to my investigations," he explained, "you must be Jotham Kidd. You served as a sergeant with the British forces deployed against Napoleon Bonaparte and his French army at the Battle of Waterloo in 1815."

The old man nodded slowly. "There is no point in trying to deny the fact."

"And from that battlefield, you carried away with you a trophy."

Old Jotham Kidd fixed the Frenchman with his steely gray eyes. But said nothing in reply.

"It was the hand of an ancestor of mine," the Frenchman continued. "My great-grandfather, to be precise. You severed the hand from his dead body and took it away with you."

"There were many trophy-hunters on that field of battle, Monsieur le Comte," replied Jotham Kidd, "and some treated the remains of the dead with far less respect than I did. But be assured, I wasn't the man who killed your ancestor. I discovered him as I led my men away from that field of slaughter. He was already dead. We all considered ourselves extremely lucky to have escaped with our own lives that day."

"That isn't the issue, Mr. Kidd," said Count Henri.

"Then what exactly is the issue?"

"My great-grandfather has lain in his grave for the last seventy years with part of his body missing. After such a long time, the family and I wish to reunite the two."

"You wish me to give the missing hand to you. Is that correct?"

"Indeed."

"That sounds simple enough," opined Holmes, who until then had remained unusually quiet, "but there is something in this business that neither of you gentlemen is telling me."

Both Kidd and Count Henri turned their attention to Holmes.

"Somewhere in this business there lies a secret element," he continued.

"How do you come to that conclusion?" growled Kidd.

"Ever since I first heard the story of the missing hand, as told by His Grace here, I have had the feeling that the main point is missing. I ask myself, 'What is kept upon a hand?' Again I ask myself, 'Why would anyone wish to steal such a hand?' The answer is always the same: A ring."

Kidd stared at Holmes, as though expecting him to say more.

Which he did. "But first of all, Mr. Kidd, we need to find the box in which you placed the hand that you took from that dead man. Can you tell us where it is now?"

"No, I cannot do that."

"Why ever not?"

"A great deal of water has passed beneath the bridge since 1815. I no longer have possession of the box and its contents. The responsibility of looking after it was taken over by my son, Michael – that is, Adelaide's father."

The young woman's face took on a grim aspect as she added, "And my father went missing."

"Missing? How long ago was that?"

"It must be ten years ago now," she replied. "I was only twelve at the time that my father absented himself from our home, and he hasn't been seen since. But I remember him very clearly. He told me he was going on an adventure. At first I was excited for him, but then, when he failed to return, I fell into a deep depression from which I haven't yet fully recovered. After that, I buried myself in the life of the Manor here, and in looking after my grandfather."

We all looked to the old man in the bed. "Do you have any idea what happened to the box, Mr. Kidd?" Holmes asked him.

"None at all. But I feel certain that it didn't leave this house."

"I am sure you are right, Grandfather," said Miss Kidd. "It must be hidden within the building somewhere."

There was clearly considerably more going on in this affair than we had first imagined.

"Miss Kidd," said Holmes. "Where was your father in the habit of spending his time when he lived in this house?"

"One place in particular, as far as I remember," she replied. "The library."

"Then we must begin our search there. Lead on, Miss Kidd."

Leaving the old man, the young woman led the way to the well-stocked library. I looked around, bemused by the array of volumes. Where to begin? But Holmes had no doubts. At once, he began to search the rows of books.

Then he stopped. "All of these books are typical of a modern professionally arranged library."

"I remember that a professional librarian came in here when I was very small," said Miss Kidd. "I was fascinated watching him work."

"The books also possess numbers identifying them," continued Holmes, "so that if you want to find any particular book, you only have to visit the index in order to locate its place upon the shelves. But here the tops of the books aren't on the same level, and neither is the numbering system in order. These books have been pulled out, and replaced without due care."

"But could that really have happened all those years ago, without it ever being put straight again in the meantime?" I asked.

"Since my father left, we have rarely ventured into this part of the house," said Miss Kidd, "so it is certainly conceivable."

Holmes then proceeded to pull out the offending volumes to reveal a brick wall behind them.

Someone had to take up the challenge to investigate what lay there, and it was Count Henri who volunteered. He rolled up his sleeve and plunged his right arm into the darkness behind the bookshelves. For several minutes, he used his sharp knife to scrape away at the mortar between the bricks. Eventually he pulled away first one brick, and then another, and laid them both down on the floor. The Frenchman then reached into the dark void left by the brickwork and pulled out a wooden box. It measured approximately eighteen inches in length by twelve in both height and width, and had a tightly fitting lid.

"I can hardly imagine this box has been lying here untouched for the last seventy years," said Count Henri.

"I am quite sure it hasn't," said Holmes. "Would you care to open the box so we can see what exactly lies within?"

Holding the box in one hand, Count Henri looked around at us and gave a nervous smile.

We all watched on in eager expectation as he pulled away the lid.

Inside the open box, we saw a black leather glove – and something else.

"Is that the glove that belonged to your ancestor?" Holmes asked him.

"That is hard to determine," said Count Henri. "But it certainly appears to match the one I saw in a painting of my great-grandfather that now hangs in our *château*."

Holmes nodded. "I think we need to consult the one man who is able to tell us more – Miss Kidd's grandfather."

Upon our return to the old man's bed-chamber, we once more gathered around the bed and showed him what we had discovered.

"Of course. My son must have hidden it in the library."

"You aren't surprised?" said Holmes.

"Not really. It is the sort of thing he might have done."

"A workman needs to come and repair the damage," said Holmes. "Unless, of course, you wish first to return the box to its hiding place."

"That will not be necessary," came a voice from the far side of the room.

We all turned to face the open French window. There, silhouetted against the daylight, we saw three men. Two of these were the men Holmes and I had confronted the previous day in the middle of Baker Street – the men who had attacked Count Henri, and whom we had sent packing. One of the men was wrapped in a voluminous coat, and wore a shapeless black hat on the back of his head. The second man, who remained in the background, wore a short jacket, a straw boater hat, and carried a black ebonized walking cane. The third man slipped almost unnoticed back outside.

"Jean Clemice," breathed Count Henri.

"Indeed," replied the more prominent of the two as he removed a handgun from his coat and turned it toward the man lying in the bed. "And you remember my brother, Hubert." He nodded toward the second man. "We arrived here much earlier, but we wanted to allow you to find the box before we made our presence known. We were sure that Mr. Holmes would be able to locate it for us. We were also confident that the old chatterbox, Clark, would never be able to keep his mouth shut."

"It is as I imagined," said Holmes. "That performance in the street yesterday morning was entirely for my benefit, in order to arouse my curiosity and make sure that I turned up here today."

Jean Clemice confirmed the matter by giving a sneering grin.

"I wondered when you were going to turn up again," said Count Henri. "I suppose you have come for the box."

"No," said Jean Clemice. "Merely the contents." The man looked around at the gathering. "Where is it?"

"I have it," replied Holmes, holding out the wooden box.

Jean Clemice snatched the box from his hand, and wrenched open the lid. From inside, the man took out the glove that we had seen earlier. It was a leather gauntlet of a large size which fitted the left hand. This agreed with the Count's assertion about the loss of the left hand of his ancestor on the field of battle. Around the ring finger of the glove sat a ring, made extra-large in order to fit over the gloved hand. It carried a jewel, an emerald of impressive size.

We all gazed at the ring.

"And this is what you here came for?" asked Holmes.

"No, it most certainly is not what we came for," growled Jean Clemice. He then withdrew the glove from the box, and pulled it back to reveal its contents. A mummified human hand, with skin even more diaphanous than that of Jotham Kidd himself. This grizzly object held the attention of each one of us. Jotham Kidd watched on with narrowed eyes. Miss Kidd covered her mouth in horror. And I, though no stranger to seeing human remains, felt spell-bound by the sight. Even Holmes watched on with a detached fascination.

It was Jean Clemice who broke the silence. "Well, where is it?"

"Where is what?" demanded Count Henri.

"You know very well what I mean. There. The ring finger. It's bare. The ring isn't on it."

A chilling silence followed as all eyes turned to the man on the bed.

Kidd's eyes glared back at Jean Clemice. "You didn't think you were going to get your hands on it so easily, did you? Thieves! Pirates! Brigands! That's what you are. You have no right to the treasure. Any argument on that subject, if indeed there is one, is entirely between the Count and myself."

The old man turned to his granddaughter. "Adelaide, kindly bring me my pillow."

With a knowing nod, the young woman reached behind her and collected a large white pillow, which she then carried to the old man and placed into his arms.

As Miss Kidd stood back, Jean Clemice tossed the box aside, snatched hold of her, and leveled his gun at her head.

"The matter is now simplified," he growled "Tell me where the true ring is, or I shall blow her brains out."

"Take your filthy hands off my granddaughter, you monster!" croaked Jotham Kidd. "Drop your gun, or I shall kill you where you stand."

Clemice laughed as he turned both his attention and his gun away from the woman and toward the bed.

During that brief moment when the gunman was turning, Jotham Kidd lowered the pillow in his lap, to reveal a gun in his hand. It was one of the ancient military holster pistols, but of the later type, fitted with a copper powder detonation cap. Kidd immediately squeezed the trigger, and the pistol roared, sending a round ball into the middle of the gunman's chest.

Carrying an expression of intense surprise, Jean Clemice dropped to the floor like a stone.

I hurried over to him, just as his lifeblood was ebbing away onto the stone floor.

It had been a matter of self-defense on the part of Jotham Kidd, and we all recognized that.

Or most of us did.

The slain man's brother, Hubert, let out a loud cry and ran over to the body of his sibling, thrusting me to one side. Then, with eyes on fire, and a heart burning with rage, the man seized his walking-cane and withdrew from it a long and sharp sword. With this, he approached the man in the bed, as though determined on running him through.

While Hubert Clemice was struggling with his rage, Jotham Kidd looked at Count Henri, and then up to the crossed swords mounted above the fireplace. The French Count read the message in the old man's eyes and grasped hold of one of the swords. To the amazement of all, he managed to pull it away from its place on the wall with little difficulty.

With this weapon, Count Henri took his place between Clemice and the sickbed, so that the two swordsmen now faced each other.

Clemice lashed out with his steel blade. Count Henri used his blade to parry the attack, and then went himself on the offensive. Clemice stood back so that the other man's blade swung wide of its target. Both men seemed quite familiar with the art of swordsmanship, and the sharp sound of steel clashing with steel filled the room. The sword-fight progressed, with first one and then the other seizing the advantage. In time, it was Clemice who proved the better swordsman, and, as Count Henri showed signs of tiring, his attention was distracted by the door opening and the butler coming into the room. In that instant, Clemice made a move that showed him to be the more proficient and level-headed of the two. He sliced into the other man's forearm, forcing Count Henri to drop the sword, and retreat to the other side of the room.

With the quickness of a lightning bolt, Adelaide Kidd hurried over to him, and threw herself into his blood-stained arms, protecting him from any further injury. The Count had proven himself to be her hero.

Within the space of a heartbeat, Holmes picked up the dropped sword, and turned to face Hubert Clemice. Again the swords clashed. Within seconds, he had disarmed his opponent and stood with the tip of his sword pressed against the other man's throat.

Clemice visibly wilted in defeat.

"You are a better swordsman than I am, Monsieur," he admitted.

Without turning to him, Holmes called upon the newly arrived butler to send for the local constabulary.

In the meantime, the third man outside had vanished.

With the butler pointing a blunderbuss at the defeated swordsman, and Miss Kidd focusing her attention onto Count Henri's injured arm, all other eyes turned to the man in the bed.

"Jotham Kidd," growled Holmes, "I believe you owe us an explanation."

Kidd dropped his gun and looked up at him. "Very well. As you already know, I was the one who cut off the hand of the Count's great-grandfather. People were looting the bodies of other men. It was the thing that victors did after such a victory. I wouldn't have bothered otherwise, only I was attracted by the ring on the glove. So I quickly cut off the hand at the wrist. I had a suitable container constructed, an almost airtight wooden box, and I kept the gloved hand inside that box. I took the hand back home with me, as a grizzly memento of that atrocious battle. I later examined it in greater detail and discovered the other ring – the one which appeared to give the location of a hidden hoard: A treasure of great worth."

"That's right," added Count Henri. "A store of valuables had been collected by my family before the Revolution, and again during the many other conflicts into which Bonaparte led us. My family kept their heads by moving to Austria. Later, they returned and increased their wealth. But after my great-grandfather's death, they could never find the resting place of those valuables, though they searched for many years. It was clear that the key to their location had to lie in that missing ring. But others also learned about the treasure."

"The Clemice brothers."

"Just so. They pretended to be friends of the family, but they were working only for their own interests."

"But Jotham Kidd managed to locate the resting place of those riches," said Holmes.

"I kept that ring for many years," Kidd explained. "I was curious about the inscription, and managed to decipher it. It gave a map reference to a place in southern France. I can no longer remember the name of the town, but the ring led me to believe that the treasure was hidden in a vault beneath the church. My memory fails me concerning the details, but I remember that I traveled there and found the treasure. I took only a portion, and left."

"How did you gain access to the vault, Mr. Kidd?" Holmes asked him.

"I failed to mention before that I also took something else from the corpse – an official document which identified him. That document was proof enough for the priest to lend me the key to the vault and allow me to go down there. In my youth, I had received some training as a locksmith, so I was able to take a wax impression of the key. I made a replica which I placed in the box alongside the glove."

"So that if ever you decided to return, you would never again need to trouble the priest," concluded Holmes.

"Indeed," Kidd continued. "But I remember there was great danger there. That was sixty years ago now, and my memory is failing. But I know that many years after my own visit, my son, Adelaide's father, decided to go after more of the treasure. He was greedy. He studied the ring and he took the key, and made his plans without consulting me. He went but never returned. If he'd told me, I could have warned him – about the danger."

"What danger?"

"With the passage of time, the details have faded from my mind. Some things I remember, Others I have forgotten. But I do remember there is real danger lurking there."

"Where?"

"In that vault."

"And the ring," Holmes demanded. "You made a point of saying the ring was studied, but the key was taken. Where is the ring now?"

Kidd turned his eyes upon his granddaughter. She reached behind her head, unhooked a fastening, and pulled her necklace from her bosom, together with the attached ring. This she removed it and held it out to Holmes, who took it and began to examine it through his magnifying glass.

"Why did you never go in search of your father, Miss Kidd?"

"My grandfather said it was too dangerous. I could never locate the reference on any map, and he refused to help me."

"Then let us take a look."

In the library, Holmes laid out a variety of maps on France. "The mystery lies in the fact that the Prime Meridian as recognized by the French passes through Paris – at least, until last year – so that it runs a couple of degrees east of the Greenwich meridian. If we use the Paris Meridian as our reference point, we can identify the place your grandfather visited: Cluce-le-Pont."

Miss Kidd nodded. "I was simply using the wrong reference longitude."

"Of course," said the old man a few minutes later. "I remember it now. But there is danger there."

"All memory of that village had been entirely lost to our family," added Count Henri.

Holmes looked around at all of us. "How do you feel about a trip to the Continent? The south of France, perhaps."

Looking down at the fallen Clemice brothers, Count Henri said, "We need to deal with these men first."

"Scotland Yard will take over custody of them," said Holmes, "so long as we each provide a statement of what has happened here today. Then we may leave for France."

The old man seemed to wither before our eyes. Soon he was asleep, dreaming of something the rest of us could only imagine.

Miss Kidd had remained close to Count Henri, and now looked up at him with adoring eyes. "I want to come with you," she declared.

"But your grandfather?"

"I know a nurse who will stay with him until we return."

"*If* indeed we return," added Count Henri. "Remember, your father never returned from his visit there."

"That is precisely why I wish to go," said Miss Kidd. "I need to find out exactly what happened to him."

"Then we must each make our preparations," concluded Holmes. "I see no reason why we need to delay our departure beyond tomorrow."

A groan arose from the bed, and Jotham Kidd awakened and sat up, his eyes staring. "The door! A deathtrap!" he declared. "Beware the door!"

But in spite of our questions, he could tell us nothing more.

For much of our journey from London, Holmes sat in a deep reverie, sometimes watching the countryside, and often enwrapped in tobacco smoke. Having taken a train from there to Dover, a ferry to Boulogne, and an express to the South of France, we finally alighted at the station nearest to our destination. A horse and carriage took us the rest of the way and dropped us off at the only hotel.

After settling into our rooms and enjoying a restorative evening meal, the four of us met to take council together in the lounge.

"The matter seems simple enough to me," said I. "We locate the vault, open the door, and retrieve the treasure."

"If only it could be that simple," replied Holmes.

"Whatever is there to stop us?" demanded Count Henri.

"It's the door, isn't it, Mr. Holmes?" said Miss Kidd. "There is something about the doorway to the vault that worries you. I recall the very last words my grandfather said while you were visiting us. 'Beware the door!'"

"Precisely so. Having studied the ring and attempted to decipher its meaning, I agree with your grandfather in sensing great danger there."

The Count stood up and stretched his long legs. "It has been a tiring day, so I intend to retire early in order to prepare for a new and demanding day tomorrow."

Miss Kidd expressed a similar opinion and departed along with the Frenchman, leaving Holmes and me to make the most of the rest of the evening.

Holmes stood up and reached for his coat. "While it's still light, I shall take a turn around the town."

"And call in at the church, no doubt," I added, following his example and joining him outside in the main street. "After all, we no longer have Kidd's key."

Cluce-le-Pont was a small community nested in a bend of a river. The town was centered on the market square surrounded by civic buildings, a cafe, a couple of shops, and the small church.

Holmes examined the graveyard, taking particular notice of the land on which the church had been built.

"It's too dark to do much here," said a voice from close behind us. We turned round to find Miss Kidd standing not far away. "I couldn't rest," she told us. "If my father really is lying here somewhere, I would like to know as soon as possible."

"But not tonight," replied Holmes. "The daylight has gone."

"I noticed a light on in the presbytery," she countered.

"Then we must disturb the reverend gentleman," concluded Holmes.

As he listened to our tale, the priest's demeanour altered from annoyance at being disturbed to intense interest. He willingly agreed to lend Holmes a lantern so that he alone could enter and wander around the church itself.

He returned not long after, looking satisfied with his investigations, but saying nothing.

Before we left, the priest promised to meet us on the following morning outside the church, and agreed to bring with him the key to the vault of the De Sancoubrey family. But he warned us that there might be a problem with the entrance, adding that he would also bring with him a couple of men whom he called the "Nephilim", or giants, to accomplish any strong-arm activity that might be required.

Before he finally turned to leave, Holmes said, "I would be obliged, Father, if you could also arrange for a crowbar to be available for my use in the morning."

"A crowbar?" came the astonished reply. "Of course."

The four of us returned to the church on the following morning, at the time determined by the parish priest.

He greeted De Sancoubrey warmly.

"It is amazing," said the Count. "All these years, nobody in the family knew about this place. But why do we need to bring these two strong men along with us?" He indicated the two burly fellows who were standing with the priest.

"You will see," replied the priest. "Come."

We followed him round to the side of the church building, where we descended a flight of stone steps down to a lower level. There, hidden among the untamed undergrowth, we came to a halt in front of a solid wooden door which was built into the structure of the building itself. It was braced shut by a large stone block, shaped like a lintel, which was lying apparently unmovable upon the ground.

"Judging by the grass growing up around it, I should estimate that this block of stone has been lying here unmoved for the last ten years," said Holmes. "No less, and perhaps not much longer."

"That would be about the time that my father went missing," declared Miss Kidd, her face now distorted by the horror she imagined lying beyond the entrance. "He must have gone in there, and this stone fell down and blocked his escape."

"Horrible," said I.

"That would be a reasonable deduction to make," concluded Holmes.

"But why couldn't he simply open the door and step over the obstruction?" asked Miss Kidd.

"That we shall have to discover. But first, we have to move the stone."

The priest stood aside, and the two strong men stepped forward. "We can lift it, Father," said one of them.

"Very well," said the priest. "Do whatever you can."

The two Nephilim set about lifting the block. As the stone rose, we heard the rattle of iron chains, indicated that a counterbalance somewhere inside the walls had relaxed its strain. This, together with the efforts of the men, added to the sound of stone grinding against the stone grooves which held it in place on either side of the doorway. Eventually, the men managed to raise the block until it was level with the top of the doorway. The wood of the door was old but not decayed, and it now became clear that it was hinged so that it opened outward.

"That would explain why nobody on the inside would ever be able to open it," Holmes explained.

"How unusual," I replied.

While the two strong men continued to hold the block at head height, Holmes grasped the door-handle, turned it, and pulled the door open. Something inside the stone structure to our left clicked, and the two strong-men felt the weight of the lintel lift from their shoulders. They relaxed.

"Very interesting," declared Holmes. "As you can see, the door is already unlocked. There is no need for the key. Whoever unlocked it last never came out again."

"My father," gasped Miss Kidd.

While we looked at each other, trying to decide who should be the first to venture inside, the young woman proved the most intrepid. She took one of the two lanterns, turned up the wick, and stepped into the darkness, followed closely by Holmes, the French Count, and me. The parish priest and the two men were close behind.

"Where is the danger?" I asked.

"I'm not sure about that," said Holmes, "but whatever you do, make sure you don't close this door."

The underground vault was divided into two parts: First an outer room, and then an inner chamber secured by another heavy door.

The outer chamber contained a small number of stone coffins, each bearing the name of some member of the De Sancoubrey family. None was less than eighty years old.

"A few of my ancestors, lost in the mists of time," declared Count Henri, as Miss Kidd clung to him.

By the light of the two lanterns, and the daylight filtering in through the open doorway, we made a careful search of that chamber but found no sign of any treasure in that part of the vault.

Then we turned to the inner chamber. One of the Nephilim heaved open the inner door and stepped aside.

Adelaide Kidd swallowed hard and stepped into the darkness, followed immediately by the Count.

I went next, only to find Miss Kidd standing stock-still, struck dumb by the horror of what she saw there.

In the light of the lantern she was holding, I looked down and found a skeleton, still dressed in the clothes of an ordinary traveling Englishman. Beside the body lay a solid iron key. "Is that your father, Miss Kidd?"

She clung to Count Henri and nodded.

Indeed. Who else could it be?

It was only now that I noticed Holmes was no longer in the vault with us. Where had he gone? No doubt he was about his own business.

Keeping a respectful distance from the skeleton, we examined the rest of the inner chamber. It was smaller than the outer one, and it contained nothing apart from two wooden trunks. One of these lay open, revealing gold and silver ornaments, many decorated with precious stones – but it looked as if half the contents had been removed.

"My grandfather must have taken the rest of it back home with him," declared Miss Kidd, detaching herself from the Count.

"Then your father came out here," I reminded her, "looking for the rest of the treasure."

"And he found it," she replied, pointing to the second trunk, which Count Henri had now opened, to reveal a box full of similar precious objects.

"Your father found all of this," said the Count, "but it did him no good when he became locked inside. Even with the key."

As he was speaking, we all heard the unmistakable sound of a door slamming shut, and of a heavy weight grinding stone against stone.

We hurried back to the entrance, only to find that the wooden door was now closed, and was presumably blocked on the far side by the stone lintel which had once more fallen into the place it had occupied for the previous ten years. We were trapped.

Each in turn, we hammered upon the wooden door, but no answer came. I looked for a door handle, but could find none on that side of the door.

Back in the inner chamber, the young woman stood looking down at the remains of her father. "At least we shall lie here together," she said, with tears sparkling in the flickering lantern light. "Perhaps for all eternity."

"We must not give up all hope just yet," I told her. "After all, Sherlock Holmes is still out there somewhere."

"But what can he do?" asked the priest. "After all, we have the strongest men in the village in here with us, and there is nothing they can do now."

In that blackness, I tried to remember everything I had learned from the years I'd spent with Holmes. I tried to examine the situation logically as I looked around at the solid stone masonry. I was now standing at the far end of the inner chamber, fighting the temptation to give up all hope, when I heard a sound coming from the roof above me. It might have been a crowbar lifting a slab of stone. I looked upward, and watched as daylight gradually began to filter down to illuminate our Stygian darkness.

This noise attracted the others, who hurried to join me in the inner chamber. Then, as we all stood looking upward, a hole appeared in the ceiling, and Holmes's face looked down at us.

"Thank you for the loan of the crowbar, Father," came his encouraging voice. "I knew the vault had to lie directly beneath the north aisle of the church, and last night I managed to establish the most likely spot."

After widening the hole, Holmes reached down and began to help us each in turn to climb out of that pit of horrors. Count Henri himself reached down for Miss Kidd, who paused to look back into the darkness. "We shall have my father's remains removed and buried properly – back at home."

On returning to the outside entrance to the vault, we found a man lying on the ground, tied up and unable to move.

"This is the fellow who shut the door on you," explained Holmes. "He acted as coachman for the Clemice brothers back in Baker Street. He was the third man we saw at Goodluck Manor who slipped away almost unnoticed. This is the third of the Clemice brothers – Vincent Clemice. With his brothers now out of the way, he followed us all the way from London, doubtless intent upon revenge. Did you not see him on the train?"

I shook my head.

We all stared at the man on the ground. How had we failed to realize the truth?

"I was too late to prevent him from locking you all inside," continued Holmes, "and I was unable to raise the stone lintel myself."

He turned to the two Nephilim who sighed and set about the task of once more raising the lintel until it again clicked into place.

Holmes carefully examined the newly opened door. "This really is intriguing," he told us. "Look. You can see a hole in the stone jamb, which corresponds to a metal prong projecting from the wooden door on the edge farthest away from the lock. Although I have no intention of demonstrating it here and now, I believe that when the door is closed, and the projection enters the opening in the stone jamb. Whatever mechanism is holding the stone lintel in place will then release its load, preventing the door from being opened from inside."

"Fiendish," said Count Henri.

"Ingenious," said I.

"But how was my grandfather able to enter and leave without himself being caught by this trap, and entombed inside?" asked Miss Kidd.

"Now that is the really diabolic part of this whole business," replied Holmes. He turned to me. "Look carefully at the door, Watson. Do you not see it? No? Then put your hand on the projection."

"Oh yes," I exclaimed. "It pushes in when I press it. It must have a strong metal spring attached to the inside. And just below the projection, I can feel a metal plate. This seems to be hinged in some manner."

"And your conclusion?"

"You can lift the plate up so that it covers the retractable projection in the door, thus preventing it from entering the hole in the stone jamb when the door is closed."

"Quite so. And preventing it from activating whatever mechanism is hidden within the stonework. In that way, the door can be closed without allowing the stone lintel to fall down and block the entrance."

"But anyone not aware of the trigger mechanism would allow the metal plate to fall," said I, "thus trapping them inside. The building is so solid that any cries for help would not be heard."

"The church and the vault must have been constructed before the Revolution," explained Holmes.

"You are undoubtedly correct, Monsieur," the priest replied. "I knew nothing of this!"

"And at the same time, the family privately constructed this vault beneath the church."

"I suppose," said Count Henri, "we must blame my ancestors for creating such a cunning device to safeguard their riches."

"But they had to issue a warning to the family," said Holmes.

"Hence the message on the ring," concluded Miss Kidd.

"Then the secret and all records of the tomb were lost," I said, "with the only evidence lying upon the battlefield. When Count Henri revealed the existence of the lost ring, others sought access to the tomb as well."

"Now," concluded Holmes, "with the three Clemice brothers out of action, the family may safely retrieve their treasure."

Henri, Comte de Sancoubrey, removed his family treasure from the vault and showed his gratitude toward those who had helped him in his quest. He rewarded the village strong-men handsomely and made a generous donation to the church. He made sure that Adelaide Kidd could return home with a substantial gift for her grandfather, along with the body of her father, who could now be buried with due dignity in the land of his birth.

Holmes refused to accept any reward from the Count, insisting only that he meet the agreed fee, along with the expenses incurred by the two of us during our time assisting the French nobleman in his quest.

The hand, which had been removed from the nobleman's great-grandfather on the battlefield of Waterloo, was returned to the family for burial alongside the man's interred remains in his grave near the *château*. He could finally rest in peace.

It came as no surprise to me when, a couple of months after our return from France, Holmes read the announcement of the death of Jotham Kidd, aged ninety-six years, who had passed away peacefully in his bed. In the same edition, an article gave notice of the betrothal of Miss Adelaide Kidd, and Henri, Comte de Sancoubrey.

"I hope they will be very happy together," I replied.

"As do we all," added Holmes. "And I fancy that Goodluck Manor will shortly be on the market."

"Minus a mummified hand."

"Indeed."

Count Henri made me the gift of a pair of gold cuff-links, each bearing my own initials. My wife insisted that I wear them while penning this tale. A small gesture, but one I am delighted to make.

Pit of Death

The day might have started out as a bright summer's morning, but this optimistic beginning was not reflected in the darkness shrouding the countenance of Mr. Sherlock Holmes. My friend wasn't pleased at having his peace disturbed by Scotland Yard's Inspector Lestrade so early in the day. The manner in which he held his smoking pipe, and the way he kept glancing between the open window and the morning newspaper he had hurriedly put aside at the arrival of the policeman all spoke volumes about his annoyance.

"Now, listen here, Lestrade," he snapped. "If you are asking me to take part in a search for a couple of men who have gone missing, then all I can say is that the police are much better equipped than I'm for finding these unfortunates. People go missing all the time. It is a sad fact of life, but it isn't a matter likely to engage my own professional interest."

Lestrade didn't appear to be deterred by this cold reception. From his facial expression and the way he held his body, I could tell that the inspector was also struggling to maintain his own composure. "I can assure you, Mr. Holmes, there is more to this business than simply a few men going missing. A body has now been found."

"Down the pit?"

"That's right."

"I'm sorry to have to admit the fact, Lestrade," continued Holmes, "but that isn't a particularly unusual tragedy in the coal mining industry, even today."

"Perhaps, but the Durham Constabulary have already been making inquiries into that man's death, and the more they investigate, the more they realize they are dealing with something extremely dark. For one thing, the corpse shows signs of having been crushed to death, but upon interviewing every single man on the shift during which the man died, they can find no satisfactory explanation for his demise. No machinery was being used in the locality that would account for the death, and no altercation had taken place which would satisfactorily explain human involvement in the tragedy."

Holmes shrugged. "But you hardly need my assistance with that."

"You aren't listening to me, Mr. Holmes," the policeman retorted. "I'm telling you that I *do* indeed need your assistance. There is something very strange about these disappearances. Extremely odd, and that's no exaggeration."

"Indeed, I have been listening to you, Inspector," replied Holmes. "You are telling me that these men went missing in County Durham, and that this mysterious death also took place there. That is nearly as far away from your customary haunts as anywhere in the entire country."

"I must concede the truth of that."

"Then why on earth can the Durham Constabulary not deal with the matter themselves?"

"That is something I'm trying to discover," continued the inspector in an exasperated tone of voice. "But all I can tell you at the moment is that the local constabulary are crying out for my help. And though I hesitate to admit the fact, they are crying out for your help as well."

"How have they heard of me?"

"Your reputation has spread far and wide – even to the slums and hovels of those poor working miners and their families."

"But why should this have anything to do with us down here?"

"Because the trail begins here in London."

Holmes steepled his fingers and thought deeply for a few minutes. "Very well, Lestrade," he concluded. "I shall give you the rest of this morning in which to convince me to travel with you up to Durham."

"I'm much obliged to you, Mr. Holmes."

"In that case, where do you wish to take us first?"

I could sense the inspector relax in a perceptible manner before he rose to his feet and retrieved his hat.

"To the home of Sir Archibald FitzMorris," he declared. "The owner of the County Durham mine at the center of our investigation."

Holmes and I exchanged glances of frustration. We both imagined that we were about to waste the rest of that glorious summer morning in pointless and mindless gossip – a wasted day in anybody's calendar.

We joined Lestrade outside, where he was waiting for us in one of Scotland Yard's four-wheelers, and together we trundled away along Baker Street and across town in the general direction of Chelsea.

The carriage drew to a halt outside an elegant Georgian townhouse, with a short flight of steps leading up to a solid front door, flanked by marble pillars.

"Coal mining is an extremely lucrative business," I opined as we stepped out of the carriage.

"For the bosses, perhaps," said Lestrade.

"But what about the ordinary working men?" asked Holmes. It was a long-discussed question which hung unanswered in the air as Lestrade rang the front doorbell, and we waited to be admitted into that glamorous building.

"We're here to see Sir Archibald," Lestrade told the maid as she opened the door. "He is expecting us."

After a hurried curtsey, the young woman led us into a cheerless side-room and left us there. She immediately turned and clattered away along the stone-paved corridor toward the rear of the building.

I looked around the room. I was surprised that I could identify very little which might connect the owner of the property with the coal-mining industry. Instead, it appeared evident that this man had spent some time in the Far East.

A man appeared in the doorway.

"Good morning, gentlemen," he began. "I am Sir Archibald FitzMorris. I know Inspector Lestrade, but you other gentlemen are new to me."

Holmes stepped forward. "I am Sherlock Holmes," he said, "and this is my associate, Dr. John Watson. I'm a consulting detective, and we're here at the behest of the inspector."

All eyes turned to the Scotland Yarder.

"May we talk with you in more congenial surroundings, Sir Archibald?" the policeman asked.

"Certainly, Inspector," said Sir Archibald, as he turned and led the way along the corridor and into a comfortable withdrawing room.

I now had time to observe the colliery owner himself – a habit I had picked up from so many years spent with Sherlock Holmes. Here was clearly in his middle years. His head, which was amazingly round in shape, was almost completely bald. This lack of hair on top was made up for by a neatly trimmed beard and sideburns, though any further facial hair had been carefully shaved away.

In attire, Sir Archibald was neatly dressed in a suit of dark gray cloth, evidently custom-made by a firm of bespoke tailors situated in the street of Savile Row in Mayfair.

Sir Archibald smiled and invited his three visitors to sit down.

"Now, gentlemen," he said, "how may I assist you?"

"You are the owner of a coal mine in County Durham," stated Lestrade.

"That is correct, Inspector," replied our host. "The Nanking Mine. It is a rather odd and somewhat exotic name, I must admit. My grandfather decided on it when he took over the working of a much-more ancient mine and sank the first new shaft. He thought the name would help to give the place a touch of class – a taste of the Orient. But that was more than fifty years ago now."

"And is the mine productive?"

"Very much so," said Sir Archibald. "Those old pit workings were abandoned long ago as worked out, but the new shaft was cut to a much lower level, where a far richer seam was discovered. That pit now supplies a good quality coal for household use, and it sells at a decent price."

"Providing you with a decent level of income, I see," added Holmes.

"That is true, Mr. Holmes. But of course that is nothing to be ashamed about, since I own the mine and its operations and, as a good capitalist, I believe I should be the one to enjoy the fruits of its success."

"Naturally," concluded Holmes, in a tone which made the mine owner purse his lips.

"I hope, Mr. Holmes," he said, "that you aren't one of these Socialists who believe the working man should share the profits of his labors."

"Perish the thought," replied Holmes, with a hint of sarcasm. "I merely feel that your workers should be paid a decent and fair wage for their toil."

"I pay as well as anyone else in the industry," replied Sir Archibald, clearly annoyed by the comment. "Now, may we please get down to the purpose of you visit here?"

"Certainly," said Lestrade, once more taking control of the discussion. "You will no doubt be aware that miners have gone missing in recent months."

Sir Archibald nodded slowly. "I'm of course aware of that fact," he said. "But I see nothing strange in it. After all, people do go missing from time to time, for their own particular and various reasons. Often they emerge again years later in some other part of the country. Sometimes even with another family." He laughed. "Having abandoned their former spouse, or after a falling out with their fellow workers."

"True," said Lestrade. "But you have lost five men in the last couple of years."

"I haven't been keeping count," admitted Sir Archibald, "but I see no reason for it to become the subject of a police investigation."

"But now a body has been discovered," added Lestrade.

"Again, I am aware of that fact," said Sir Archibald. "But coal mining is a dangerous occupation, Inspector. Tragically, men do die in the mines of our country. As in many other industries. We have attempted to introduce the latest safety measures for our miners, so once again, I see no reason for this to be a matter of concern for the police."

"It is merely that the coroner in Durham isn't satisfied with the *post mortem* examination, and has asked us to investigate the matter further."

"Well," said Sir Archibald, "I have told you all I know about the matter. Unless you imagine that I have been spiriting away these men and hiding them somewhere down here in London." He chuckled.

"Not at all, Sir Archibald."

"And as for the dead man, I'm confident that it will be shown to be an ordinary accident in a dangerous occupation."

Indicating that our interview was now at an end, Sir Archibald FitzMorris stood up and headed for the doorway.

"Wait a moment, Sir Archibald," said Holmes, sniffing the air. "I detect a slight musty scent in the atmosphere. Are you, by any chance, a collector of exotic animals?"

Our host brightened up at the mention of a subject which clearly was close to his heart.

"Oh, yes, Mr. Holmes. I have a collection of reptiles."

"May we see them?" asked Holmes.

"Why, of course," our host replied, and led the way through one of the connecting doors, into a room lined with glass vivarium tanks. These contained a selection of reptiles of various kinds.

"Lizards, skinks, and a number of small snakes," said Sir Archibald. "It is my obsession."

"Am I correct in thinking," said Holmes cautiously, "that all of these specimens originated in Southern Asia? French Indochina, perhaps?"

"You seem to know a great deal about reptiles."

"Not at all. Merely a passing interest."

"I began to acquire these animals during my travels in Southeast Asia, in the very area you mentioned. I was visiting there partly on business, organizing coaling depots for steamships across the Empire, and partly for pleasure. I spent a couple of years out there, and came back with a small collection of animals, which has expanded over the years."

"How long ago was that?"

"Oh, let me see now – it must be about twenty-five years ago."

Once more outside in the bright morning air, Holmes turned to confront the inspector.

"Well, Lestrade, you certainly seem to be in possession of a most intriguing mystery here. What do you intend to do now?"

"I intend to go up to Durham tomorrow, in order to help clear up this matter. It will allow them time to organize themselves in preparation for our visit. Will you come with me, Mr. Holmes? Dr. Watson?"

Holmes looked to me. "What do you say, Watson?" he asked me. "Will you be free to join us?"

"You know you can rely on me," I replied. "I'll certainly come along with you."

"If nothing else," continued Lestrade, "you might enjoy the Miners' Gala, which is due to take place in Durham City on this coming Saturday. The locals call it the Big Meeting because, for many people, it is the only time in the entire year when families are free to meet together. It's a day of games and competitions, along with speeches by Trades Union officials. Oh, and there's to be a service in the Cathedral as well, for the first time in the history of the event."

The following afternoon, we alighted at Durham's main-line station, courtesy of the North Eastern Railway. The view from the viaduct, which we crossed immediately before reaching the station, has always been for me, on the few occasions when I have traveled that way, one of the most spectacular of all railway views. The solid castle and the majestic cathedral are spectacular, particularly in the light of the afternoon sunshine. Inspector Lestrade also sat transfixed by the sight, although Holmes paid little or no attention to it.

On the platform, we were greeted by a small group of policemen.

The senior of the group introduced himself as Inspector Cragbrook, welcoming us to the City and the County of Durham.

We followed him outside the station to where an enclosed carriage was waiting for us.

"It's good of you all to come at such short notice," said the local man. "But this is also a particularly busy weekend. However, I have managed to arrange accommodation for you all – even though we could only find one hotel bedroom. That I have reserved for Mr. Sherlock Holmes."

Holmes nodded his thanks.

"Inspector Lestrade will be the guest of myself and my wife, whilst Dr. Watson has been invited to stay at the home of my sergeant."

I noticed one of the other policeman smile. He seemed affable enough.

"But first, Mr. Holmes, I imagine you will want to view the body of the victim."

"That is indeed my wish, Inspector," replied Holmes. "And without delay, if that is possible."

The carriage drove off. "In that case, we must travel to Police Headquarters at Aykley Heads."

We were soon there and ushered inside, to be taken down to the morgue, where the police surgeon was waiting for us.

"Ah, Mr. Holmes," said the police surgeon. "I have heard so much about you, and I'm sure that, if anyone can solve this strange conundrum, then it has to be yourself."

Without comment, Holmes turned to the slab in the middle of the room and indicated the white cloth covering it.

"Is this the body?"

The surgeon removed the covering with the utmost care.

"Here he is – Amos Williamson."

The body of a man, perhaps in his mid-thirties, lay before us. Apart from signs of the usual *post mortem* inspection, there seemed to be little wrong with the corpse.

"In every other respect," said the surgeon, "he is a fit and healthy man, even taking into account the nature of his employment. The mining industry is dangerous and life-shortening for many men."

"And what is your conclusion, Doctor?"

"He died of asphyxiation, Mr. Holmes. The air has been squeezed out of him. You can see some bruising to the upper abdomen. The man sustained a number of broken ribs, with one of them having pierced the right lung."

Holmes looked to me for comment.

"Yes, that is a most likely reason for his death," I said after examining the body. "I have seen it many times when I was on service in Afghanistan. Men crushed by a horse or a gun-carriage. If you can reach the man soon enough after the event, it is sometimes possible to breathe life back into him again."

The surgeon nodded.

"But how was the injury inflicted in this case?"

"It seems to me that there are three possibilities," said the police surgeon. "The first is that he was crushed by machinery. The mine authorities have looked into that possibility, and confirm that at the time, no such equipment was being used in the area where he had been working."

"And the second possibility?" asked Holmes.

"That the crush by a human stampede in the confines of the mine could have caused the death."

"And was such a stampede reported on the day of the accident?"

"None of those later interviewed remembered there being any such incident."

"And third possibility?"

"If it wasn't an accident," continued the police surgeon, "then we're left with the possibility that it was murder. That the man had been grasped from behind by somebody stronger than himself and had the air squeezed out of him."

"Is that possible?" asked Holmes.

"Theoretically," said the police surgeon, "but it would take a very strong individual to kill a man in that way."

"Even a physically active man like a coal-miner?"

"Even so."

"And which of these three possibilities do you consider the most likely?"

The surgeon gave us each a cold stare. "None."

"But what other possibilities are there?" I asked.

"That is what we're hoping Mr. Sherlock Holmes will be able to discover for us. That is the reason for you being here, is it not?"

"There is still the other matter," continued Holmes. "The business of the disappearing miners."

The police surgeon shrugged. "Without a body, that matter is outside my province. All I can tell you is that the coroner wishes to release this body as soon as possible for burial. As you can imagine, mid-summer isn't a good time to be keeping the dead from their final resting places."

"Then let us try to expedite the matter," said Holmes. He turned to Cragbrook. "I should like to see the place where the body was found, and then pay a visit to the dead man's family."

"Certainly, Mr. Holmes. But those matters will have to wait until tomorrow."

With thanks expressed to the police surgeon, we each made our way to our assigned overnight accommodation.

Holmes turned to the local police inspector. "I should be obliged," he began, "if you could let me see the statements made by the men who were working down the mine during that man's last shift."

"Certainly, Mr. Holmes. I'll have them delivered to your hotel room within the hour."

As far as I was concerned, Sergeant Allerwick and his wife were the best hosts I could have expected. Their two children – a boy aged seven years and a girl of ten – seemed well behaved and friendly enough.

I slept well and was awakened early, in time for breakfast and personal preparations for the day ahead.

A knock at the front door announced that a carriage was waiting for the sergeant and myself out in the street, with Sherlock Holmes already on board.

"I trust you had a good night's sleep," I said by way of greeting.

My friend appeared distracted. "Indeed. Thank you, Watson. My mind was much taken by this case. At first I had a handful of possible solutions, but they are gradually diminishing in number as I consider them each more closely."

"Then perhaps this morning will move matters along for you," I suggested.

"The colliery is inevitably the place where we must begin our quest for the truth."

The exotically-named Nanking Mine lay at the end of a half-hour's journey along rough roads. The closer we came to the place, the less I liked the look of it. The entire valley in which the colliery lay appeared grim, to say the very least. The pithead winding gear rose like some huge beast above the colliery yard, dwarfing the surrounding area. There I could discern dwelling places: Humble homes of a most depressing nature. Some lined the streets of the adjacent village, while others lay within the yard itself, cheek-by-jowl with the mining operations. Above all of this, even the winding gear, stood the huge spoil heap. This black mountain hung with a menacing presence above the lives of the people in that small community.

"What a dreadful place to bring up children," I said with a sigh.

"Indeed" returned Holmes. "But the backstreets of London possess their own horrors. Our concern at the moment is with the underground workings."

Suspicious glances glared at us from all around. Dirty faced children looked up from the cobbled streets. Raggedly dressed women paused in hanging out their clothes, as they turned to watch us drive by. I wondered how clean those clothes would be when once they had been dried by such a dust laden atmosphere.

Our carriage pulled to a halt in the colliery yard itself and we all climbed out. The place was full of noise. The coal dryer hummed and the grader rattled as it sorted the different sizes of coal, while the railway wagons waited in line while they were filled noisily from a hopper above.

A man in a brown suit approached us from the official office. His face presented us with the only smile we would find there all day.

"Good morning, gentlemen," said the friendly face. "My name is Giles Ravenstone. I'm the colliery manager here. I know Inspector Cragbrook and the sergeant, but not you other gentlemen."

Cragbrook stepped forward. "It is indeed good of you to agree to meet us here today, Mr. Ravenstone. These gentlemen with me are Mr. Sherlock Holmes, from London, and his associate, Dr. John Watson. They are here to assist us in solving the mystery here at the Nanking Mine."

"Mystery?" queried the manager. "We have no mystery here. Only a few missing men, and another who has died in a mining accident."

Holmes stepped forward. "In that case, Mr. Ravenstone, you will have no objection to showing where the body was discovered."

"If you feel it would help you in any way, Mr. Holmes," said the manager, "then I'm sure we can oblige. Have you been below ground before?"

"Not in a coal mine," replied Holmes. "Although I have been to some very unusual places during my career. So I'm sure I can endure and indeed value this new experience."

Mr. Ravenstone led us to a wooden building close beside the mine operations and the winding engine shed.

"Now, gentlemen," he began. "We have here a set of coveralls for each of you, together with a helmet and a Safety Davy Lamp for each. Its purpose is to give warning of bad air down there. Keep the lamp close to the ground. When it burns low, it will be a visual warning of the presence of the invisible choke-damp gas. It will certainly choke you if you pay no heed to the warning. You must come out as soon as you can when the flame burns low. But have no fear, gentlemen, I shall be with you at all times, and I shall be carrying the lamp to illuminate your way. You will be safe with me. Now, I suggest you prepare yourselves for the descent into the mine."

A few minutes later, each dressed in the somewhat unfamiliar attire of a coal-miner, Holmes, myself, and the two Durham policemen stood beneath the huge winding-gear.

Inspector Lestrade took a deep breath and joined the rest of us as we followed the pit manager into the metal cage suspended over the top of the shaft. The manager informed us that we would be descending a total of eight-hundred feet to the bottom.

"We each need to be issued with a tally," said Mr. Ravenstone. "A disc with a number on it. This will be checked off when you return to the surface. It allows us to make sure that everybody is accounted for."

"So there must be a few of these tallies which have never been returned," noted Holmes.

"That's right, Mr. Holmes. Over the last year or so, several tallies were never returned. Each time that happened, we made a thorough search of the mine workings."

"And found no trace of the missing men," said Holmes.

The manager coughed nervously. "We have no idea what happened to those men. They might have come up with the rest of their shift, and then have left the village."

"Or they might still be down there."

"There is no direct evidence for that. They simply vanished. Alive or dead, nobody knows."

As the cage descended, we passed through a realm of utter darkness, aware only of the presence of each other in the gloom.

"This is as black as Newgate's knocker," muttered Lestrade, referring to London's notorious prison – a Cockney phrase for "pitch black".

We kept going down.

Occasionally, we passed openings in the wall, which appeared even more intensely dark than the shaft down which we were now traveling.

"Those lead to the older workings of the mine," the manager explained. "Some of the earlier much-shallower seams were worked out many years ago. Then they were abandoned and blocked off when we extended the shaft deeper into the earth."

"So no one ever goes in there," noted Holmes.

"That's correct, Mr. Holmes. If they did, they would soon become lost in a warren of passages. Go in there, and you would never come out again."

After several minutes, during which it was impossible to say how fast we were descending, we finally reached the bottom of the shaft and the cage jerked to a clattering halt.

Mr. Ravenstone stepped out. "Now, gentlemen, kindly follow me, and I will show you where the dead man was discovered."

We followed him into the darkness, passing men and boys engaged in their various activities in the workings. Some of the boys held jobs which merely to keep the air circulating through the mine – a humble but essential part of the operations.

I was glad to be wearing a stout pair of boots, as water was dripping from somewhere beyond our sight, and I had to avoid stumbling over the steel rails along which the mine's wagons, or tubs, were taken before being transferred to the surface.

The air was filled with the harsh noises of the working mine, and the atmosphere felt surprisingly hot and humid.

With nothing to guide us apart from the manager's lamp, I was completely lost when we came finally to a halt.

We gathered around a dark corner of the working area of the mine, into which Mr. Ravenstone shone his lamp. I could see nothing significant, but Holmes showed that he was intensely interested in this location.

"There," declared the manager. "That is the place where Mr. Williamson was discovered just a few days ago. There can surely be no mystery about his death. It was an accident, I tell you, like so many, caused by him being crushed against the rear wall by a passing tub on its way to the shaft. Those things can be extremely heavy when full of coal and can carry a considerable momentum when being pulled along by the ponies."

Without responding, Holmes began to explore the surrounding area, paying particular attention to a dark opening in the angle of the trackway.

"Where does that lead?"

"Lead? It doesn't lead anywhere. It least, not nowadays. It's one of the access shafts which were blocked off many years ago. I told you that there are ancient workings around here, and that shaft used to give access to the other levels above where we're now standing."

Holmes drew closer to the blocked-off shaft. And sniffed.

"What do you make of that smell?" he asked me.

The air was heavy with the odours of men, ponies, and industrial machinery. And yet, there was something familiar about it. Something that recalled another place and another time not so long before.

Holmes held his finger to his lips, so I remained quiet.

"I have seen all that I need to see down here, Mr. Ravenstone," he announced. "I think it's time for us to return to the surface. I would like now to pay a visit to the family of the dead man."

"Certainly, Mr. Holmes," said the manager.

The Durham policemen nodded that they could see no further reason to be down in the mine workings, so we headed back to the shaft, and to the cage that would take us back to the surface again.

The home which Amos Williamson had shared with his wife and family until his tragic death turned out to be a humble and yet well-cared-for property. We found his widow, Sarah, surrounded by her two children and her sister, Julia.

"I'm very sorry to hear about your loss, Mrs. Williamson," said Holmes. "I'm here to help the police to find out what really happened, and how your husband was died."

Sarah Williamson glared up at Holmes with her blue eyes, rimmed with red from so much crying. "His death was no accident!" she told him. "All his friends say that he was nowhere near the tubs at the time. That can mean only one thing: My husband was killed – *Murdered!*"

"But the police have interviewed everyone who was on that shift. I myself have read the statements, and they all seem to say the same thing: Nobody working that day was responsible for his death."

"That is nonsense!" declared the grief-stricken woman. "I know he was killed by somebody. And I want you to find out who that person was."

Holmes shook his head sadly. "The police have nothing to go on. No names. No suspects."

"But you are a clever man, Mr. Holmes," returned Sarah's sister, Julia. "I've heard about you. No matter how difficult, you are the man who can discover the truth."

"Even if the truth turns out to be something that neither you nor the police nor the mine officials have ever considered?"

The two women looked at each other for a moment.

Then Julia looked him in the eye. "Even so, Mr. Holmes. You have to find out for us."

With nothing further to discuss, it was clear that it was time for us to leave. I turned and followed Holmes out into the afternoon air. On the way out, I noticed Holmes, almost unobserved, leave a silver coin on the mantelshelf.

Saturday saw the Durham Miners' Gala, known as the Big Meeting, when mining families from across the coalfield descended upon the ancient city. It was a day for speeches, marches with banners, and a service at the Cathedral led by the Dean. Afterward, everybody returned to the Racecourse, where families and friends met together to share the food they had brought along with them.

"For many of these folk," said Sergeant Allerwick, "this is the one time in the year when they can get together. They all look forward to the Big Meeting eagerly."

Holmes and I wandered among the people, watching the children playing and the parents deep in conversation, until we heard somebody call our names.

"Mr. Holmes. Dr. Watson."

It was Julia. The sister of the dead man's wife.

We went across to join her and her own family.

"I have something for you, Mr. Holmes," said Julia, as she waved a piece of paper.

"What is it?"

"A list of the men we consider most likely to have killed Amos."

Holmes took the paper and looked down at it.

"Having read their statements, I see no reason why suspicion should be attached to any of these men," he told her. "Do the police know about your list?"

"I gave a copy to Sergeant Allerwick, but they're bound to have those men on their own list of suspects. Especially the one at the top: George Slimthorpe. He's a real character. Shady as well. And Mr. Holmes, he is a big man. Capable of crushing another to death with his own bare hands!"

"That's very interesting," replied Holmes. "Thank you for this."

"But you must act upon it, Mr. Holmes! Bring that beggar to justice."

As the day wore on, Holmes and I wandered through the streets of the old city and ended up in a small public house, filled with coalminers who were already halfway to intoxicated oblivion. Considering the harsh working conditions they had to endure almost daily, who could blame them?

We sat in a corner with a couple of glasses of ale in front of us, trying to remain unnoticed, but watching everything.

The door opened and another man came in. He was big, powerful, and sported a shaggy mane and brown beard. If anybody could ever be described as a bear, then it was surely him.

The bear scanned the tables, fixed his gaze upon the two of us, and advanced in our direction. His staggering gait showed that he had already drunk more than was good for him. Or perhaps for us as well.

He stood before our table and glared down at Holmes.

"So you are the famous Sherlock Holmes, are you?"

"I am Holmes."

"And you think I killed Amos Williamson."

"No."

"What do you mean by that? Am I not at the very top of the list of suspects?"

"If you are George Slimthorpe, then you are indeed at the top of *a* list. But not the list of my own suspects. Admittedly, you are probably strong enough to have killed the man by crushing the life out of him, but I don't think you did it."

Looking surprised, Slimthorpe sat down opposite us and accepted the offer of another drink.

When we were all settled, the miner rested his elbows on the table and stared at Holmes.

"Tell me, Mr. Holmes," he said. "Have you ever heard the legend of the Lambton Worm?"

"I have heard of it," said Holmes. "The Lambton Estate isn't far from here. But I should like to hear the legend told by yourself. There is obviously some reason for you to mention it, and I should like to hear what you have to tell me."

"Very well. Many years ago, John Lambton, heir of the Lambton estate, and a man with little respect for man or beast, one day went out to fish in the River Wear. He couldn't even do that right. Caught nothing all day. So he uttered a curse. Loud and long. Then he finally made a catch, but it turned out to be the ugliest and most vile worm you have ever seen or could imagine. It wasn't particularly big, but it was the most evil-looking creature anybody had ever seen."

"A worm?"

"So the legend tells us."

"Please carry on."

"In disgust, the young John Lambton threw the Worm down a nearby well, and paid it no further attention. But that worm grew, Mr. Holmes, and soon it emerged from its well and began to terrorize the entire neighborhood. It slaughtered livestock. It killed people. It grew in size until the people called upon Lambton to do something about stopping it. Well, John realized he had done wrong in unleashing this monster upon the local community so, in order to atone for his sins, he left the country, and went as a knight on Crusade to fight the Saracen."

Slimthorpe sipped his ale thoughtfully for a moment.

"Almost given up for dead, after seven long years, Sir John returned home. There he found the matter far worse than he had left it. During the time he had been away, brave knights had tried to kill the great Worm, but each time, the creature had ended up either killing or maiming every one of them. It was now time for Sir John to risk his own life. He took counsel from a local witch, who explained to him how he could defeat the monster – but there was a price to pay. The price was that, on his return from killing the Worm, he must kill the very first thing that came out to meet him. So he set out and slew the monster, but the first person to come out and congratulate him was his own father. Sir John refused to kill the old man, and thus brought down a curse upon the family which lasted for seven generations. No head of the Lambtons would ever die in their beds."

"This is all very interesting," said Holmes. "But why are you telling me this today?"

"Because, Mr. Holmes, the Worm has returned. She is back again. A huge monster."

"How do you know this?"

"Because I have seen her with my own eyes!"

"You're drunk," I told him.

"That's right!" he cried, running a hand across his face. "I am drunk. If I was sober, I would never be able to tell you this story. The very memory of that hideous face would strike me dumb."

Holmes seemed much more sympathetic. "Where did this happen? Tell us exactly what you saw."

Slimthorpe again leaned forward and looked from one to the other of us.

"It was a few weeks ago. Down in the area not far from that mine, in the vicinity of the Old Grange. I have always been a small-time poacher. I have often taken rabbits for the pot, and pheasants for a special treat for my wife and family. Occasionally, I even ventured into that part of the countryside. I know the farmer there, and he has always been ready to look the other way whenever I've been out with my snares at night. But recently, even he has been nervous, sensing a terror among the local animals, and among his own livestock – as though something was wanting to kill them. And if the poor animals thought that, then they were right to be terrified. That farmer, along with others in that area, has lost livestock. Not to any wolf or big cat. No. They simply disappeared without trace."

"What exactly did you see on the night in question?" persisted Holmes.

"I'm telling you. It was the Worm. Lengthy. She was so long that I couldn't measure her. I was alerted at first by the sound of slithering among the undergrowth. I lay still and looked. The head appeared first. Evil, with big eyes and a huge mouth. I watched her for a while, but when that head turned in my direction, I knew that she had me in her sights. That was enough for me, I can tell you. I took to my heels and ran for my life. I didn't look back, in case the Worm took me. I haven't been back to those parts since that night. Even in the daylight."

Two other men now entered the bar-room and came to stand behind Slimthorpe.

"You haven't been boring people with that story of yours, have you, Geordie?" said one of them.

"We've come to take you home, you old fool!" said the other. "Your wife's worried about you."

As the two newcomers escorted away the man who had been telling us his tale, Slimthorpe turned with one final message for Holmes. "The men are all scared of going down that pit, Mr. Holmes. They're afraid they might not come up again. They go because they have no choice. That mine is known as 'The Pit of Death'."

When the three men had gone, Holmes turned to me. "The time has come for me to return the hotel. I have some thinking to do."

Within ten minutes, I had left Holmes sitting in his room, with the smoke of pipe tobacco swirling around his head.

The following morning, I returned to the hotel bedroom to find Holmes still asleep, and the room so thick with tobacco smoke that I would hardly see across the room. So I sat. And waited. Eventually, I heard him call my name.

"Watson."

"Yes?"

"Do you have your service revolver with you?"

"Indeed I do," I reassured him.

"Good. Because today we're going to either solve this mystery, or else die in the attempt."

"What do have in mind?"

"After luncheon, we must travel to the area of the Old Grange. But first I need to consult a plan of the old mine workings – the ones from before the present enterprise."

Later that morning, the manager shook his head. "We have no plans that go back that far, Mr. Holmes. All we know is that we need to keep well away from those old workings. Some of them came perilously close to ground level. Claims have been made against us for damage caused by subsidence, but we have always claimed that such liability has nothing to do with us."

"And the Old Grange?"

"The Old Grange is a large country house which belongs to the colliery owner, Sir Archibald FitzMorris. His grandfather built the place. Later, Sir Archibald's father lived there, and as soon as the old man died, the son moved away to London, left me in charge of the colliery, and leased out the old building."

"Who has the lease at the moment?" asked Holmes. "Who lives there?"

"A Scotsman has lived for many years – a man by the name of Rockall. I believe he used to be a Big Game Hunter somewhere in Southern Africa, but there's never been any big game around here for him to hunt."

"Until now." Holmes raised his eyebrows. "May we go and visit him?"

"Indeed. He prefers his own company, but he might be prepared to welcome you."

"But first, we need to examine the surrounding area."

The two local policemen grew bored of watching Holmes making his detailed exploration and went about their other duties. This left the pit manager, Inspector Lestrade, Holmes, and myself to continue our investigation of the area around the Old Grange. The countryside consisted of a wide but steep-sided valley, consisting of relatively rich pastureland.

Holmes spent much of the following hour examining the side of the valley nearest to the mining operations. "The original mining must have been not far from here."

"That has to be true, Mr. Holmes," said Ravenstone. "Behind that cliff-side. Somewhere."

"In fact," continued Holmes, "I can detect signs of the subsidence that you were telling us about. If I'm correct in my conclusions, there must be an opening from here giving access to those ancient workings."

We kept searching, until Holmes pulled aside a clump of shrubbery, stood erect, and pointed to a dark opening.

"I have never noticed that before," said the manager.

Holmes turned to me. "What do you make of this?"

I drew closer. "It certainly looks like the opening to a passageway."

"And the smell?"

"It's the same musty smell we came across inside the mine."

"Precisely. And where else have we come across it?"

I had to think carefully. "In London. At the Zoological gardens. The herpetological section."

"Come, come. You're evading the issue."

"We came across it at the home of Sir Archibald."

"I knew you would get to the point eventually."

"But what does it mean?"

The opening to the hole was large enough for a man to crawl into. And Holmes did just that, disappearing into the darkness for a couple of minutes, and returning with an expression of satisfaction on his face, and his lighted pipe in his mouth.

"Now, it's time for us to go and meet the Great Hunter. The man who lives at the Old Manor. Rockall."

The building was perhaps a hundred years old and somewhat poorly maintained, but the man himself was at home and answered Holmes's insistent knock at the front door.

"Good afternoon, gentlemen," said Rockall.

The hunter was a tall man with fair hair and a face of freckles, adorned by a rich red beard.

"Mr. Ravenstone, I know," continued Rockall. "And you must be the famous Sherlock Holmes and Doctor Watson."

"And Inspector Lestrade of Scotland Yard," added our accompanying policeman.

"I'm indeed pleased to meet you. Sir Archibald sent me a message telling me that you might be calling on me in the near future."

"And you are the hunter that people are telling us about."

Rockall nodded graciously. "Come inside," he said. "The afternoon is drawing on, and it must be nearly time for tea. As I live entirely by myself, I have to look to such things on my own."

Our host led us into a large living room. The walls were decorated with photographs of the man himself, standing over certain animals, mostly rhinoceros and elephant, which certainly looked to be dead. There were also the heads of various animals which had been expertly mounted and impressively displayed.

"This is quite a collection," Holmes said as Rockall returned to the room a few minutes later, carrying a tray of light refreshments.

"I'm retired now, Mr. Holmes," he replied as he laid out the small table in the middle of the room. "I exist mainly on the income from the books I write – relating the exploits of myself and my companions over many years in the wilds of Africa."

As we sat together, drinking tea, our host sat back and looked at my friend.

"Your arrival here suggests that you know something of my story, Mr. Holmes, although perhaps very little in the way of detail, so I shall now provide you with a little more in the way of explanation."

"Please carry on," said Holmes.

"A couple of years ago, after many years in Africa, I arrived back in England, determined to live out the rest of my life in quiet isolation. But at the time I had nowhere to live. It just so happened that, one day I was at a social gathering where I met Sir Archibald FitzMorris – the man you met in London."

Holmes nodded.

"He told me that he owned an old manor house in County Durham – this house. He told me that he no longer used the building, but that he would be happy if I would like to come and live here, at a peppercorn rent, for as long as I wished."

We remained silent, patiently waiting for something more to emerge.

"There was of course more to the matter than simply providing an impoverished hunter with a house. Sir Archibald told me that the people who lived in the area of the Old Manor were subject to an illogical superstition about a dragon being on the loose. They called it 'The Worm'. Apparently this Worm was in the habit of taking livestock, and occasionally people as well, but few people had ever seen this monster, and nobody had ever been able to capture or to kill the creature – if it really existed. He felt that the presence of a game hunter in the area might provide some measure of reassurance for the local people."

"And what makes you think that my presence here has anything to do with this mystery?" Holmes asked him.

"You are too modest, Mr. Holmes. It all began with the mysterious disappearances of men from the pit, and now the police have the body of a man who has been crushed to death. That is the sort of mystery that would inevitably intrigue you."

"Do you think that these scare stories are based upon some reality?"

"They are certainly based upon the existence of something real – something which perhaps emerges from time to time in order to kill livestock and feast upon the abundance of men in the mine."

"Well, you certainly seem to think that is true."

"I merely entertain the possibility."

"Such a creature, if it exists, must be cold-blooded," added Holmes. "And where else in this cold climate might be more suitable for such a creature to live as in the abandoned tunnels inside a coal mine – a place which maintains a steady temperature throughout the year."

Giles Ravenstone leaned forward, clearly paying close attention to the discussion.

"And what do you think this mystery might be, Mr. Rockall," asked the manager.

"The very same thing that has occurred to Mr. Holmes."

"My own opinion is that, having considered all the other possibilities, whatever is left, however improbable, has to be the truth."

Rockall nodded. "As a man who has spent many years hunting in the wild, I have in my possession a gun such as will deal death to any creature I may encounter. Large or small. I'm talking of an Elephant Gun." He pointed to a rife resting against the wall in the far corner of the room. "A real beast of a thing," he said. "Two barrels, all cleaned and oiled. I need only load the gun, and it will be ready to go hunting." A gleam entered the eye of the hunter. "But will the dragon emerge from her hole tonight?"

"I'm certain that she will," replied Holmes, calmly. "I have myself ventured into the creature's lair and left there my scent, along with a strong smell of the tobacco I use. If she is cold-blooded, then she will need to eat only rarely, but the creature must be hungry by now. She was deprived of her last meal, and was forced to leave her prey dead but uneaten in the mine workings. The discovery of that body is the reason I was invited to come here. I believe that the creature will emerge from her burrow after dark and come looking. For me. Tonight."

"Do you really think it will be tonight?" asked Ravenstone.

"We can only wait," said Holmes.

"In the high latitudes of this part of the world, the twilight comes on later than in places farther south," mused Rockall, "so as we have some time yet to wait, I would like to invite you gentlemen to join me in sharing my simple Sunday evening supper. Cheese and bread."

As the time drew near for us to set about our quest, Rockall stood up and looked Holmes over.

"Speaking as a man experienced in the art of hunting," he said, "I think you may need a little extra help to defeat the monster. Every knight needs his armour."

"Armour?" I asked. "Is this really going to be so dangerous?"

"Without doubt," he replied.

Rockall disappeared for a moment and returned carrying a thick leather jacket, reinforced with metal padding.

"You must wear this, Mr. Holmes," he said, holding it out. "It may save you from the teeth of whatever vicious creature is out there."

The garment made Holmes appear much more bulky than normal but, in view of the undoubted danger, he offered no objections. This turn of events made me wonder what kind of peril the hunter was envisioning for my friend.

Darkness was beginning to creep across the landscape and settle over the fields like a great cloak. The scents of night were hanging heavy on the still evening air as together we made our way to the opening we had discovered earlier in the side of the cliff.

"Is your service revolver loaded, Watson?" asked Holmes.

"Indeed it is," I replied. "All this talk of a giant Worm makes me feel I could well need it tonight."

We gathered at the opening in the cliff.

The pit manager was keeping his distance. I could hardly blame the man.

"It's quite clear now," said Holmes, as he turned to look around him at the undergrowth, "that the Worm has already left her lair. Look at the grass. It has been pressed down flat by something huge. Believe me, the monster is out here, somewhere. Looking for me."

"But what exactly is this creature?" I asked.

"I imagine we are going to find that out very soon," said Holmes. He wasn't going to enlighten me at that moment.

As my pulse began to race even faster, I struggled to remain calm. I fumbled nervously with my service revolver. This simple action took me back to my days in the Army serving in Afghanistan. Many a night I had kept watch out in the wilds of that faraway land, waiting for death or danger to descend upon myself and my companions.

For several minutes we stood and waited. Our senses were on high alert, and becoming ever more attentive to each sound and smell, straining to distinguish the unusual sounds from the more customary nocturnal noises. But a strange silence had gripped that entire area of countryside. Nothing was moving. Even the usual evening birdsong had been stilled. The usual rustle of small animals in the undergrowth was absent. A sense of impending doom hung over everything. By instinct, the wildlife sensed danger. Something was out there.

Holmes now stepped into the open, offering himself as bait for the monster. His pipe sent the familiar acrid smell of its tobacco curling about him in the light breeze. If the creature was hunting, she would soon make her appearance.

A rustling sound attracted my attention, but it was only Lestrade, moving closer to Holmes. Our friend from Scotland Yard appeared to be completely out of his depth in this unusual environment, but his courage was no less diminished. He had often been with us, or sometimes against us, during so many of our encounters with crime and evil, but here he joined us in facing something even darker than we had encountered before.

In the silence, each of us harbored his own thoughts, unable to share them, and that only increased the tension. I waited. Holmes waited. The manager waited. Lestrade and

Rockall waited. And somewhere amongst that long grass, the monster waited.

The crisis, when it arrived, took us all by surprise as the creature made her move.

So many things happened at the same moment that I had little time to think.

The first thing I noticed in the half-light was a huge head with a vicious mouth, rising above the undergrowth. The olive-green skin was a perfect camouflage amidst the night-shaded shrubbery.

My blood froze.

Lestrade let out an oath.

The manager stood frozen to the spot.

Only Rockall remained calm.

Then, before I could even comprehend the speed in which it occurred, Sherlock Holmes was now gripped between the jaws of that monster, his body being quickly encircled by the crushing coils of a gigantic snake.

The creature had taken the bait.

But time was extremely short.

I knew what I had to do. I raised my revolver and, trying not to hit my friend, I fired at that monstrous head. My action distracted the Worm's attention for one vital moment. Or was it perhaps that she wasn't happy with her grip on the armored jacket? She loosened her teeth from their grip and turned those cold-blooded eyes upon me.

Perhaps the snake sensed danger.

The Universe held its breath.

Then Rockall, the Big Game Hunter, stepped forward, raised his elephant gun, and fired off both barrels at once.

The sound, exploded across the land, and echoed back to us like rolling thunder.

The devil-creature's head immediately disintegrated.

The hunter joined forces with myself and the pit manager to immediately tear Holmes away from the writhing clutches of the dead snake's coils. I examined him but, apart from some bruising to his ribs, he appeared to be unharmed by his close encounter with death.

Together we sat in the gathering darkness, all dazed and trying to make sense of what had just happened.

I felt physically sick at the memory of what I had been watching, the sight of snake's head, and now its gore, and the thought of what might have happened if Rockall had missed his mark.

All I could do was to breathe a word of thanks to the man with the elephant gun. Without him, my friend Sherlock Holmes would certainly have been crushed to death.

"It really is a great shame, you know," said Rockall, as he cradled his rifle.

"What is?" I asked him.

He indicated the dead snake. "No head to add to my collection. But the skin might yet be of some use."

"Perhaps it's edible," I told him.

Ravenstone shook his head vigorously. "I can't imagine anyone wanting to consume this animal after it has fed on the flesh of their loved ones."

"True," I conceded.

Then I turned to Holmes. "What have we here, then?"

"A python. Perhaps twenty-five to thirty feet in length."

"But how has it managed to live here almost entirely unnoticed?"

"Mr. Ravenstone tells us that the older workings of the mine are very ancient. Left to itself, such a monster would find plenty of room in there to live and grow. We have already discovered that underground tunnels maintain an even temperature, warm enough to allow her to live in relative comfort, and with a ready supply of food – both miners inside the workings, and animals in the fields around here. She had access to both."

"But where did she originally come from?" I persisted.

"Oh, that. You remember the smell we encountered at the home of Sir Archibald in London? The musty smell of reptiles in general, and of snakes in particular." Holmes relit his pipe. "I imagine that many years ago, when the family lived here at Old Grange, Sir Archibald's father, or perhaps even his grandfather, also kept reptiles as a pastime. Perhaps that is how Sir Archibald developed his own interest in the subject. It seems likely that one day, one of the snakes escaped and took up residence inside the mine. That must have been many years ago now – time enough for the python to have grown slowly but steadily to such a great length."

With our work in Durham completed, and with the monster having now been slain, Holmes and I joined Lestrade and headed south once more to London. And to home.

The sight of that huge python's head and mouth sometimes haunt my sleeping hours to this day.

Life in Durham returned to relative normality, and we have retained contact with many of the people we met there – not least the Big Game hunter, who emerged from his quiet life, becoming a famous local hero. Rockall never again had to pay for his own drinks at any bar in the entire county.

Then, a few months later, Holmes received a parcel. It turned out to be a pair of snake-skin shoes.

Holmes was never likely to make use of such a gift, and instead he passed the shoes on to his brother. Mycroft Holmes proudly wore those shoes when he traveled to Balmoral in Scotland to attend an audience with Queen Victoria. Her Majesty was much amused at the idea that "Saint George" had finally slain the dragon, with an Elephant Gun.

The Dark Tavern

As a result of the professional and personal demands being made upon my life during those darkening days of October, I was relieved that I could find nothing in the national or local press to add to my concerns. On the other hand, neither could I see anything that was likely to bring Sherlock Holmes out of his current gloomy shell. I thought that perhaps he ought to be allowed to browse the dearth of interesting news for himself. Perhaps he might find some mindless article to amuse him. It was for this reason that I passed the morning newspaper over to my friend, with a comment to that effect.

A few moments later, he tossed the journal back to me, with renewed urgency in his voice, and a corrective comment. "Look at the '*Stop Press*', Watson."

I looked. The brief article at the foot of the back page mentioned that a couple of mud larks, while scouring the briefly revealed banks of the low-tide Thames in search of items that they could sell, had discovered the body of a man. The police had not yet managed to identify the corpse.

"That is hardly a novelty," commented Holmes, "but I suppose that is the reason why Lestrade is at this moment climbing the stairs to the landing outside our rooms."

I had failed to hear the tell-tale sound of the inspector's familiar footfall upon the stairs, so I was alerted by the sound of a knock upon the door and the turning of the door-handle. I looked up just in time to watch the inspector enter the room.

"Ah, Lestrade!" said Holmes. "What a refreshing surprise it is to see you this morning. It seems this is becoming something of a habit of yours. Kindly take a seat here beside the fire. You look as if you need warming up."

"Thank you, I'm sure, Mr. Holmes," said Lestrade. "The weather certainly has taken a turn for the colder."

"Now," said Holmes, sitting back in his chair and observing the policeman over his steepled fingers, "what can we do this morning in order to assist the crime-fighting efforts of Scotland Yard?"

"Have you seen the latest in the local newspapers?"

"Reports of the unidentified corpse, you mean? We have indeed seen the article – brief as it is. However, I have usually considered the identification of such victims to be the province of the police. In which case, how do you imagine I may be of assistance?"

"I have to admit, Mr. Holmes, that you have proven to be of some help to us in the past. And it was for that reason that our thoughts turned to you on this occasion."

"Please carry on."

"We are entirely without a lead in this case. We can find no one who recognizes the man. And we can find no means of identification upon his person."

"In that case, how do you suppose I might be able to help?"

"You have your methods, and I merely thought you might be willing to use them to assist us on this occasion."

Holmes smiled. "To help identify the dead man?"

"The circumstances are somewhat perplexing, I have to admit. He was discovered on the mud banks of the Thames at low water. That is all we have to go on."

"Is this matter of any particular importance?"

"Without identifying the man, it is of course impossible to tell. However, I know that you enjoy unscrambling a conundrum, so before consigning the poor victim to a pauper's grave, we thought that perhaps this one might appeal to your turn of mind."

Holmes thought for a moment. Then he pushed himself to his feet. "You have transport for us, I presume."

"Indeed. A cab is waiting for us outside."

"Splendid. Very well, Inspector. Lead on. Watson, are you joining us? This might prove to be in your line of work."

"My appointments diary does appear to be rather full at the moment," I said, "but I suppose I could call upon one of my colleagues to cover my immediate obligations." I stood up reluctantly, grasped my hat, coat, and cane, and followed.

I found the morgue at Scotland Yard to be as cold and clinical as I ever remembered it. The scent of death pervaded every brick and tile of the place. I might be a medical professional, used to dealing with the realities of life and death, but I have to admit that I often feel a slight shudder pass through me on such occasions.

At Lestrade's instruction, the clinician wheeled out the corpse, placed the trolley it in the middle of the room, and removed the shroud to reveal the mortal remains of this unfortunate individual.

Holmes commenced his examination of the body.

"He was a young man, perhaps still in his twenties. The cause of death is obvious."

"Indeed," said Lestrade. "His throat has been cut."

Holmes examined the injury through his magnifying glass. "With the use of a knife which possessed a singular blade – one with a serrated edge, from which a number of teeth are missing. Distinctive. I am sure I would recognize the instrument if I ever saw it."

Lestrade raised an eyebrow in wonder, and perhaps some doubt, at such a confident statement.

Holmes continued his examination of the body. "He looks to be physically fit. Although clearly not a working seaman, his hands show that he has been involved in some kind of manual work, but only in recent days. He has been in the habit of paying particular attention to his own appearance, and his personal care. What do you think, Watson?"

181

I took off my coat, rolled up my sleeves, and examined the body. "I can add nothing further to what you have said," I told him. "I can only describe this crime as cold-blooded murder."

"Without a doubt."

I stepped back again and retrieved my coat.

"As you say, Inspector," said Holmes, "there is nothing on the body to assist us with identification."

The policeman nodded, relieved that his own conclusion had now been confirmed.

"Now we must turn our attention to whatever the man was wearing when he was discovered," said Holmes, glancing at Lestrade. "Can you show us his clothing?"

"Come. I'll show you." Lestrade led us through a plain green door into the next room. The clothes lay upon a steel table. "As you can see, these would suggest that he was a working seaman, but you have already dismissed that idea."

"Hmm." Holmes carefully sorted through the garments one by one. "Wool underwear. Linen shirt. Cotton trousers. Heavy cotton jacket. Leather sea boots. And a leather cap which might or might not have accompanied the rest." Holmes looked up. "Anything else?"

"That was everything," Lestrade confirmed. "Except that he had been weighed down by having an iron bar strapped across the torso."

"Then why isn't he now at the bottom of the Thames?"

"It seems that the body was dropped over the side of a ship while it was in port, possibly during the gathering darkness, but the pressure of the ebbing tide forced the corpse up against a series of wooden pilings. A group of mud larks found him while they were searching along the foreshore late last night."

Holmes nodded and began to sort through the young man's trouser pockets.

"We've already looked through those," said Lestrade.

Holmes nodded. "It is always worth gaining a second opinion."

We all watched as Holmes pulled out a small and tightly pressed fragment of paper.

"Must have missed that," grouched Lestrade.

"It was pressed well down."

"But I don't see much hope of finding any useful information from it."

"That is to be seen," returned Holmes as he searched through the trouser turn-ups. From these, he poured out a small quantity of clumped white powder, still there after submersion in the river.

Holmes tasted the powder, and examined it more closely through his magnifying glass. "Alum."

"Is that significant?"

"That also remains to be seen. But together with the crumpled paper, it might provide an indication. May I take this paper fragment and see what I can make of it?"

"Certainly, Mr. Holmes. If you can find out anything about this man, then it might be of the greatest help in our search for what happened to him, and why."

"And another thing."

"Yes?"

"I need a list of all the vessels that have visited the docks here in London during the past few days. Where they came from, where they were bound for, and what cargoes they were carrying."

"Do you have any idea how many hundreds of ships and boats pass along the Thames every single day?"

"Certainly I do. But you may confine your search to those which have been trading in both alum and scrap iron. I need that information. I need it quickly, and you are the only organization capable of acquiring it for me in short order."

"Very well, Mr. Holmes," said Lestrade with a sigh. "I'll get every man I have onto the job for you."

Back at 221b Baker Street, Holmes settled himself down to examine the small wad of paper he had discovered. He began by gently teasing the bundle out to its full extent. After several minutes, a small and ragged fragment lay flat upon the table.

He stood back and studied it thoughtfully. Then he examined it at closer range and in greater detail, first using his magnifying lens, and then progressing to placing the paper beneath his microscope.

"Hmm."

"What have you found?" I inquired.

"It appears to be a receipt from a shop in Newcastle-Upon-Tyne. A gentleman's outfitters. The name of the establishment has faded away, but a number appears at the top right-hand corner."

"The number from a receipt pad, perhaps?"

"Precisely. That is the clue we must follow. And we must do it as quickly as possible."

"I wonder how many such businesses there must be in Newcastle," I mused.

"And how many have issued numbered receipts in the recent past?"

A hurried visit to the local Reference Library produced a list of such gentlemen's establishments and their addresses. Holmes sent telegrams to each of these shops, mentioning the receipt number and asking for the name of the client and, if possible, a description of the man concerned.

Holmes received a single positive reply within the hour.

"Now," he declared as he stood before the fire, "at the very least, it seems we have a name."

"Will it be of any help to us?" I asked.

"Possibly. The receipt was given to a man called Richard Cadmus, upon the purchase of a pea-jacket."

"That sounds unusual," I replied. "Was he a military man?"

"Perhaps. But that name – *Cadmus* – rings a bell in my memory."

"The letter you received a few days ago," I said, recalling that Holmes had set it aside after initially dismissing it. "Wasn't that from a man called Cadmus?"

"You mean, the fish-monger?"

"That's the one."

"Whatever became of the letter?"

"It probably became lost among your chaotic filing system," I suggested. "I can only imagine that you put it to one side for future reference, but I have noticed that you often hide such correspondence in the pocket of your purple dressing gown."

"Was I wearing it that day?"

"In all probability. It will take only a few seconds to check the contents."

After a search through the said pockets, Holmes emerged triumphant, clutching several letters, including the one from the fish-monger. This he set about reading with much greater interest than on the previous occasion.

"Here we are. It seems that the writer's name is Joshua Cadmus, and he asks for my help in locating his son, with whom he has lost contact in recent days. He sounds worried. I was busy at the time, but perhaps now is the right moment to respond to his call for help. Ah, now I remember him. Cadmus owns one or two of the stalls down at the Billingsgate Fish Market."

"A businessman," I concluded, "rather than a mere street-corner shopkeeper."

Joshua Cadmus was nearing the conclusion of a particularly busy day when we arrived at the Fish Market in Lower Thames Street. The streets around the market were busy, and at this time of day the traffic consisted of horse-drawn wagons carrying barrels and wooden boxes, emptied and washed, for conveyance to the various railway stations, and thence returned to their home fishing ports. Cadmus was supervising the loading of the final cart leaving for Paddington Station.

On hearing that his son might have been found dead, Cadmus dropped everything he was doing, handed his work over to a subordinate, and insisted on accompanying Holmes and myself back to Scotland Yard in order to make the official identification.

In the gloom of the early evening, the morgue felt even more oppressive than it had on our previous visit earlier in the day. This heavy atmosphere clearly added to the weight of Joshua Cadmus' despair, as he positively identified the body on the trolley as that of his son, Richard. A mixture of emotions crowded through the man's heart and mind, and these showed upon his face until they burst out in a cry of anger which could be heard throughout the building.

"Who did this?" he demanded.

"We have no idea," said Lestrade, his face displaying its usual downcast aspect.

"We thought you might be able to throw some light onto the matter," said Holmes. "After all, you did send me a letter saying that you were concerned for the safety of your missing son."

"And I was right to be concerned, wasn't I?" shot back the fish-monger, as his red and angry eyes riveting Holmes. "But you were too late in offering to help me. The least you can do now is to investigate the matter and help bring the villain who killed my son to justice. Or do I have to do it all by myself?"

"It wouldn't be wise to take the law into your own hands, Mr. Cadmus," said Lestrade. "Now that we have the man's name, we can begin to investigate the matter in earnest."

"Begin? Have you done nothing at all so far?"

"We have these," said Lestrade as he placed a pile of papers on the desk in front of us. "Mr. Holmes, you asked for a list of all the vessels to have passed along the Thames during the past day or two. Here they are. Even down to the smallest barge."

"Thank you, Lestrade," said Holmes.

"And we have noted especially those vessels which have been transporting alum or scrap iron."

Holmes collected the bundle of papers and, as the police morgue attendant tidied away young Cadmus' body, he took them into an adjoining room in order to study them without interruptions from the rest of us.

I joined Lestrade and Mr. Cadmus in another side-office, where the inspector interviewed the grieving father in greater detail. Joshua Cadmus told us that his son had been working with the Coast Guard and law-enforcement officers along the northeast coast of England, keeping an eye open for any illegal smuggling activities.

Lestrade leapt into action, sending out a couple of runners. One he sent to the Admiralty in search of someone who could give further information about the work of the Coast Guard. The other was instructed to deliver a call for an individual from the Foreign Office.

Both officials arrived in short order, in time for Lestrade to outline his case to them. This he finished just as Sherlock Holmes arrived once more upon the scene.

"Well, Mr. Holmes," said Lestrade. "Have you found anything of interest?"

"A schooner, called the *Craster Bay*, arrived from the northeast the day before yesterday, with a cargo of alum."

"Alum? You mentioned that before."

"A salt of potassium sulphate, used in the dyeing industry, paper manufacture, and waterproofing of fabric, amongst other uses."

"And when did she leave?"

"Earlier today."

"Where was she going?"

"If this is indeed the right vessel," said Holmes, "the documents mention Holland. Vaguely."

"That is very interesting," said the official from the Foreign Office.

Holmes turned to the Admiralty official. "Since the Coast Guard are under the authority of the Admiralty, what can you tell us about the young man Cadmus, and the work he was involved in?"

"He was investigating a renewed activity amongst the smuggling community of northeast England," said the official.

"But I thought large-scale smuggling was a thing of the past," I stated.

"True enough," said the Admiralty Official. "Spirits and tobacco no longer bring the financial returns they once did. So these people must be dealing in something else. Something more lucrative."

"That's what we are afraid of," said the man from the Foreign Office.

"What sort of commodity might be attracting them?" Holmes shot back.

"That is the question that Richard Cadmus was investigating He gave us little in the way of feedback, but he felt sure he knew exactly what they were doing. And it all had to do with a certain man living in Northumberland, by the name of Gorgoson."

I had heard of that individual before, so I watched Holmes for some sign that he also recognized the name. His face remained a masterpiece of impassivity. "Whatever they're involved in smuggling," said Holmes thoughtfully, "it seems to be under the cover of a small boat, bringing alum down from the northeast coast, and transporting scrap iron across to the Netherlands."

"Or somewhere else along that coast of the German Ocean," added the Foreign Office man.

"And where might this schooner be at this precise moment?" asked Holmes.

All eyes turned to the man from the Admiralty.

"With the way the tides are running at the moment, and with a contrary wind blowing in from the sea, she is probably at this moment no farther downriver than Gravesend."

"Very well," declared Holmes. "Lestrade, send word down river to hold the schooner for examination, possibly on the pretext of studying her manifest. Meanwhile, get us down there in time to board her before she sails again. If this is indeed the vessel we're looking for, then I might be able to discover exactly what is going on here by posing as a member of her crew."

"You will have to take great care, Mr. Holmes," said Lestrade.

"I have every intention of doing so."

Sherlock Holmes instructed both myself and Joshua Cadmus to pack our bags for a few days away from home, and to meet each other again at King's Cross railway station at our earliest convenience.

Back at our rooms, Holmes gave me his clear instructions. "I want you, Watson, to take Cadmus with you – he may prove to be useful – and travel up to the coast of Northumberland. Wait for me there. Although, as we have already agreed, large-scale smuggling is very much a thing of the past, there is still one place which retains a particularly dubious reputation from those old days: A coastal tavern called The Wheelhouse Inn. Also in that area resides a man who is known to me through a family connection. He's the man we've already heard about: Harold Gorgoson. I suspect him of being at the very heart of this business. Be wary, and be sure to take your service revolver with you whenever you make contact."

"And are you really going to join the crew of that ship?"

"I shall attempt to board the vessel and inform the captain that I'm acting on instructions from Gorgoson, sent to replace the unfortunate Cadmus. If he accepts me, then it will confirm for us three important and significant facts, which will determine the course of this investigation: First, Gorgoson really is the man at the middle of this intrigue. Second, young Cadmus was indeed murdered by one of the crew, most probably by the captain himself. And third, the murder had been planned in advance. That it was cold-blooded and premeditated. Whatever happens, Watson, I want you to wait for me at that tavern. Our paths will surely cross again there."

"And we still have no idea what exactly these people are smuggling."

"None whatsoever, although a number of possibilities come to mind."

Holmes had already left by the time I had packed my traveling bag, pulled on my heavy overcoat, and hurried down the stairs once more.

As planned, I met Joshua Cadmus at King's Cross. There he revealed himself to be dressed and prepared much as I was, and yet he was in a state of mind somewhat different from my own. His face appeared clearly set with the determination of a man intent upon justice at any price.

We took seats on the late-night service on the East Coast line to Edinburgh, although we were due to leave this leg of our journey earlier, at Newcastle-upon-Tyne.

We journeyed north.

Through the darkest hours of that October night, I listened as rain occasionally rattled against the windows, making me glad that at the very least I was under cover. Lights occasionally flashed past us, places which were impossible to identify. Cadmus proved to be a poor traveling companion with little to say, although much seemed to be going on inside his mind.

We stepped down onto the dark platform at Newcastle-upon-Tyne in the early morning of the following day, and I had a painful crick in my neck. I looked around for the connecting train which would take me on to my next stop. Cadmus suddenly announced that he was going to leave me at this point and make contact with a representative from the Coast Guard.

"It was with them that my son was working when he died," said Joshua Cadmus. "At least that's what I understood from what Richard had told me."

"Very well," said I. "In that case, I shall make my own way to The Wheelhouse Inn, exactly as planned. Perhaps we shall meet up again later."

"I am sure we shall, Dr. Watson," he said as he turned his back on me and made his way toward the exit.

From this point, my own route was clear. I was obliged to take the mail train north along the main line, stopping at almost every junction, until we reached the historic market town of Alnwick. I had visited this place on a previous occasion and had been deeply impressed by the magnificent castle which dominates the town. This time, however, a study of that fortress would have to wait – at least until we had successfully dealt with the present crisis.

Standing on the railway platform at Alnwick, just visible in the half-light, I discovered a tall figure in a gray overcoat. My acquaintance with policemen meant that I was able to identify him readily as an officer of the law – not that there were many other people on the platform, apart from several employees of the railway company.

"Dr. Watson?" he inquired.

"Indeed," I replied, grasping his proffered hand. "I am Dr. John Watson."

"I am Inspector Nathaniel Bewick of the Northumberland County Constabulary. I wish you to be assured, Doctor, that we are prepared to provide you with all the support that we have available. Scotland Yard made that matter abundantly clear."

"I am indeed most grateful, Inspector."

"Were there not supposed to be two of you?"

"Two of us did indeed set off from London, but my companion, Mr. Cadmus, has decided to continue with his own inquiries at Newcastle. It is the death of his son that we're investigating."

"Of course."

"My instructions are to check in at The Wheelhouse Inn until Sherlock Holmes makes his appearance there."

"In that case, I have a horse-and-trap waiting to take you to your destination. It isn't very far away."

"Thank you. But one more thing – "

"Yes, Doctor?"

"Does the name 'Gorgoson' mean anything to you, Inspector?"

"Gorgoson? Indeed it does. He used to be high on the list of suspects involved in the smuggling trade. We could never catch the man, but we're sure that he still has his hand in questionable activities, even to this day."

We parted, and I stepped onto the vehicle he had procured for me, headed in the direction of the coast. We passed cold gray fields on both sides, where men, women, and animals were already beginning to emerge and take up their daily work. At that time of the year, the wind was biting as it blew in from the gray and cold waters of the German Ocean. I was tired after a night of failing to find much sleep on the train, and my mind was turning to my friend, Sherlock Holmes. Had he managed to board the schooner? Had he started to unravel this mystery? I thought also of Joshua Cadmus. What were his plans, having left me alone in order to pursue his own investigations? I felt annoyed at being left in the lurch like this.

I was so tired that I was nodding off as we trundled along, but a jolt roused me from a shallow slumber. I felt decidedly unsettled as I realized that we were approaching my final destination.

The prospect on every side had hardly improved. I could see the ocean, but no jetty or quayside. Rather, I could see a line of small, clinker-built fishing boats, or *cobles*, that had been dragged up onto the shingled foreshore. A row of fishermen's cottages overlooked the cold and depressing sea. Here was undoubtedly one of the bleakest places I had ever had cause to visit. Or was that merely a reflection generated by my own grim state of mind?

Our horse-and-trap drew up at the far end of the village road, in front of a solid-looking building which displayed a sign proclaiming it to be *The Wheelhouse Inn*. The building appeared to be constructed of the same gray stone as both the adjacent fishermen's cottages and the other village buildings. Not that there were many of those. On the other hand, this tavern seemed to be the largest building in the village, and sported a roof of red terracotta pantiles – the only color I could make out. In need of some warmth and a decent meal, I hoisted my bag out of the vehicle, paid the driver, and walked toward the front door of the inn. I could see nothing welcoming about the place. Not yet at any rate. The place appeared to be enveloped in a gloomy darkness as I entered.

A man seated at the reception desk looked up at me as I made my way inside. His look of bored disinterest turned to sullen hostility when he noticed that I was a stranger there.

"Yes?" he challenged me.

"My name is Doctor Watson, and I should like a room for the night. Or possibly for more than the one night."

Without looking down at his visitors' book, he sniffed. "All the rooms are full."

I looked around at the barren lounge with its empty chairs and tables. "At this time of the year?"

"At any time of the year."

"In that case, how do you manage to make a living?"

"That's my concern, Dr. Watson. What business do you have here, anyway?"

My mind went back to the instructions Sherlock Holmes had given me. "I am hoping to meet a friend. Harold Gorgoson."

At the mention of this name, an auburn-haired young woman who had been cleaning behind the bar looked up at me and frowned. The attitude of the man also altered considerably.

"Well," he said, "any friend of Mr. Gogoson is welcome here." He consulted his book. "Ah, now that I look more closely, I see that we do indeed have a room for you, Doctor."

He handed me a key.

"The most prestigious room in the place," he added. "With a sea-view prospect. And luncheon will be served in here at noon."

I acknowledged his welcoming comment with a smile. "That would be ideal."

After I had rested for a while, catching up on a couple of hours' lost sleep, I consumed a veritable feast of a midday meal and decided to explore outside. Not that there was much out there to see.

With my coat buttoned up against the cutting east wind, I wandered along the seafront. The only thing I could discover was a great deal of mud, a number of rocks, and the smell of ozone.

Not wanting to risk dampening the turn-ups of my trousers, I returned to the road and decided to continue my explorations on the following day.

I found that The Wheelhouse Inn tended to come alive every evening. It was then, at the end of an arduous working day, that the place would fill up with fishermen and local farm workers in search of companionship and liquid refreshment. Having a fresh audience to hear their tales, namely myself, these people were quick to include me in their conversations, and so I learned a great deal about the local situation and people. I heard of many things: About the legend of a man, one of several, who had been known as "The King of the Gypsies", and who had been involved in smuggling goods into southern Scotland not so many years before.

"But nothing like that is going on at the moment!" declared one man.

"Rubbish," said another, with a look of warning. "Something is going on here – but the truth is that we aren't involved in it."

"It's that fellow Gorgoson," said another, in hushed tones. "And we all know it!"

The atmosphere turned colder, as though some dark truth was being revealed. All eyes turned to the doorway, where a man had just come in. Here was a tough-looking fellow whose appearance brought a look of fear to the eyes of my companions. One man in our company rubbed his face, heavily bruised by some encounter with a weighty object. The message to me was clear: A heavy hand was taking charge of events in this community.

The morning following my first evening at the tavern, when I was much refreshed by another decent meal and a good night's rest, I continued to explore the village and the seafront. I watched the ebb tide. Before long it revealed a truly horrific sight: With the sea having retreated, I could see whole stretches of shoals and reefs of sharp limestone, littered with huge boulders, which had previously been hidden by the water. Here was danger sufficient to rip the bottom out of any ship which struck these underwater hazards.

Farther along, this death trap gave way to a kind of lagoon, or haven, which was protected by yet another obstacle which stretched like a finger out into the ocean, almost entirely surrounding the haven with a promontory of hard, vicious rock. I watched as a gang of men set about unloading a moored fishing boat of its catch of crabs and lobsters, and then hauling the vessel up above the high water line.

I heard a voice behind me. "Dr. Watson, I presume."

I turned, and immediately noticed a man standing a few feet away, watching me intently. His face displayed a disarming smile. He was tall, dark, with graying side-whiskers, and dressed in a smart suit. I failed to recognize him.

"Indeed."

"Allow me to introduce myself. My name is Harold Gorgoson. I understand we have a friend in common."

"Sherlock Holmes?"

He nodded.

"Certainly," I replied.

"In that case, I should like to invite you to visit me, to join me for dinner. I shall send a carriage to collect you at seven. Would that be convenient?"

I had been caught out with a lie, since I wasn't yet acquainted with this man. I felt obliged to remedy that error. I couldn't think at that moment of any convincing reason why I shouldn't be able to attend the appointment. "Seven, you say?" I nodded. "Thank you. I shall be ready."

"Splendid," said Gorgoson, before turning and heading back in the direction of the inn.

Everything and everybody seemed to be quite innocent. Was more going on than appeared on the surface? Perhaps Holmes had been right about shady activities occurring here. But there was no sign of this just yet. The only way I was to discover the truth was to join the man for dinner.

Harold Gorgoson's house was something quite amazing. And yet chilling. It gave the impression of being a small but well-formed country house, a manor house perhaps. Situated only a couple of miles from the ocean, and it stood out on a rise above the small fishing village. Beside the main front door I noticed a nameplate, with the name of the place carved into a slab of white limestone: *The Furze*. The interior of the building was splendidly furnished and fitted out. The dining table carried silver cutlery and best quality crockery. A series of oil-lamps lined the walls. I wondered how much of this had been paid for from the ill-gotten gains of the smuggling trade.

"Food from the sea which lies not far away," Gorgoson explained as the first course appeared. "Lobster and herring."

"Perfect," I replied, wondering why it was that Holmes had warned me against this man – and why the men of the village seemed to fear him. To me he appeared harmless enough.

"I live here alone," Gorgoson explained. "I have no wife and family. Never have had. So my housekeeper has brought in a few helpers from the village."

In the shadows, I immediately recognized the young woman I had first seen behind the bar at The Wheelhouse Inn. I tried to smile at her, but she remained grim-faced.

After these initial pleasantries, and after the first course of our meal had been cleared away, Gorgoson came to the point of our gathering. "What exactly are you doing here, Dr. Watson? What brings you to this wind-swept place so late in the year?"

"Me? I am waiting for somebody."

"Mr. Holmes, I imagine."

"How perceptive of you. Yes. He told me to stay here until he arrived."

"And when will that be?"

"I suppose that depends upon the tides and the winds."

"He is at sea, then?"

"I really don't know where he is at this precise moment."

"And what exactly is his business?"

"You'll have to ask him about that when he comes. But it has something to do with a body being discovered in the River Thames."

"London? Many miles from here. What would that have to do with me?"

"I'm not sure it has anything at all to do with you, Mr. Gorgoson."

He appeared to be relieved by this statement. And gave a benign smile.

"Sherlock Holmes has a mind," I told him, "which is sometimes difficult to comprehend."

Gorgoson nodded. "He and I have long been acquainted, so I'm well aware of his unfathomable turn of mind."

We sparred with each other for the rest of the evening, he trying to extract from me any further information I possessed about this case, which wasn't a great deal, while in turn, I tried to learn from him anything I could about his involvement in whatever it was that was going on here. And, in passing, I asked about the smuggling trade.

"Be assured, Doctor," he said as I prepared to take my leave, "large-scale smuggling of valuable goods has all but finished now along this coast. It's no longer worth our while to run such risks with the prospect of so little financial gain."

I declined the offer of a carriage back to the inn, and opted instead to walk the couple of miles down toward the coast. I had things to think about. What was he hiding?

Outside, I stood for a while in silence, looking back at the house. What was really going on here? Gorgoson might not be married, but he was clearly devoted to some enterprise in which he was presently involved. But what exactly that was, I still didn't have any idea.

As I stood in the darkness, I noticed figures moving about – men and women walking away from the back of the house. Trudging. The very set of their bodies told me that something was wrong.

Then I became aware of somebody standing close beside me.

"Who's there?" I whispered.

"It's only me," came a young female voice. "Annie. From the inn."

"Oh, hello. You shouldn't be out here alone at this time of night."

"Have no fear for me. I can look after myself, thank you."

I nodded toward the people moving in the darkness. "Who are those people? Where are they going?"

"Those are the latest consignment that Gorgoson and his men are smuggling."

I suddenly felt confused. "People? Is he dealing in illegal immigrants?"

"Illegal, yes. But not willing immigrants. This is a business which is very different from helping migrants. Something really terrible is happening here. Something extremely evil. Something that has to be stopped."

"But aren't you working for these people?"

"I thought *you* were working for them. You said you were Mr. Gorgoson's friend."

"Not me," I told her.

"Yes, I've been working here, but I'm not one of them. Somebody has to find out what's going on in this place."

"What have you done about it so far?"

"I was the one who told Richard Cadmus about what they're doing."

"Cadmus? That makes sense. And now he is dead," I added thoughtlessly.

"Is he?" she gasped in horror.

I realized how shocking my careless revelation had been. "And that is why I am here," I added quickly. "Waiting for my friend, Sherlock Holmes, to arrive and help solve this problem. He'll know what to do."

"Richard was such a nice young man. I got to know him quite well. I didn't know he was dead. I'm extremely sorry about that, but that makes it all the more important for *you* to do something. You're the only person here who can do anything now. You'll find that the entire village is on your side."

"Me? What do you imagine I can do?"

"When does your friend Mr. Sherlock Holmes get here?"

"When the schooner that he's on arrives."

"So, he's on board that accursed boat."

"Yes. When does it return?"

"Tomorrow night. It will be dark and moonless – ideal for moving contraband . . . and people. The vessel will anchor offshore during the darkest hours of the night, and a small boat will bring their consignment ashore."

"You say these rogues are smuggling people. But why?"

"It's a way of making money, of course."

"The notion of slavery is somewhat out of date," I suggested. "The American states fought a war over it not very long ago, and it is outlawed throughout the British Empire.

"It would be naïve to suggest that there is no slavery today, Dr. Watson," said Annie. "There are many things that enslave people: Poverty, illness, disabilities. Heartless crooks like these."

"Could you not tell the whole village about what you've discovered and organize them to put a stop to it?"

"The men of the village are convinced that something is going on here, but they aren't sure what it is. These criminals are ruthless people. If the village rose up against them, there would be a bloodbath. One or two of us have already suffered physical attacks for even suggesting it. Far better to let the police and law enforcement people deal with the matter rather than taking the law into our own hands."

The following day, the village appeared to be going about its daily routine, unhindered by thoughts of what might be going on in their midst. Fishing boats went out to their work, and came back again loaded with crab creels and lobster pots.

I turned away from the coast and back toward Gorgoson's house. I wanted to find out a little more about those people I had seen leaving from the rear of the building. Had they been legitimate workers or slaves?

Acting as though I were taking a casual saunter through the countryside, I went along the footpath I had shared with Annie the night before. Gradually, the house came into view. Even in the light of day, the place retained a forbidding appearance.

Not seeing anyone else, I worked around to the other side of the building. There I discovered an entrance, closed by double doors made of stout wood, and fastened with an iron bar across them. I decided to explore, so I lifted the iron bar and pushed open one of the doors, revealing a storage room of some kind.

I stepped across the filthy threshold.

The stale air from inside struck me with what felt almost like a physical blow. The stench of unwashed and uncared-for humanity pervaded the entire place. Iron chains hung from the walls, and the evidence of recent human occupation was unmistakeable. But I found that the place was empty.

"This is a stable," came a voice from behind me.

I turned, to find myself confronted by the owner of the house himself. Harold Gorgoson.

"Stable?"

"Certainly. That smell is a combination of horses, together with various other contributors. We sometimes have vagrants calling at the house here. We even had some call upon us here last night, so we provide this place as a kind of refuge for these unfortunate gentlemen of the road."

I began to doubt myself. Was this explanation enough to account for the existence of this place? And sufficient to explain the people that I'd seen moving about in the darkness on the previous evening? No, I concluded. He was clearly lying.

"I came here to say thank you once again for the excellent dinner you provided me with last night," I told him.

He gave me an innocent smile. "But when you arrived here just now, you were diverted by the sight of this building. Of course you were. Any companion of Sherlock Holmes could be expected to do nothing less."

"With my curiosity now satisfied," said I, "perhaps it's time that I left."

"Quite so, Dr. Watson."

Feeling ashamed at having been caught out, and with plenty more to think about, I realized that I would be pushing my luck if I stayed any longer, so I doffed my hat, returned to the door, and departed.

Back at the inn, I took to studying a couple of the books I had brought with me from home. My attention wasn't fully upon what I was reading, so I resigned myself to waiting for the inevitable events to unfold. For someone to arrive. For the truth to be revealed.

For the rest of that day, I remained the only person at the inn, which was hardly surprising given the time of the year. The cold wind was still blowing in from the German Ocean. The sky was overcast, and it mattered little that the night would be dark, windswept and moonless.

At mealtime, I noticed Annie give me a smile. It lit up her face. Had she learned about my morning exploit? Was I now forgiven for visiting Gorgoson?

As a clouded darkness fell, I looked out toward the ocean, but could see no sign of the anticipated vessel.

The usual drinkers and gossipers gathered that evening, and they lost ourselves in storytelling. Perhaps many of these tales had been augmented over the years by vivid imaginations, but my mind was also fixed upon other matters. Finally, when it was time for the others to leave, I retired to my bedroom, with its window looking out over the sea. I could see no sign of the schooner. Of course not. Why was I expecting it to appear so early in the evening? The darkness made it impossible to see anything or anybody out there with any clarity. These were just the right conditions for landing smuggled goods – or smuggled people.

The landlord unexpectedly brought me a mug of mulled wine and advised me to drink it all down. A good night's sleep would do me a world of good, he told me. I was delighted at his thoughtfulness.

But when he had left, I wondered about the man's motive. I suspected that the wine might be drugged. It would certainly suit the purposes of the present operation if I slept through the night, with no chance of interfering with their plans. I poured it out.

I remained in my day clothes, extinguished the lantern, and waited. As far as I could tell, the rest of the inn was enveloped in darkness. Then, at nearly two o'clock in the morning, I heard movement farther along the landing on which my room was situated. I moved quietly to the door, but found that it had been locked. Just then, before I could try to pick it, I heard footsteps. I heard somebody coming along the landing toward my own room. The light from a lantern spilled beneath the door.

I hurriedly climbed back into my bed, pulled up the counterpane, and feigned sleep.

The lock turned, the door opened, and a figure walked in – Careful. Silent.

The figure placed the lighted lantern onto the floor, and unfastened the wooden shutter, and placed the lantern on the windowsill. The darkness of the night appeared even more intense.

In the light of the lantern, I saw a face – no one that I recognized. I wondered about the staff of this tavern, and how deeply they were involved in this conspiracy. Or whether they all, as it appeared to me, being kept in order by Gorgoson's thugs

The man finished his task, returned to the doorway, slipped out onto the landing, and turned the lock closed again, before his footsteps disappeared along the wooden floorboards.

The light, still shining out from the window, was clearly intended to be a signal, a sign to somebody outside, perhaps at sea. It seemed that the arrival of the schooner was certainly now in the offing. Or was it already here?

I crept to the window and peered outside. Against the near blackness of the night, I noticed the dim outline of masts and spars, obviously belonging to some kind of ship, standing out in the ocean. Beyond those cruel and vicious rocks. I also saw movement. Even in the blackness, I could see a couple of small boats going and coming.

Several minutes passed, with people moving about downstairs. Then I heard a noise – footsteps – once again approaching my bedroom door. I dived back into bed.

I heard the lock click open, and the handle turn.

A figure entered. Not the landlord. Not the man who had last visited my room.

"Watson? Are you awake?"

"Holmes? Thank Heavens you're here!"

In the dim light of the lantern, I would never have recognized my friend if not for his voice. He was dressed in the manner of a sailor – and a tough one at that. But I was glad to see him all the same.

"We must be busy," he told me. "This entire business is about to be exposed."

"And about time too."

"Are you dressed?"

"I am."

"Then follow me."

So saying, he grasped hold of the lantern in the window and led the way back out and along the landing.

Holmes stopped at the next doorway and used a bent wire to turn the lock. The door opened, and inside we discovered the entire staff of The Wheelhouse Inn, cowering in the darkness. Annie threw herself at me, and held on tightly to my arm. Then she looked up. "Is this the Mr. Holmes you were telling me about?"

"It is."

"Then we must hurry."

The landlord bustled out onto the landing. "I'm glad you decided not to drink that mulled wine I gave you, Doctor," he told me. "It was Gorgoson's idea. It was drugged with a sleeping potion."

"Naturally."

"His people are taking over the place," he said, "but now we must alert the entire village. With the cat now well-and-truly out of the bag, we must mobilize the fishermen to take action. Quickly now – there is a back staircase we can use that will take us safely outside."

No one else seemed to be around so, as the others went about rousing the village, I followed Holmes toward the entrance hallway.

"This old building must be full of hidey-holes, used in the past for storing contraband," said Holmes. "But the present consignment of smuggled goods is being held down in the basement."

We descended into the depths of the building, where Holmes once more opened a locked door.

There, in the light of the lantern, I saw a sea of eyes, all looking up at me. None made a sound. I recognized the expressions of despair on the faces of the people huddled there in the darkness. Men, woman, and a few children.

"This is Gorgoson's cargo, Watson."

"Slaves," I replied.

Holmes nodded. "Homeless people. Stateless. Hopeless. People from across Europe, unable to afford their passage to a new life across the Atlantic. Swept up, like dregs, to be exploited by these evil people for their own selfish ends."

"The poorest of the poor," I concluded.

"Quite. Now, do you have your revolver with you?"

"I have it in my pocket."

"Capital. Now let us go up and meet these rogues. They will no doubt be waiting for us when we emerge."

He turned toward the staircase, leaving the door open. I followed.

At the top of the flight of stone steps, we emerged once more into the front passageway of the inn. There, as Holmes had predicted, we found that we weren't alone.

Half-a-dozen heavily built seamen stood around us. I noticed a couple of black eyes amongst them, and supposed this to be the work of Holmes in defending himself at some time during the voyage. A couple of lanterns lit up the faces of the two other men who were waiting for us there – one in particular.

"Good evening, Mr. Sherlock Holmes."

"Ah, Harold," said Holmes, standing to his full height, no longer the stooping seaman he had at first appeared. "I am ashamed to admit it, Watson, but this man is an acquaintance of my family."

"This fellow told me his name was Sigerson," said one of the sailors.

"A name he also uses when convenience requires it," said Gorgoson.

"Ah, Sutherland," said Holmes, addressing the man standing beside Gorgoson. "The captain of the schooner, and the man who murdered Richard Cadmus. He threatened me with that knife of his, Watson – the one he had used to kill the young man. And, as I predicted, I recognized it immediately as the murder weapon."

"Gorgoson is the man at the center of this web of intrigue," I noted.

"That was quickly confirmed when Sutherland allowed me to join the crew of the schooner. I rapidly learned the full story from the other members of the crew."

"When you reached Holland," said Gorgoson, "Sutherland sent me a wire to let me know that you were aboard, Holmes. You see, he never really trusted you. I knew immediately what was going on."

"And at the same time," said Holmes, "I sent a communication to Scotland Yard, who are about to descend upon this village in order to dismantle your evil schemes. It's time for you to surrender to the law-enforcement authorities."

Gorgoson raised a small but deadly-looking handgun, and pointed it at Holmes.

"I really have no wish to kill you," he said, "but you are in my way."

"And you are trading in human beings," said Holmes. "People who have been made vulnerable by their poverty, and now enslaved by you and your thugs here. Why?"

"I'm not as inhuman as you might think," said Gorgoson. "England has been made rich through trade, and the use of an industrial workforce provided by the poor working people of our land. Now that the trade unions are gaining power and demanding fair treatment and an increase in wages for their workers, we need a supply of people for our factories who will bring a smaller drain on the profits of our industrialists. These people are vital to the future prosperity of our country. We're merely supplying where there is a need."

"Nonsense!" snarled Holmes. "You're merely exploiting the poor, and being well paid for it by your corrupt cronies. You must surrender yourselves to the authorities and accept the consequences of your crimes. The hangman's rope is awaiting all of you."

A door opened, and we all turned to see Annie standing in the doorway. "There is a man here to see you, Mr. Gorgoson," she said.

Joshua Cadmus walked into the room and stood facing our two main opponents. "Which one of you two is responsible for killing my son?"

The captain looked up and gave a nasty grin. "And any moment now, you will end up as dead as he!" cried the man. "He was poking his nose into our affairs, and was about to go to Scotland Yard, so we had to deal with him. It was just everyone's misfortune that his body was discovered so quickly. Otherwise, we could have continued our business in peace."

"I think not," returned Cadmus. "The men of this village have finally discovered what you've been doing here, and they're coming together at this very moment to stop you. This building is currently surrounded by them, waiting to watch you leave – one way or another."

Gorgoson looked around at the thugs who were standing close behind Sutherland. "Go outside and check."

"Right you are," said one of them.

We waited in silence. Shortly afterwards the sound of shouts and scuffling reached us.

One of the thugs stumbled back inside the inn.

"You'd better think about leaving," he said to Gorgoson. "The fishermen we can deal with, but the village is at this moment filling up with armed men. Too many for us. We're going back to the ship."

Gorgoson looked around at the rest of us. In the confusion, I had taken the opportunity of removing my service revolver from my pocket, and was now pointing it at his head.

"I see we've reached an impasse," he declared. "I can barely say I'm surprised. I'm prepared to offer a solution. As I said, I have no wish to kill a family friend, nor do I relish having my head own blown off. I certainly don't wish to have my neck stretched by the law. If I swear to leave and never return to this village, will you let me go? Otherwise, there will be a bloodbath."

I was prepared to take the villain into custody regardless, but to my surprise, Holmes said nothing in reply.

"You can use your schooner," interrupted Cadmus.

"Go," added Holmes. "And never return."

Without a word, Gorgoson turned, and he and the ship's captain followed their crew, leaving the building quickly and heading for the seafront. From there they took a small boat out across the mounting seas to their vessel, where it was lying beyond the rocks.

As we all watched them go, catching whatever view we could of them in the near pitch blackness, I turned to Holmes. "How can you just let him escape?"

Without answering me, Holmes turned to Cadmus. "Did you accomplish your task?"

"That ship is definitely not seaworthy," said Cadmus, nodding.

This was a different aspect to the situation. "How can you be so certain?" I asked.

"Some of the locals helped me open the sea-cocks on that ship, and to make it impossible to close them. In this rough sea, the schooner will ship water and not be able to pump it out again."

"I estimate that they'll probably sink within the hour," added Holmes.

The police soon descended in number upon that small Northumberland village, where they spent the rest of the night interviewing, asking questions, and taking statements from almost everybody in the village.

Coast Guard vessels and locally owned fishing boats scoured the inshore and offshore waters for any sign of the escaping criminals. Police in the Netherlands closed down that end of the smuggling stream, and set free those unfortunate people who had been the victims of this cruel activity.

Scotland Yard still has an open book on the criminal activities of Gorgoson and his cronies, as the ship and crew were never seen again, but there is little chance of them ever finding the final resting place of the crew of the *Craster Bay*. The official opinion remains that the ship foundered somewhere in the middle of the German Ocean.

By the time daylight broke, we were all exhausted, and I was ready to return home to London.

I was standing on the shoreline with Sherlock Holmes at my side. We were both watching the village emerge out of the darkness of night. The gray skies had rolled back, allowing the first rays of the sun to rise out of the ocean and shine fully upon The Wheelhouse Inn. This gave a magical, almost innocent appearance to the place. And, as I was about to turn away and follow my luggage aboard the horse-and-trap that would take us back to the railway station at Alnwick, I noticed a figure standing on the balcony of the tavern. I recognized the figure that of as Annie, the young woman who had risked her life to inform me of the smuggling activities taking place around her.

She waved, and I waved back.

"Always an eye for the ladies, eh, Watson?" asked Sherlock Holmes.

I gave a chuckle. "It seems to me that perhaps that Inn is not quite such a dark place after all."

"Your morning letters, if I remember right, were from a fish-monger and a tidewaiter."

– Dr. John Watson
"The Noble Bachelor"

211

Umbrella Trouble

The month of October can often be one of the most depressing periods of the year – at least as far I am concerned. Especially when the weather is wet. That day, a gloom hung over our shared rooms in 221b Baker Street. The rain outside continued with a persistent intensity which seemed to allow for no respite.

My friend Sherlock Holmes was sitting much agitated, glaring toward the drawer which housed his syringe and supply of cocaine. I recognized the expression on his face. He was resisting temptation with practically the same intensity that Odysseus must have used when he resisted the death-call of the Sirens. And gradually losing the struggle.

I picked up my copy of the local morning newspaper and scanned the advertisements.

"I see an exhibition is being held at the Town Hall in Camberwell," I said.

No reaction whatsoever came from Holmes.

"Quite apposite to the day," I continued, trusting that my friend was indeed listening. "The exhibition concerns wet weather gear." I put down my newspaper. "Which reminds me: You really must purchase another umbrella."

"An umbrella?" Holmes sounded horrified as he looked round at me with irritation evident in his eyes.

"Certainly. In order to protect you against this insufferable downpour."

"Watson," he said in a tone which suggested disapproval, "the very idea of going outside in this weather, merely in order to purchase such a protective contraption, is totally illogical. The most appropriate time to purchase an umbrella, if indeed such a time ever does exist, has to be when it is, in fact, not raining outside."

"But everyone is carrying an umbrella nowadays," I replied. "Come rain or shine."

"Everybody? Surely you exaggerate."

"Not by much."

My friend's face now took on a defiant expression – which, in contrast to his former appearance, made a refreshing change.

"I bought an umbrella not long ago," he said. "A matter of a couple of months, in fact."

"Yes, I remember. And you left it on a Fulham omnibus – or so you informed me later. You never did find it again."

"It is all a matter of habit," said Holmes as he continued to fix me with his thoughtful gaze. "If my mind is engaged with other more important matters, I can hardly be expected to pay much attention to what other items of apparel I'm supposed to be carrying with me. It's rather like having a child with you and having the responsibility of keeping an eye on him or her. While I cannot speak for others, an umbrella, as far as I am concerned, is a sheer waste of time, and of good money."

"But you never forget your hat."

"Now that is a different matter altogether," he said. "I hardly need to think twice about what is on my head. My fore-and-aft hunting cap is quite sufficient for me, thank you very much. After all, it has a peak at the back as well as at the front. And that keeps the rain from dripping down the back of my neck."

"As you say," I retorted, "it is all a matter of lifestyle familiarity. Habit. In which case, I hardly think that I, myself, could ever become used to wearing such a cap on a regular basis."

"Which is why you own an umbrella, while I, at the moment, do not."

"*Touché.*"

"And besides, the first gust of wind would inevitably turn the thing inside out and force its owner to engage in a jolly dance. Comical, but hardly practical – at least in fulfilling my chosen profession."

He chuckled for a moment at the image he had conjured up. Then he turned to look out of the window and gave a long, heartfelt sigh.

"You certainly cannot stay in here all day long," I told him. "It's already been raining for the last two days, and shows little sign of ending just at the moment."

"If Scotland Yard could come up with some case worthy of my intellectual talents," said Holmes, "that might prove to be a better reason for venturing outdoors than going in search of an umbrella."

I stood up and reached for my coat, hat, and cane.

"Are you coming?" I asked.

"For what purpose? In order to purchase an umbrella?" He sighed and forced himself to rise from his chair.

"We can at the very least take a look at what the shops have on sale."

"Very well," he said with a sigh. "If I must. But I insist that we take a cab."

We alighted from the hansom in the middle of Regent Street and immediately ducked under the arcading, in search of shelter from the unrelenting downpour.

As fortune would have it, we had arrived directly outside the premised of Messrs Baldersby and Jones, Milliners, being the precise establishment we were seeking. They claimed to sell, and even rent, hats and other items of clothing and goods to the more discerning of customers, and we had both been patrons of the place during recent months.

"I suppose there is no escaping the fact that you wish to visit this establishment," sighed Holmes. "But I enter without any obligation or intention to purchasing anything."

Immediately inside the front entrance, a display of umbrellas and parasols attracted our attention.

"I see the proprietors are enjoying a brisk trade in these protectors from the present spell of weather," I said.

Holmes remained stubbornly silent.

As we were entering the shop, a young woman in a dark coat burst out through the front entrance, pushed past us, and unfurled her newly purchased umbrella above her head. She then scurried across the road, narrowly dodging an omnibus and a brace of cabs.

In her wake, both Holmes and I heard something fall to the ground.

On closer investigation, we noticed that an item of jewellery had fallen onto the roadway directly in front of us.

Holmes bent down to retrieve the article.

"It appears to be a woman's diamond bracelet," he said as he looked carefully at the object. "Expensive."

"The bracelet must belong to that young woman," I concluded, nodding in her direction. "There is nobody else around us who might have dropped it."

I then raised my arm and waved and shouted to the young woman. But she had already gone, and my words were drowned out amidst the cacophony of the morning traffic.

As he continued to examine the bracelet with great care, Holmes ventured with me into the milliner's shop, almost colliding with one of the sales staff.

"Good morning," said the man in a smart suit. "It must be Dr. Watson and Mr. Sherlock Holmes."

"Ah, good morning, Mr. Baldersby," said Holmes, suddenly taking an interest in the events taking place around him, and brightening up considerably.

"I recognize the deerstalker cap," said the shop owner. "Purchased from here, no doubt."

"No doubt."

"There you are, Watson," said Holmes as he turned to me. "Yet another reason to celebrate my sartorial individuality."

I chuckled.

Baldersby nodded, and the matter was dropped. "How may I help you, gentlemen?" asked the shop owner.

"The young woman who just left these premises in such a hurry," said Holmes. "It seems that she has dropped an item of jewellery into the roadway. This bracelet, in fact. We picked it up immediately outside your front door."

"Oh dear," said Baldersby, furrowing his forehead. "I have no recollection of having seen it before, and it was certainly not on her wrist when she purchased the umbrella. Otherwise, she would have made a noise by rattling it as she opened and closed her purse. I notice these things."

"I happen to know that you are assiduous at keeping records of those who purchase items from your establishment," said Holmes.

"That is quite right, Mr. Holmes. It really is important to us to record the contact details for each of our customers – if only to provide the patron with a proper receipt."

"In that case, you must have been particularly busy this morning."

"Run off our feet, I am pleased to say."

"Then you might be able to help us communicate with the young lady, in order to find out if the bracelet really does belong to her."

"I fully understand," said the man in the suit, "but it is our policy never to reveal details of our customers to any third party."

"Then you must also understand," said Holmes, "that in this particular case, the alternatives are either for us to notify the police, or for yourself to visit the young lady instead."

"On a day as hectic as this, that would be impossible," said Baldersby. "And it would be against our professional interests to be seen to have a policeman calling here."

"As we picked the bracelet up outside in the street," mused Holmes, "it is possible that it really has nothing to do with your business here."

"True. Well, if there is no alternative, and if it really is a matter of returning lost property, then providing you with her name and address would perhaps be an act of public service."

"Precisely."

Armed with the name and address supplied by Mr. Baldersby, Holmes and I took a cab to Cumberland Court, a suite of townhouses some half-a-mile away from Regent Street.

In answer to our knock, using a large and impressive brass knocker, the front door was opened by a young woman in a maid's uniform.

"How may I help you, gentlemen?" she asked. "I am sorry to have to tell you that the family are out for the day."

Holmes touched his hat. "We are looking for a young woman by the name of Agnes Smithercote."

The maid appeared surprised by this news. "Well, if you have any business with Agnes, then you'd better go round the back, to the servants' and tradesmen's entrance."

"Is she is a member of staff here, then?"

"She certainly is. Senior housemaid, in fact. A bit above her proper station if you ask me. This morning has been her half-day off, so she will probably be back again by now."

The same maid answered the back door when we knocked there a moment later and called upon us to step inside.

"You will find Agnes Smithercote in the servants' quarters," the maid told us. "Down the corridor, and first door on the right."

We knocked upon the door she had indicated, and a female voice from inside invited us to enter. There we found Agnes, a tall, slim, fair-haired young woman sitting in a corner of the room, reading a daily newspaper.

"Miss Smithercote?" inquired Holmes.

She looked up. "Yes?"

"My name is Sherlock Holmes, I am a private consulting detective, and this is my friend and colleague, Dr. John Watson."

"How may I help you, gentlemen?"

"Less than an hour ago, you visited a shop in Regent Street."

"Indeed I did. You might perhaps consider it inappropriate for a mere housemaid to be doing her shopping in such a thoroughfare."

"That is your business entirely," countered Holmes.

"I was there in order to purchase an umbrella."

"From Baldersby and Jones?"

"That's right. I like to purchase top quality goods whenever I can."

"Indeed. You hurried out, pushed passed us, and rushed across the road."

"Did I?"

"And, as you unfurled your newly purchased umbrella, something fell to the ground. Do you remember that?"

"I seem to recall feeling something brush past my shoulder, but I was running late and had no time to stop and look around me. I didn't consider the matter particularly important at the time."

"It seems that the item which fell to the ground was an item of jewellery."

Agnes laughed. "I can assure you, Mr. Holmes, that I am not wealthy enough to own any jewellery."

"But you could afford to buy a new umbrella."

"I have been saving up my money for many month in order to buy one. While we as a family were never well off, my mother always insisted that we purchase goods of the highest possible quality."

"Which you did."

She nodded. "I am convinced that my new purchase will serve me well for many years to come."

"So, you are not missing any pieces of jewellery."

"That is what I have already told you."

He held out the bracelet for the young woman to see. "Have you ever seen this before?"

"Certainly not! Is this the item you found fallen onto the ground?"

"Yes."

"Then I think, if I owned such an item, I would treat it with much greater respect and care than the person who lost it."

"I too should hope so," continued Holmes, "but it seems that the bracelet must have fallen to the ground when you raised the umbrella in order to open it against the rain."

"So it seems."

"Did you not think of opening it while you were still inside the shop, before parting with your hard-earned money for it?"

She laughed.

"Mr. Holmes, you obviously do not yourself own an umbrella. Are you not aware that it is commonly believed that opening an umbrella inside a house is risking bad luck?"

"Of course. I had it had slipped my mind for a moment. But how do you imagine the bracelet might have found its way into the folds of your umbrella?"

"I imagine somebody must have dropped it in there."

"On purpose, or by accident?"

"You're a detective, Mr. Holmes, and a good one – or so I have heard. What do you think happened?"

"It is far too early in our investigations to determine that." He stood up. "Well, thank you for answering my questions, Miss Smithercote. If a reward is offered for the return of this bracelet, then I shall certainly put your name forward to receive it."

She smiled. "That is very kind of you. Even in my present job, life can be somewhat limited by the price of everyday expenses."

Once outside, Holmes and I consulted on our next step.

"I have a number of errands to run," I told him. "One or two elderly ladies require my professional attention from time to time, and today is my day for visiting them. Although one particular old lady is now confined to her own home, she is well known among the privileged classes of London. If I could take the bracelet along with me, she might be able to help identify its owner."

"Splendid," replied Holmes, handing it to me. "Meanwhile, I shall have to call into the offices of *The Evening News*, and then return to Regent Street, in the hope that I can persuade Baldersby and Jones to let me have a list of all of their customers during the past week or so."

My old ladies always looked forward to my visits, and loved to have somebody there with whom they could chat. The lady I had in mind was surprised when I showed her the bracelet.

"That is a most beautiful piece of jewellery," she told me. "Wherever did you get hold of it, Dr. Watson?"

I told her the truth: That we had found it dropped in the street and were now looking for the owner.

"Then I hope you manage to find her. I am quite sure that the owner would be delighted to have it returned to her again."

"Have you ever seen it before?" I asked.

"You know," she told me, looking more closely at the bracelet, "I think I have . . . ."

When I returned to Baker Street later that afternoon, the rain was still torrential. As I loitered on the opposite side of the street from our rooms, waiting for the late afternoon traffic to clear sufficiently for me to cross in safety, I felt a hand touch my arm. I turned and found myself facing Sherlock Holmes.

"I believe we have visitors," said Holmes as he looked up at the windows of our apartment.

"So I see," I replied as I observed a police four-wheeler waiting outside our front door, and two silhouettes passing in front of the window – both men.

"How did your afternoon progress?" he asked me.

"Productive, I hope," I told him. "That old lady I was telling you about did remember the bracelet. She had seen it before, at an evening gathering some months ago. She is convinced that it belongs to Lady Leonora, the wife of Sir James Bullingworth-Webb, the Member of Parliament."

"Interesting."

"That's what I thought, but how it connects with the present investigation, I really have no idea."

"Perhaps we shall find out within the next few minutes. Come, Watson. It's time for us to discover exactly who has pressing business with us, and what that business might be."

Now heedless of the traffic, we both ran across the road, in through the front door, and up the stairs in double-quick time.

Without knocking, Holmes burst in, turning the heads of both of our visitors abruptly in our direction.

"Ah, Lestrade!" said Holmes in a tone which appeared brighter than the weather.

"There you are, Mr. Holmes," said the inspector. "I'm glad you have finally arrived."

"I was hardly expecting you."

"But you did put that enigmatic notice in the evening newspaper reporting that a certain item of ladies jewellery had been found."

"Ah, yes. The first edition seems to come out earlier every day. Still, I'm glad you're here in response to it."

"We are here also because we're engaged in a rather delicate business, and we are in need of your assistance. That entry in *The Evening News* shows us that we're certainly on the right track."

"Indeed?" said Holmes, as he invited us all to take seats around the room.

"This gentleman," continued Lestrade, "is Mr. Hamilton Bullingworth."

"The brother of Lady Leonora Bullingworth-Webb," added Holmes.

"That's quite right!" said Mr. Bullingworth, rather surprised. "Inspector, I can see now why you told me that this gentleman was exceptional."

"Purely elementary, I assure you," replied Holmes, with a smile.

"But now to business," said Lestrade.

"And it has something to do with Mr. Hamilton's sister."

"Correct."

"Kindly elaborate."

"It seems that on the night before last, the Bullingworth-Webb household suffered a burglary. A break-in, during which a certain item belonging to Lady Leonora was stolen from her jewel box."

"A certain item? A diamond bracelet, perhaps?"

"Precisely."

"Watson."

Taking my cue from Holmes, I reached into my inner coat pocket and brought out the bracelet which had been at the heart of our investigation.

"Great Scott!" exclaimed Bullingworth. "You've found it!"

"But how?" demanded the inspector.

"It fell from a newly purchased umbrella in the middle of Regent Street earlier today," replied Holmes. "I feel that, if any reward were to be offered for finding it, then the money should go to the young lady who purchased the umbrella in which it had been concealed."

"Certainly, certainly," agreed Bullingworth.

"I shall provide you with her name and address later, but first I should like to hear a detailed description of what occurred."

"Correct me if I'm wrong, Mr. Bullingworth," said Lestrade. "But it seems that during the evening, a man climbed up the outside wall of the house, broke in through the upstairs window, entered the lady's boudoir, opened her jewel case, removed that bracelet, and left by the same method."

"And how do you know that it was a man?"

"A large sized muddy footprint was found on the carpet flooring of the bedroom. It was larger than that of any normal woman."

"Or perhaps of any medium-sized man."

"That was our conclusion."

Holmes allowed a pensive expression to spread across his face.

"During the following day," said Holmes, "the thief obviously found the bracelet to be a little too hot to handle. Indeed, he tried his best to lose it by pushing it down into the folds of an umbrella which was being offered for sale in a certain shop in Regent Street."

"And you have been trying to return it to its rightful owner throughout the day."

"Indeed. But that was yesterday's crime," said Holmes. "Why have you come to visit me today?"

"A second break-in, almost exactly the same in every respect as the first, took place only yesterday evening."

"And what was taken this time?"

"Forty pounds in cash," said Hamilton Bullingworth. "Eight five-pound notes."

"And how do you know that it was the same thief as on the previous occasion?"

"Another footprint was discovered."

"Exactly the same as before?"

"That is the way it appears."

"An oversized boot, leaving a muddy footmark?"

"Yes. Precisely that."

Holmes tried hard to suppress the guffaw of laughter which was welling up inside him, but he failed, and let out the sort of laugh which might have been heard as far away as Whitehall.

"Forgive me, gentlemen," he said a moment later, "but this all sounds somewhat farcical to me."

"Farcical! Do you have an idea who the thief is, then?"

"I have a good idea. But first I would need to examine the scene of the break-ins."

"Of course," said the policeman.

"Very well, Lestrade. Kindly take us there."

Crammed together into the police vehicle we had passed earlier, the four of us rattled through the streets until we entered a gateway which led up along a gravel pathway to the front entrance of a particularly fashionable upper-class house on the north-eastern edge of London.

One of the maids answered our knock upon the front door and ushered us all into one of the front reception rooms. There we met Lady Leonora, a middle-aged woman, whose extraordinary personality filled the entire room with the sense of her presence.

"This is Mr. Sherlock Holmes," Inspector Lestrade explained to the lady, "and Dr. Watson."

"They are here to assist with the investigation into the theft of your diamond bracelet," added Hamilton Bullingworth. "And I am delighted to say that they have already managed to retrieve it."

"That is excellent work," declared Lady Leonora. "Who was the thief?"

"So far," said Lestrade, "he has not been identified."

"That is extremely unfortunate," she replied. "And what about the theft of the money?"

"We assume it was the same person who broke in on both occasions," said Lestrade, "but we're still in the dark as to the identity of that culprit as well."

"On the other hand," explained Mr. Bullingworth, "Mr. Holmes thinks he might know the name of the thief."

"Then who is it?"

"It would be a grave error to jump to such conclusions before examining all of the evidence at first hand," added Holmes. "I think we should like to begin by visiting the location of the crime – or crimes."

Lady Leonora, together with her brother, Mrs. Williams the middle-aged housekeeper, Lestrade, and myself all stood in the doorway to her inner bedroom – watching – while Holmes examined the room where the robbery had taken place.

As he examined the carpeted floor, Holmes complained that he would have also liked to examine the scene of the first break-in. "It is a great shame, but you assure me that it is much the same as the second."

"And the carpet had been brushed and cleaned after the police had examined the scene on that first occasion?"

"That is correct," said the lady of the house.

"That's right," said the housekeeper. "We are proud of the way we keep a clean and tidy house."

"As far as you are concerned, Lestrade," asked Holmes, "can you confirm that?"

"I can indeed, Mr. Holmes."

"And I understand that a large muddy footprint was discovered on the carpet in the middle of the room."

"Yes, sir. The chambermaid spent a great deal of time scrubbing it away."

"But the same footprint, or a similar one, has appeared during last night, and is here before us now."

The housekeeper nodded.

"Can you confirm that it is the same or similar imprint, Mrs. Williams?"

"As far as I can tell, yes," replied the housekeeper. "You'd have to speak to the chambermaid about that."

"I intend to do that as soon as I have finished here," replied Holmes.

He next stepped over to the window and examined it carefully. He discovered that it was currently unlocked and standing slightly open to the outside atmosphere. He pushed open the window and looked outside. Then, with a grunt, he closed it again and returned to continue his examination of the floor area. Finally, he declared that he was satisfied and invited those of us standing in the doorway to come inside the room.

"Lady Leonora," he said, "I would be grateful if you could please show me exactly where the bracelet was kept before it was stolen from this room."

"Certainly," she replied, as she wandered over to where her personal items were positioned beside her bed. "I have always kept it in this small wooden box. It was kept locked at all times, and remained in the drawer beside my bed."

"But it is no longer in that drawer."

"That is evident."

"And where do you keep the key?"

"Oh, the key has always remained on the chatelaine which I keep in the same drawer."

"So that if anyone knew where to find the bracelet, they would have no difficulty in locating the key. All they would need is a knowledge of your personal habits."

"I suppose you are correct, but where I kept my jewels was never any secret. I expect everyone in the household knows about it. I merely expected everyone to respect my privacy."

"But that has been returned to its rightful place," Lestrade said.

"Thank you for your help, Lady Leonora."

"So," said Mr. Bullingworth, "the culprit could have been anybody."

"I hardly think so," replied Holmes. "But I think the time has come for us to have a conference of everyone in the household."

"We could meet in the drawing room," said Hamilton Bullingworth.

"That would be ideal," replied Holmes.

"The evening meal will be served at seven o'clock," said Lady Leonora. "Immediately after that would seem to be a suitable time for the meeting."

Everyone nodded.

"And I trust that our visitors will join us for our meal," added Lady Leonora.

"Splendid," replied Holmes. "But first I need to confer with the chambermaid."

I sat with Holmes as he interviewed Annie Longtown, the chambermaid.

"I have a few questions to put to you," he began. "If you're willing to help me out, that is."

"Certainly, Mr. Holmes," said the pretty auburn-haired young woman. "What would you like to know?"

"I'm referring to the two break-ins that took place in Lady Leonora's rooms recently."

"Yes?"

"I understand that you were the one who cleaned up the bedroom after the first burglary. Is that so?"

"Presumably you mean the muddy footprint. Yes sir, I cleaned that up the first time. After all, it is part of my job. It took a great deal of effort to make it clean again, I can tell you. And I shall no doubt be the one to clean up this time as well – now that you have finished examining the place."

"Quite. In which case, can you tell me about the window? Is it always kept shut, or is it sometimes left unlocked, or even left open?"

"The window, sir? No. Her Ladyship always insists that it is kept shut at all times, except perhaps in the middle of summer, when the heat is oppressive. But the window doesn't have a working lock, so it wouldn't be very difficult for somebody to open it, even from the outside."

"What you are saying is that both last night and the night before, the window was shut. Is that right?"

"Probably, sir. At least as far as I am aware."

"But you say it could have been opened from the outside."

"Yes, sir."

"Now, I want you to tell me about the first footprint – the one you had to clean up yesterday, apparently identical to the one you will be required to clean up today. What can you tell me about them?"

"What sort of thing do you want to know?"

"Was the footprint large or small?"

"It was big, sir, very big – just like the second footprint. It must have been made by somebody with an extremely large foot."

"Or perhaps a rubber waterproof boot."

"Yes. I suppose so."

"That is very interesting, Annie. Thank you."

The young chambermaid seemed relieved. "I'm glad that was helpful to you, sir."

"Now, tell me, who has the largest feet in the entire household?"

The girl giggled. "Well, I suppose it has to be Isaac Sudbury, the gardener. Although what he might have been doing inside the house, wearing those big boots, I really cannot say."

"Might he have been breaking in?"

"To steal her Ladyship's jewels? It is just possible, but I hardly think so. I can hardly imagine him climbing up the foliage outside and then climbing in through the window. Have you met our gardener?"

"Not yet. Why? Is he getting on in age?"

"He must be at least a hundred years old if he's a day."

"And have you any idea who has the smallest feet in the household?"

"The smallest? Of the men, I would imagine it would be Ambrose Bullingworth, Lady Leonora's nephew. She has quite a large family of siblings, you know. Down in the servants' quarters we often joke about how small his feet are. Almost like those of a woman. He also has a slight gap between his front teeth. Otherwise, he's quite attractive."

"Does he know that you talk about him?"

"No. But if he has any understanding of the life of servants, he will have a good idea that we do."

"Is he intelligent?"

Annie pulled a face. "Not really. His main interest is in gambling. The horses, you know."

"And does he get himself into debt?"

"Oh, yes, sir. I happen to know that a couple of bookmakers are pressing him for payment at this very moment."

"And one more thing."

"Yes?"

"Do you know if anybody in the household has purchased a new pair of cuff-links recently?"

She thought for a few seconds. "I'm not sure, but I think Ambrose has been talking about getting a new pair. Though how he could manage to afford them, I really couldn't say."

"Thank you, Annie," said Holmes. "Now, where might I be able to find Isaac Sudbury at this hour of the day?"

"He'll be in or near his potting shed, I should imagine."

Isaac Sudbury was sitting in his potting shed when Holmes and I arrived there. He was drinking a large mug of tea. He did appear to be somewhat elderly, perhaps well over the age of sixty, but looking vigorous for his many years.

"I am Sherlock Holmes," said my companion. "And this is my friend and colleague, Dr. John Watson."

"Well, good afternoon, gentlemen," he began. "Would you care to join me in a cup of tea?"

"Thank you," replied Holmes. "It might help warm me up on such a depressing day.

"And you, Dr. Watson?"

"Yes," I replied. "I think we all need cheering up today."

A moment later, we were all sitting together in the shed, looking out at the rain.

"I heard you were in the house," said Sudbury. "News travels quickly in a small community like this. They're all a load of nosy-parkers around here."

"I can imagine," replied Holmes.

"Now, gentlemen, how can I, in particular, help you?"

"We're here concerning the theft of Lady Leonora's bracelet," replied Holmes.

"I had no doubt about that. And am I one of the suspects in this case, Mr. Holmes?"

"Certainly not in my mind," replied Holmes, warming up his hands by wrapping them around the hot mug. "But a large footprint was discovered at the scene."

"Is that so? And it's well known that I have the largest feet of anyone on the property. Are those the grounds for any suspicion?"

"Not your feet, but perhaps your waterproof boots."

The gardener reached over to a corner of the shed, which was obscured in shade, and brought out a pair of rubber boots. "As you can see, these are impressively large, but when I'm working outside, I need them to be both waterproof and capable of taking a pair of thick woollen stockings."

"Indeed."

We sat together in silence for a moment. Then Isaac Sudbury looked Holmes square in the face. "Go ahead, Mr. Holmes. Ask the question you seem so eager to put to me."

"Very well," said Holmes. "On the evening before last, did you discover that one of your boots was missing?"

Isaac nodded. "I certainly did. One of them, at least. I thought that was a bit odd. If somebody was trying to steal my boots, why would they not take both of them?"

"Indeed. Was it the right foot or the left foot?"

"The right foot only."

"And when was it returned to you?"

"That's rather difficult to say exactly, but it was in its proper place the very next time I looked in here. Certainly by the following morning."

"That's all very useful information," said Holmes. "Thank you. But then there occurred a second break-in – yesterday evening, in fact – when somebody entered the same room, employing the same method of entry, and this time removed a certain quantity of cash."

"So I heard."

"A second footprint was discovered on that occasion. Much like the first time, or so I am told. Did you find your boot missing again last night?"

"Indeed I did. I thought it was extremely impertinent to violate a man's possessions for a second time."

"I think I'd feel exactly the same," said Holmes.

"But we both know the identity of the culprit – isn't that so, Mr. Holmes?"

"I'm still in the process of amassing information," replied Holmes. He rose to his feet. "Come, Watson. We must prepare for the family meeting later this evening."

The evening meal was generous and enjoyable, but a nervous tension remained in the air throughout. It felt as though some people would have liked to have the serious business of the evening dealt with as quickly as possible, while others wanted to delay it for as long as they were able. For some reason, Ambrose Bullingworth, Lady Leonora's nephew, needed to leave the table part-way through the meal, and was absent for quite some time. However, no one seemed to notice this, let alone show any concern over his absence.

The gathering of the household, immediately after the meal, involved just about everyone. Lady Leonora, her brother Hamilton Bullingworth, his son Ambrose, Annie Longtown the chambermaid, the housekeeper, and even Sudbury the gardener, now wearing a respectful pair of shoes.

With the evening lights now lit, and with the odours of the meal still lingering in the air, the room now held an air of expectation.

Holmes stood up in the middle of the gathering.

"Ladies and gentlemen," he began. "I hope not to detain you here very long, but this business needs to be dealt with before the end of this evening."

Most of those present appeared to agree – or at the very least, they remained silent.

"The theft of the bracelet, and then of the money, would seem to have been perpetrated by someone in the household. Someone here now."

A low muttering of surprise ran around the gathering.

"But who is it, Mr. Holmes?" demanded Lady Leonora.

"Let us clear one thing up immediately," said Holmes. "There was no break-in. When I examined it, the window showed no sign of having been forced open, and the foliage outside showed no indication whatsoever of having been disturbed by somebody climbing up. That means that the intruder entered the bedroom from the hallway, simply by the use of a key. In which case, I need to ask: Who had access to a key to your bedroom, Lady Leonora?"

"I suppose just about anybody could find a key if they really wanted to," replied Lady Leonora.

"Hmm. We must leave that for the moment. Let us now reconstruct in our imagination exactly what must have happened during the theft. Late on the first evening, the thief took one of the gardener's boots, dirty from his working outside, opened the door to the bedroom, and entered – and all of this during the hours of darkness."

"I have to admit," said Lady Leonora, "I heard nothing at all, even though I was asleep in the same room. The very thought that someone was there makes my blood run cold."

Holmes continued. "The thief then placed the muddy boot onto the carpet, where it left a soil-stained impression. Next, the thief took out the box of jewels, extracted the key, and used it to open the box. Then, having taken the bracelet out of the box and replaced it, the thief opened the window, in order to suggest that a burglary had occurred and that the thief had left that way. That person then left the room by the door, in order to return the boot to its owner."

"Diabolical," declared Hamilton Bullingworth.

"Later that following morning," continued Holmes, "the same thief took the bracelet along to the shop of Baldersby and Jones, the milliners in Regent Street. There, unobserved by the management, the burglar dropped it into the folds of an umbrella set amongst those being offered for sale."

"Who do we know who was in Regent Street that morning?" demanded Hamilton Bullingworth.

Holmes took a sheet of paper out of his inside pocket and opened it up.

"I have here a list of all the people who purchased items from Baldersby and Jones on that day."

"And?"

"The name of Ambrose Bullingworth is on the list."

All eyes turned to Lady Leonora's young nephew.

Ambrose seemed to turn a more ghastly shade of white.

"I didn't steal that bracelet!" he declared with passion. "I swear it!"

"Let us continue," said Holmes. "The second break-in, which again, as we have seen, wasn't a break-in at all, followed the pattern of the first. Once more, the thief had ready access to the bedroom, although this time her Ladyship had taken the precaution to sleep in one of the guest bedrooms.

It seems that the burglar knew exactly where her Ladyship kept her cash, and removed forty pounds from her wallet."

"Forty?" demanded the chambermaid, before she could stop herself.

"It was your plan all along to take cash from her Ladyship," Holmes said, with his eyes fixing the chambermaid as with a gimlet. "Is that not so? You took the bracelet purely in order to distract attention away from your intended theft, which was that of taking the money the following night. You knew that Ambrose had gone to the milliner's shop in Regent Street, in order to purchase a pair of cufflinks, so you followed him shortly afterwards and dropped the bracelet into its hiding place, precisely in order to point the accusing finger at him. Your name is also on the list of clients given to me by the shop's owners, so there is no point in you trying to deny it."

"But I do deny it!" said the girl. "At least, I deny being the thief."

"No. This entire farrago has been your doing."

It was now girl's turn to grow unnaturally pale. With all eyes now riveted upon her, Annie Longtown found that her legs would no longer support her, and she slipped to her knees, covered her face with her hands, and began to sob.

"So," said Lady Leonora, her voice now turned cold as ice, "it really was you, Longtown."

"You knew that your privileged position would keep you quite safe from suspicion," said Holmes. "But as chambermaid, you had ready access to her Ladyship's jewels and cash anytime you wanted. The rest was simply drama, in order to cast suspicion onto other people. The muddy boot, which suggested the gardener was responsible, was ridiculous. You had probably already taken the bracelet earlier on the day of the first supposed burglary, and the money on the second occasion, so on neither night would you have had to risk alerting the sleeping Lady Leonora."

"I needed the money!" sobbed the girl desperately. "I needed it in order to pay for my mother's medical care! She is dreadfully sick."

"You could have come to me," said her Ladyship. "I would have helped you. You didn't have to steal my money."

"I wasn't thinking!"

"I imagine you were indeed thinking, Longtown," said Holmes in a tone which implied grave accusation. "The plan was well considered, though somewhat amateur in nature."

"But I took only *twenty* pounds," she said between sniffles.

The tense atmosphere remained, until Hamilton Bullingworth broke it with a cough.

"I think that is enough for one evening," he declared. "We all need to take this matter away, and think carefully about it."

"The facts are clear enough to me," said Lady Leonora. "But I suppose you're right. We will need a level head in order to decide what to do with this young woman. I suggest that we adjourn this meeting until tomorrow, immediately after luncheon. In the meantime, Inspector Lestrade, I would be obliged if you would take this young woman into custody and bring her back here tomorrow in order to learn my considered decision about her fate."

Holmes and I found a cabbie who knew us and was quite accustomed to our returning home at such an hour, and had become something of a friend to both of us.

The moment the cab stopped in Baker Street, Holmes and I disembarked, and immediately noticed a group of three thugs emerge from the shadows. They were brandishing heavy sticks as they slouched toward us.

During my time in the army, I had been trained in effective methods of self-protection, and I held my stick so as to be ready to fend off any attack. Holmes, I already knew, could prove himself to be an effective street-fighter, and held his own cane ready to defend himself. As we waited for the thugs to begin their assault, the cabbie joined us, holding a heavy stick. We were ready.

"What do you want?" demanded Holmes, as he addressed the thugs.

"We have a message for you, Mr. Holmes," said the leader of the gang.

"What is your message?"

"Tomorrow, you must remain at home, and spend your time nursing the bruises we're about to give you."

"Very well, do your worst," Holmes challenged him. "If you can."

This seemed to provoke the thugs into aggressive action. They stepped menacingly forward in order to confront us as we took up our position beneath a street gas-lamp.

Three against three. That seemed fair enough. And as we continued to exchange blows for several minutes, it was the thugs who seemed to fare the worst of any of us.

But one thing tipped the balance decisively to our advantage. The door to number 221b opened, and Mrs. Hudson emerged. Silhouetted against the inside light, she brandished her broom-handle and launched her own assault against our three attackers.

They hardly stood a chance, and one by one, they slunk away, snarling like wolves – until just one remained, pushed up against a wall by Holmes, who held his cane pressed up against the man's throat.

"I thought I recognized you," growled Holmes. "You are the one they call 'Green Harry'."

"So?" the man croaked.

"Now," growled Holmes, "tell us who sent you."

He relaxed the pressure on the man's windpipe, sufficiently to allow him to answer.

"It was this young toff," said the thug.

"Young toff?"

The man nodded.

"Do you know his name?"

"No."

"Did this young toff have a gap between his front teeth?"

"Yeah, that's him."

"Very well," said Holmes. "Now, take yourself away from here, if you wish to avoid something worse happening to you."

"Then I shall bid you a good night, Mr. Holmes," said Green Harry. "And if you come across that young toff, tell him the fee he offered to pay us was far too small to guarantee success."

"Or was it the appearance of our landlady? I admit she can be a bit fierce at times."

The following morning, with our few bruises bathed but still painful, we discovered that the rain had dried up and the clouds were dissipating.

Holmes set out early, on his own. His mission, or so he told me, was to consult with Lady Leonora ahead of the gathering there after luncheon. Exactly what he did that morning, he didn't confide to me, even when he returned, excited but in time to enjoy a rather frugal lunch.

It was with some reluctance on my part, but with a sparkle of expectation in Holmes's eyes, that we returned to the townhouse of the Bullingworth-Webb household early that afternoon. We found the same room somewhat more crowded than on the previous occasion.

Holmes took a centrally positioned chair while I stood in one corner, from where I had an excellent view of everyone present.

The miscreant chambermaid, Annie Longtown, who was now looking unkempt and crestfallen, was seated in the far corner, attended by a robust-looking uniformed policeman. Lady Leonora was seated in her upright but well-upholstered chair, clearly the one in charge of the proceedings which were to follow. Beside her stood a man in a black frock coat, whom I recognized as her husband, the Right Honorable Sir James Bullingworth-Webb. Hamilton Bullingworth stood beside him, with a face like thunder. Other members of the household had gathered as well. Many of the servants had come to either support or to gloat over Annie Longtown's predicament. Lestrade sat in a comfortable seat beside the window, looking impatient to be about his other work. And beside the doorway stood a man who was new to me. He was thick-set in body and, beneath his grizzled beard, his face displayed the ravages of all kinds of weather. A seafarer, beyond doubt.

Having satisfied himself that everyone had now assembled, Sir James drew the gathering to order.

"Ladies and gentlemen, thank you for coming together here this afternoon. Although I wasn't at the meeting yesterday, having had business at the House, I am cognisant of the matters which were discussed here. I think I had better hand things over to my wife, who has something to say concerning the so-called break-ins that have taken place here in recent days."

Lady Leonora looked around at the gathering.

"We need not go over the details of the events which discussed here yesterday evening," said Lady Leonora, "except to say that Mr. Holmes explained to us how the theft was made of my diamond bracelet, and of forty pounds, both from my own bedroom – a violation which I find it difficult to forgive. This criminal behaviour was perpetrated by a member of my own household: My personal chambermaid, Annie Longtown."

"She is here at your request, ma'am," said Lestrade, "awaiting your decision about prosecution."

"And that brings us to the next point in our investigation," said Holmes.

"Which is?"

"Since the chambermaid denied taking the full forty pounds, but admitted to taking only half of that amount, who was it that took the other twenty pounds?"

All eyes once more returned to Ambrose, who glanced from one face to another, and saw nothing in them to offer him any consolation. Then he turned back to Holmes and waited to hear what he had to tell the gathering."

Facing Ambrose, Holmes said, "Hiring those thugs to attack us last night was tantamount to a confession. They complained that you short-changed them for the job. No doubt they will want to talk the matter over with you – not that you were short of money," continued Holmes. "But you were hard-up earlier in the day. The cufflinks you bought from the shop in Regent Street were put onto your account, and not paid for immediately. You were perhaps anticipating a windfall in order to pay for them. Also, it is well known that you engage in betting on the outcome of horse races. You are in debt. When the opportunity arose, you took it. You were one of the first people to enter her Ladyship's room after the theft had been discovered. You saw the money lying there, and you imagined that when the thief was found, that person would pay the penalty for the full amount taken."

"This is a rum business, Mr. Holmes," said Lady Leonora.

"Indeed it is, ma'am," said Holmes. "Annie Longtown attempted to incriminate Ambrose, and Ambrose, in his turn, although he didn't know the identity of the thief at the time, tried to incriminate the chambermaid."

As Holmes sat back, his story told, a great sigh ran around all gathered there.

"So," concluded Hamilton Bullingworth, "both are guilty."

"That is evident," said Holmes.

"In which case," declared Lady Leonora, "I have now reached my decision."

Not a sound could be heard from anyone present, as the expectant pause appeared to foretell doom for the two young people now accused of theft.

Lady Leonora turned her acerbic stare onto the chambermaid. "I have decided that you, Longtown, will be dismissed from my service immediately. I shall not provide you with a reference, since that would require me to include mention of you as a thief. On the other hand, I will attempt to find you some kind of employment, however menial, through my own various contacts. I shall do this in order to allow you time to repay me the money you took. You will have twelve months in which to repay that twenty pounds you stole from me. If you fail to do that within the calendar year, then you will go to prison."

Annie blinked. "How can I raise that amount of money in so short a period of time?"

"Genuine hard work," replied Lady Leonora.

Annie hung her head and stuttered a muted word of gratitude.

"Now to Ambrose: You need to grow up, young man."

"Yes, Aunt Leonora."

"This man," she indicated the seafarer, "is Captain Kilberry. He is master of a steamship which plies between Southampton and the Far East. He is known to Mr. Holmes, who recommend him to me when we talked the matter through earlier today. I have decided that you will sign up to be a member of his ship's crew, for the next twelve months. During that time, you will save up as much as you can and, at the end of a year, you will return to me that twenty pounds you stole. Succeed, and the slate will be wiped clean, so to speak. Fail, and I shall ask that your case be brought to trial, and insist that you go straight to prison. Do you understand?"

"I understand," Ambrose croaked.

Captain Kilberry's face showed that he was looking forward to knocking this young man into shape.

"Very well," declared Sir James. "The matter is now settled. Is there any further business we need to deal with at the moment?"

Holmes spoke up. "Only that I shall shortly present you with a bill for my fees, together with expenses incurred during the conducting of this case. Also, that the young lady who was responsible for discovering your bracelet should receive a reward. I can give you her name and address."

Lady Leonora looked at her husband, who nodded his agreement.

"Very well, Mr. Holmes," she told him. "And thank you for your professional assistance in resolving this case."

With that, Sir James dismissed the gathering.

Lady Leonora's chambermaid, now discharged from her position, and her nephew, now thoroughly disgraced, both left in order to collect their personal effects in preparation for leaving the house – one to return home to face the endless struggle to pay her way in life and return the money she had stolen, the other to be taken in hand by Captain Kilberry. Which of the two I pitied the most, it was difficult to decide.

"I have to say," declared Holmes as the two of us ventured out into the fresh air, with the October sunshine lighting up the western sky, "that I am glad to be out of that place. What a household, eh? Hardly a brain cell among the entire family."

"I tend to agree with you," I told him.

"Now you can perhaps see the sort of trouble that purchasing one of those contraptions can bring you."

"An umbrella?"

"Certainly. In this case, it turned out to be a veritable Pandora's Box."

"Now it's your turn to exaggerate, Holmes."

He laughed.

"Just deserts for Ambrose, perhaps," I continued.

"Oh, Ambrose is just a young fool who needs to grow up."

"And what of Annie Longtown?"

"Now there is a woman with poison in her heart, Watson," said Holmes. "I'm quite sure she has stolen from her mistress before this occasion."

"Really? She seemed such in innocent young thing."

"You are easily taken in by female beauty."

"But concern about her sick mother must have been playing on her mind," I told him. "I would dearly like to offer her family the benefit of my medical assistance."

"Watson, my dear fellow," continued Holmes. "Spare her your sympathy. A reply to a telegram I sent to the Essex Police, near to where she lives, this morning elicited the information that that young woman's mother is both alive and in a healthy condition. At this moment, she is preparing to have a severe word with her daughter."

"Then she was lying in order to gain our pity, and to soften the pain of her retribution."

"I can assure that this present situation is nemesis as far as she is concerned. She is now reaping the consequences of her duplicity – not once, but on many occasions."

"On the other hand, it all seems to have worked out well for Agnes Smithercote," I said. "The young woman who found the bracelet in the first place."

"Or who unwittingly dropped it into the road."

"She is now in possession of a smart new umbrella, and is in line to receive a reward for discovering the diamond bracelet."

"And good luck to her," replied Holmes. "I hope that Fortune and her umbrella will keep her safe from the severest downpours for the rest of her life."

"I agree with that sentiment," I replied.

A moment later, Holmes brightened up as a thought occurred to him. "A concert of chamber music is being performed this evening at Covent Garden.," he declared. "Are you free to join me there?"

"It would certainly be a much-needed refreshment," I told him. "After all we've seen during the past day or two."

"Capital!" said Holmes. "But no more mention of umbrellas."

I smiled and kept my own counsel on the matter.

MX Publishing

MX Publishing is the world's largest specialist Sherlock Holmes publisher, with over six-hundred titles and over two-hundred authors creating the latest in Sherlock Holmes fiction and non-fiction

The catalogue includes several award winning books, and over four-hundred-and-fifty have been converted into audio.

MX Publishing also has one of the largest communities of Holmes fans on Facebook, with regular contributions from dozens of authors.

www.mxpublishing.com

@mxpublishing on Facebook, Twitter, and Instagram

www.ingramcontent.com/pod-product-compliance
Lightning Source LLC
Chambersburg PA
CBHW071145260626
47162CB00003B/923